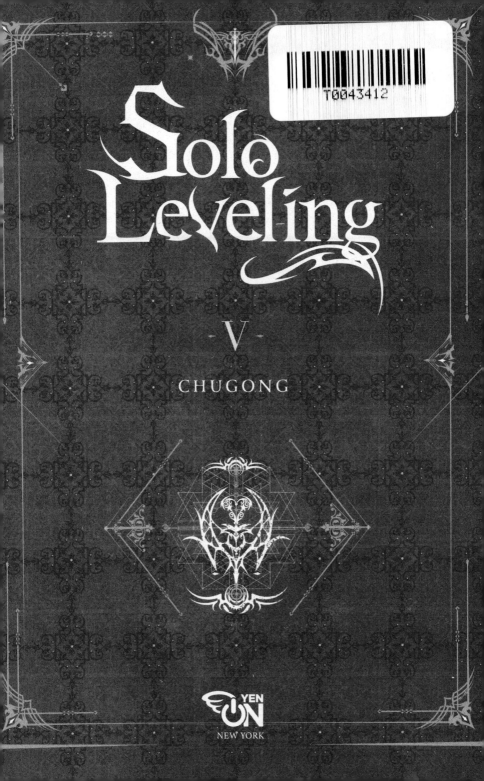

Solo Leveling

V

CHUGONG

YEN ON
NEW YORK

Solo Leveling V

CHUGONG

Translation by Hye Young Im and J. Torres

This book is a work of fiction. Names, characters, places, and incidents are the product of the author's imagination or are used fictitiously. Any resemblance to actual events, locales, or persons, living or dead, is coincidental.

SOLO LEVELING Volume 5
© Chugong 2017 / D&C MEDIA
All rights reserved.
First published in Korea in 2017 by D&C MEDIA Co., Ltd.

English translation © 2022 by Yen Press, LLC

Yen Press, LLC supports the right to free expression and the value of copyright. The purpose of copyright is to encourage writers and artists to produce the creative works that enrich our culture.

The scanning, uploading, and distribution of this book without permission is a theft of the author's intellectual property. If you would like permission to use material from the book (other than for review purposes), please contact the publisher. Thank you for your support of the author's rights.

Yen On
150 West 30th Street, 19th Floor
New York, NY 10001

Visit us at yenpress.com ◊ facebook.com/yenpress ◊ twitter.com/yenpress
yenpress.tumblr.com ◊ instagram.com/yenpress

First Yen On Edition: August 2022

Edited by Yen On Editorial: Won Young Seo, Kurt Hassler
Designed by Yen Press Design: Wendy Chan

Yen On is an imprint of Yen Press, LLC.
The Yen On name and logo are trademarks of Yen Press, LLC.

The publisher is not responsible for websites (or their content) that are not owned by the publisher.

Library of Congress Cataloging-in-Publication Data
Names: Chugong, author. | Im, Hye Young, translator. | Torres, J., 1969– translator.
Title: Solo leveling / Chugong ; translation by Hye Young Im and J. Torres.
Other titles: Na honjaman rebereop. English
Description: First Yen On edition. | New York, NY : Yen On, 2021.
Identifiers: LCCN 2020047938 | ISBN 9781975319274 (v. 1 ; trade paperback) |
ISBN 9781975319298 (v. 2 ; trade paperback) | ISBN 9781975319311 (v. 3 ; trade paperback) |
ISBN 9781975319335 (v. 4 ; trade paperback) | ISBN 9781975319359 (v. 5 ; trade paperback)
Subjects: GSAFD: Fantasy fiction.
Classification: LCC PL994.215.G66 N313 2021 | DDC 895.73/5—dc23
LC record available at https://lccn.loc.gov/2020047938

ISBNs: 978-1-9753-1935-9 (paperback)
978-1-9753-1936-6 (ebook)

1 3 5 7 9 10 8 6 4 2

LSC-C

Printed in the United States of America

CONTENTS

1

HUNTING HUMANS

1

HUNTING HUMANS

Orcs were natural-born predators. Although their intelligence level was below that of humans, they were far superior at tracking and hunting weaker prey.

And now that the door—the barrier that used to exist between this world and the dungeon—was gone, the predators spilled out.

"Grrrowr."

"Grrr."

The orcs used their feet to push aside the dead bodies of the boys who were obstructing their path and surveyed their surroundings.

Sniff, sniff.

"Grrahh."

The orcs had been holding their breath for an entire week as they sat in the darkness of the dungeon. No wonder they were so worked up by the smell of flesh and blood all around them. However, this group was just the reconnaissance team. As much as their blood boiled, they had tread carefully as, behind the circular portal, dozens of their kind awaited their report.

Straight walls lined with many doors and windows—the leader of the reconnaissance team noted immediately how the building they were standing in had a complicated layout similar to a castle.

"Grrrr." The beast's nostrils flared.

He had two choices. One was to immediately leave this hall to slaughter whatever prey they could get their hands on. The other was to kill all the humans within this castle, make it their fortress, then go forth and hunt.

It was clear which was the safer choice.

The leader barked at one of his subordinates. "Bring forth our brothers!"

He then looked up at the ceiling. The beast's ears twitched as he listened for sounds from above. One floor up, then one more, and even beyond that... The building was filled with prey.

His head throbbed from the voice echoing in his head, incessantly urging him to slaughter.

"All right." He parted his lips and bared his fangs. "We'll start by clearing out the inside of this building."

* * *

A crowd had gathered at Gwangalli Beach. Despite the gloomy clouds overhead, people's attentions were solely focused on one thing—the large gate that had appeared on the beach. The local police force and the Busan branch of the Hunter's Association had cooperated to set up a barricade prohibiting civilians from entering the area, but the number of onlookers continued to grow anyway.

"Boss!" The new employee whimpered to his supervisor, having almost been trampled by the throng. "Are we supposed to deal with this every time a gate appears?"

But the supervisor was similarly taken aback by the situation. They had never seen it this busy around a gate. "We're just going to have to deal with it. It's because this is one of the biggest gates to ever appear in Busan."

They then peeked over their shoulders at the immense hole suspended in midair. It felt like they might be sucked in if they stared at it, so they were doing their best to ignore it. Of course...

A gate can't hurt anyone unless a dungeon break happens, though......

Even so, they detested these things, kind of like how some people had an irrational fear of the ocean or outer space. That's why, whenever they were out in the field, the sole preoccupation of the pencil pushers was a fervent wish that the hunters would deal with the ominous holes.

In that vein, there was one aspect of this specific raid that put them at ease.

The same thought seemed to cross the rookie's mind. "Oh! Boss, did you hear?"

"Hear what?"

"I heard an S-rank hunter from Seoul is on his way!"

Who hadn't heard about that? The supervisor estimated that about half the crowd was here to see the gate and the other half was rubbernecking to see the S-rank hunter.

"Hunter Jinwoo Sung?"

"Yes, him!"

"Do you know him or something? Why're you so excited?"

"N-no." The rookie blushed and frantically waved his hands. "To tell you the truth, it's going to be my first time seeing an S-rank hunter, so......"

The supervisor sighed, exasperated. "Hunter Sung is a newbie just like you, so why're you so different from him?"

"Boss!"

"If you've got the energy to chitchat, why don't you make yourself useful and help out by putting in some overtime?"

"I'm taking a break because my leg hurts from being on my feet all day!"

The supervisor clicked his tongue as the rookie's reproachful glances made it clear he felt wronged. Though his superior didn't think this new guy was particularly reliable, the rookie's enthusiasm was somewhat understandable.

"I'll admit, I'm a little curious about Hunter Sung, too. Everyone's talking about him."

"You too, huh, boss?"

"I mean, he single-handedly defeated the boss of an S-rank gate."

Technically, the queen ant was the magic beast boss of the dungeon on Jeju Island. However, the battle with the monstrous mutated ant had left such a strong impression, many of those who'd watched the live broadcast of that raid mistakenly took it for the boss. Killing the boss closes the gate, so in the people's eyes, Jinwoo was a hunter who could close an S-rank gate all by himself. No wonder there were rumors Jinwoo's power was up there with the national-level hunters.

It was only natural that he was getting all this attention.

"To think, an S-rank hunter is coming! I wonder what it's like to see one in person."

The supervisor was a little unnerved by the rookie's sparkling eyes.

Did he apply to the association to stalk hunters or something?

Oblivious to his superior's petulant gaze, the rookie's eyes kept on shining, and he continued enthusiastically.

"Hey, boss!"

"What now?"

"I've heard it's super difficult to look an extremely powerful hunter in the eyes. Have you ever run into an S rank before?"

The supervisor recalled his business trip to Gwangju. "......I have."

"Wow!"

The elder man, who'd initially found this exchange bothersome, puffed up with pride at the newbie's awed response.

"How was it, sir? Were you really scared?"

"Man, tell me about it. I met Hunter Dongwook Ma of the Fame Guild last year while on official business—"

"Excuse me. I just need to get by."

"Yes, of course."

The two association employees quickly parted to let a man pass between them, then stepped back into place.

"Huh?" The supervisor looked back at the hooded figure who'd just passed them.

"What's wrong, boss?"

"Nothing. I just thought he looked familiar."

"Huh? That's weird. I thought so, too."

"Does he work for the association?"

"Hmm......"

"Hang on, where was I?"

"Uh...... You were saying about Hunter Ma from the Fame Guild?"

"Oh, right. I had a chance to meet Hunter Ma in person, and he was such a huge guy that his shoulders were this wide."

"Whoa!"

Turns out, the supervisor and the trainee were birds of a feather.

* * *

"Hunter Sung!"

Jongsu Park was so happy to see Jinwoo that he sounded nearly tearful in a way unbecoming of a man in his thirties. It reflected just how high the stakes of this raid were.

Jinwoo calmly checked the time as Jongsu greeted him overzealously and watched as the numbers on his cell phone changed from 10:59 to 11:00.

Good.

Jinwoo smiled. Although he'd taken a roundabout route using Stealth in order to avoid the chaos, he'd still arrived on time. He was starting off the raid on a good note.

He finally looked up and took in the sight of the gate.

......It's bigger than I thought.

The gate was much larger in person than it had looked in the footage he'd seen, and just as the association had informed the Knights Guild, the amount of mana radiating from it was extraordinary.

What kind of magic beasts am I going to find in there?

Jinwoo couldn't help but grin.

Beyond the gate's unusual size, nothing else about it seemed out of the ordinary. As one would expect at any raid, there were two groups of low-rank hunters standing by.

That's the collection team, and that's the excavation team.

The more knowledge one had, the more they noticed, and thanks to his time with the Hunters Guild, Jinwoo was easily able to tell the groups apart based on their uniforms and tools.

And there are guild personnel busily running around as always.

Indeed, experience was the best teacher.

"Whoa!"

"He actually came!"

"Mr. Jinwoo Sung?"

Having been called over by Jongsu, the elite hunters began gathering around Jinwoo, their faces lighting up as soon as they recognized him. As he briefly greeted each hunter, Jinwoo sized them up. He counted thirty high-rank hunters. Just as Jongsu had confidently explained, the quantity and quality of the Knights Guild A- and B-rank hunters was on par with the Hunters Guild.

Of course......

He expected no less from a guild that represented an entire region of Korea. On top of that, because everyone was suited up in either armor or protective gear imbued with mana, the title of knight fit them perfectly.

It was a shame such an outstanding guild was often underestimated simply due to a lack of S-rank members. Jinwoo understood why President Park had hastily asked him to join the Knights Guild.

By the time Jinwoo snapped out of his thoughts, he was already surrounded by the other hunters.

"Ummm......"

"Hmm."

A moment of hesitation soon turned into a competition to get Jinwoo's attention.

"Hunter Sung, the Jeju Island raid was truly amazing!"

"How do you summon those soldiers in black? Or wait, are you sure they're actually minions?"

"You're going to lead today's raid, aren't you?"

Jinwoo didn't know how to handle the barrage of questions.

"Okay, stop! Stop!"

Healer Yerim, whose idea it had been to invite Jinwoo in the first place, pushed the other hunters aside and stepped forward. "You're making Hunter Sung uncomfortable! Stop acting like a bunch of newbies."

She glared sharply at her colleagues. High-rank healers were just like den mothers who carried the weight of the team's well-being. The strike squad members bit their tongues and swallowed their complaints like children after a scolding.

Heh.

Yerim chuckled. She spun and extended her hand to Jinwoo.

"I'm Yerim Jung, the main healer of the elite strike squad of the Knights Guild." She grinned at him as she continued. "At the very least, I think the leader and the primary healer of the team should get along, don't you?"

Jinwoo's gaze shifted away from Yerim, whose eyes were gleaming with an ulterior motive, and to Jongsu. "Haven't you explained everything to them yet?"

"Oh, the thing is……" Jongsu ran his fingers through his hair, embarrassed. "My schedule's been crazy, what with all the paperwork and gathering everyone here."

He gave an awkward laugh, then looked around at the other hunters. At least everyone in the squad was assembled in front of him so he would have to explain things only once.

"I, Jongsu Park, will be the leader of this raid."

His words triggered some grumbling in the crowd.

"The president again?"

"But Hunter Sung is here…"

"Is this really okay?"

The tank Jongsu was among the strongest A-rank hunters, so it wasn't strange for him to lead a raid. In fact, except when he was under the weather, he led most of the Knights Guild raids. However, there was now an S-rank hunter in the strike squad. Common sense dictated that the strongest would take the lead.

Jongsu quickly continued his explanation for his confused subordinates. "Hunter Jinwoo Sung will be in charge of our safety and guard our rear."

This had been Jongsu's demand—that Jinwoo insure the squad's safety from the back of the party.

This was for both the security and honor of the Knights Guild. Hunters with high combat abilities usually marched in front. Those weaker and more vulnerable to sudden attacks, such as mages, healers, or support hunters, brought up the rear. Since the Knights Guild was having difficulties recruiting rookies, the survival of these hunters was a matter of the guild's continued existence.

So what if they placed Jinwoo in back? The strike squad could quickly advance without worrying about a surprise attack from behind. No, they would even welcome it because the one fielding such strikes would be him—Jinwoo Sung, destroyer of thousands of S-rank magic beasts on Jeju Island! Heck, if their enemies persistently attacked from the rear, the strike squad might even be able to clock out early.

That was the first reason for Jongsu's request. The second was more pressing......

Gulp.

Jongsu swallowed hard as he observed the swarm of reporters by the police barricade. It was proof that this raid was the center of attention. If they weren't careful, people might think the Knights Guild was riding on Jinwoo's coattails.

I mean, it's true, but......

Either way, he couldn't have the public thinking that, because the true purpose of this raid was to show people that the Knights Guild was still going strong. That's why he had been so desperate to recruit Jinwoo. And so...

"This is something Hunter Sung and I agreed on after much discussion, so I will only entertain your complaints after the raid is done," Jongsu relayed to his teammates.

But at that moment...

"Hang on, sir. I, for one, don't understand this decision." An A-rank hunter stepped forward. He was a rookie who had been recently recruited to the guild. "Are we so weak that we need someone else's protection?"

Blood drained from the faces of the senior hunters at his question.

Gah......!

H-hey, kid!

Confidence oozed from the young hunter, who looked to be about Jinwoo's age. "Is that not so, everyone?"

His attitude was understandable. He was the ace of the new crop of hunters this year, and given that the accolades he'd received had been second only to those of Chul Kim, his bravado wasn't unfounded. The only problem was that he was barking up the wrong tree.

"Mr. Jinwoo Sung, do the elite members of the Knights Guild seem that weak to you?"

......

Jinwoo suppressed his laughter and quietly listened to what the new kid had to say.

Of course, the other hunters were on pins and needles.

Where is his unwarranted confidence coming from......?

Oh man... Is this his first time meeting an S-rank hunter?

Somebody, please stop him!

He should know this isn't the time or place for spouting such nonsense......

Seeing his seniors at a loss for words and Jinwoo's silence made the rookie even cockier. "And you too, President Park!"

"Me?" Was it Jongsu's turn now? The guild master was speechless as he pointed to himself.

"I know S ranks have an extremely high net worth, but why would you agree to give him half the profits? He's just one person, not an entire guild."

"......" Jongsu looked to Jinwoo for help as his head started throbbing.

Hunter Sung... I leave him in your hands.

Jinwoo gave a firm nod.

"In any case, I don't understand the ridiculous terms of this contr—"

Just then, Igris materialized in front of the protesting rookie.

Eek!

The A-rank hunter flinched and stumbled back at the force of the magic power coming from the knight in black armor. But before he could retreat more than two steps, his back collided against something hard. Startled, the newbie turned to see a second knight a few heads taller than the first peering down at him—Iron.

"Yikes!" He gasped and broke out in a cold sweat.

Something next to him tapped his shoulder, and his head slowly swiveled to see a hooded figure in a black robe.

"A-ahhh!" The rookie's legs gave out at the dark mana emanating from Fang.

I feel bad enough for him, so I'll hold off on summoning Beru.

The three knight-rank soldiers returned to the shadows with a wave from Jinwoo. He then walked over to the trembling man and offered a hand.

"Do you understand now?"

The A-rank rookie grabbed Jinwoo's hand and clumsily got back on his feet. He nodded vigorously. And that was that.

Jinwoo and the Knights Guild strike squad moved to the front of the gate, but before they went in...

"Just a minute, please."

President Jongsu Park and Vice President Yoontae Jung performed a final check on their equipment and team members. Standing in front of the gate, their excitement tamped down, and there was only silence.

......

He wasn't sure since when, but Jinwoo had grown to like the palpable tension right before entering a dungeon. It felt like his mind was settling. In the past, Jinwoo had lived in fear of receiving a summons from the association and had avoided all phone calls. Who would've thought it'd ever be possible that he could feel this way?

"We're good to go, boss."

"All right." Jongsu nodded and walked over to Jinwoo, who was keeping his distance from the strike squad.

They exchanged looks.

"Hunter Sung."

"Yes." Jinwoo uncrossed his arms and met the guild master's gaze.

Jongsu bowed his head to Jinwoo. "I look forward to working with you." It was a short sentence that conveyed many sentiments.

Jinwoo replied in kind. "I look forward to working with you as well."

Jongsu and Yoontae entered the gate first, followed by the rest of the party. After confirming that the rest of the party was in, Jinwoo strolled through.

* * *

[You have entered the dungeon.]

As usual, the system message visible only to Jinwoo greeted him. However…

Hmm?

Jinwoo blinked in surprise.

The dungeon was made of passages big enough to accommodate lumbering giants. Although his experience in high-rank dungeons was limited, he'd luckily been able to explore one before. Based on that encounter, what puzzled Jinwoo wasn't the magnitude of this dungeon but, rather, its atmosphere.

What's going on……?

For some reason, Jinwoo was at ease here. He'd felt an ominous wind blowing in many a dungeon, but this was his first time feeling comfortable in one.

Just then…

"It's an ogre!"

Contrary to Jinwoo's senses, the strike squad ran into danger right from the start.

"A two-headed ogre!"

"Everyone, watch out!"

A magic beast that could easily be the boss of a high-rank dungeon guarded the entrance, its red eyes flashing.

"GRRAAHH!"

Two-Headed Ogres were more than twice the size of ordinary ogres and possessed Herculean strength. The average strike squad would flee in terror upon encountering one.

"Let's go!"

The elite hunters of the Knights Guild leaped into action. Jongsu the tank rushed to the front of the group with his shield raised. As soon as the ogre spotted him, it swung a club that seemed to be fashioned from a tree it had uprooted.

BAM!

The powerful impact shook the entire cave, but Jongsu, who had bulked up his muscles using a skill, braced his knees and withstood the strike.

"Boss!"

"I'm fine!"

"Then I'm going in, too!" Yoontae, the sub tank, took a firm stance next to Jongsu.

Having succeeded in getting the ogre's attention, Jongsu roared. "Attack!"

At his signal, the Knights Guild's counterattack began. Arrows, spells, swords, and spears rained down on the Two-Headed Ogre.

GRRAAAK!

The enraged monster went berserk, but Jongsu wouldn't allow it to focus on anyone but the main tank, and Yoontae moved quickly to block the occasional rogue attacks.

Stomp!

Yoontae slid backward, his feet leaving two long skid marks on the ground as he blocked a kick. Thanks to him, the other hunters sustained little to no damage.

"GUH, GAAAH!"

Little by little, the damage dealers tore into the ogre's body with exceptional teamwork.

It was clear to Jinwoo why the Knights Guild had held on to the number one spot in the Youngnam region for so long.

"GRUHH…!" Eventually, the ogre began foaming at the mouth and toppled over backward.

Thud!

The boss-level magic beast had gone down without injuring any of the humans. It was a flawless victory for the team.

"Nice!" Jongsu pumped both his fists.

Was it because they had a guest? Both he and his team were in the highest of spirits today. Jongsu wondered what Jinwoo thought of their performance.

It would be the cherry on top if our teamwork impressed him enough to join our guild.

Jongsu glanced at Jinwoo and locked eyes with him. The tank felt awkward, as if the S-rank hunter had read his mind, but after much internal debate, he eventually smiled and walked over.

"We'll continue after regrouping."

"Got it." Jinwoo nodded in understanding. He could freely replenish his mana and recover stamina using potions, but other hunters didn't have that luxury. They needed a moment's rest after fighting such a strong magic beast.

Jongsu gazed at the ogre with a troubled look. "This isn't good."

"……?" Jinwoo turned to face him.

"This raid won't be as easy as I expected. I can't believe we had to deal with a Two-Headed Ogre right at the entrance." Jongsu rubbed his chin, then grinned at Jinwoo. "By any chance, do you know the nickname for these things?"

Jinwoo shook his head, and Jongsu immediately answered.

"Grave Keepers."

Was it because of all the inevitable victims who had fallen in the face of their immense power? But Jongsu's explanation diverged greatly from Jinwoo's expectations.

"It's because…" He gazed into the depths of the cave. To him, it felt like ominous energy was wafting out from the bowels of the dungeon.

"If you come across a Two-Headed Ogre at the entrance as opposed to the boss lair…" His voice sounded worried. "It means the dungeon is filled with the undead."

* * *

The emergency center of the Hunter's Association received an urgent phone call. The voice on the other end belonged to a teenage girl.

"I-is this the association?!"

The staffer at the call center could tell by the sobs coming through the line that something was very wrong.

"Yes, it is. Please state your emergency."

"I'm a-at-at my school…… Th-there are m-magic beasts outside."

"Outside? Where are you right now?"

"I'm hiding. I was… I was with my friend, but…but my friend was… Hic! I'm in the bathroom."

It was difficult to understand the girl because of her uncontrollable sobbing, but the experienced employee was fortunately able to piece her words together to figure out what she was trying to say.

An alert was immediately sent to the main office of the Hunter's Association.

Magic beasts sighting at school. One victim confirmed. Caller in hiding.

Could there have been a dungeon break inside a school? The staffer shuddered at the grisly thought and focused on rescuing the girl.

"How many magic beasts are there? Are they nearby?"

"I don't—I don't know. Ohhh, the screams… Th-there are too many screams. Hic! Am I g-going to die?"

"Please stay calm and listen to me."

The call taker had been doing this job for a long time and knew all too well how vulnerable humans could be when their lives were in danger. In situations like this, it was imperative to remain calm. The primary objective was to steady the caller and relay instructions as needed. That was what it meant to work at an emergency call center.

"Hunters from the association are on their way now. They will do their utmost to save you, so you must keep calm until they get there. Do you understand?"

"Really? Th-then, I'm not going to die?"

The voice coming through the receiver began to sound less panicked. This was a good sign. With the student in a stabler frame of mind, the staffer proceeded to ask the most important question necessary to ensure her survival.

"By any chance…do you know what kind of magic beasts they are?"

"Yes, yes, I... I know. On TV, I saw them."

"What kind of magic beasts are they?"

If they had dull senses and relied solely on their eyes, then hiding in a bathroom was a good idea. The one taking the call prayed that's what they were dealing with.

"Uh... Th-their body looks like a human's, b-but they have ugly faces. Oh, they have green skin."

Could it be?

The staffer's eyes widened. "Are…are you talking about orcs?"

"Yes, that was the name. Orcs."

NO!

The staffer immediately jumped up and shouted, "Get out of there! Right now! Orcs are—"

Despite the desperate prayers that had been offered, the loud crack of the bathroom door being ripped open could be heard over the line, followed by a bloodcurdling scream.

"GYAAAAAH!"

* * *

The Knights Guild's raid was going smoothly. In fact, it was rather odd how well it was going.

Yet another magic beast—

"Argggh!"

A rotting creature the size of a house evaded the strike squad's attacks instead of retaliating before being captured by a mage hunter's restraining magic and meeting a miserable end. This same series of events kept recurring, so the hunters began to wonder:

"Isn't this weird?"

"Why do they keep running away from us?"

"It's like they're being chased by something, don't you think?"

The hunters kept encountering powerful undead magic beasts such as vampires, liches, dread worms, and red ghouls. The undead weren't easy opponents to deal with. Killing them was hard enough, but hunters couldn't let down their guards even after the fact because the beasts could recover or come back to life and try to even the score at any moment.

However... These particular enemies seemed to be offering up their lives to the hunters before they could use much of their power.

They seem so scared of something that they can't even consider resisting......

That was Jongsu's evaluation of the magic beasts they'd encountered thus far. The thought that he wouldn't have brought Jinwoo along had he known their opponents would be at this level popped into his head.

You really don't know what to expect in a dungeon.

Who knew raiding a top A-rank dungeon would be this easy?

Well anyway......

It looked like they could safely complete the raid without any major injuries, which was a relief. It was a satisfying conclusion despite suffering some financial losses.

On the other hand, Jinwoo was rather disappointed.

I had high hopes for this A-rank dungeon, but......

Although he could sense high levels of mana farther inside, he couldn't expect to gain much by way of experience points if this kept up. Jinwoo hadn't even had a chance to join the battle because the Knights Guild was doing so well on their own.

......

Jinwoo quietly let out a sigh…then stopped dead in his tracks.

Huh?

He looked over his shoulder.

Healer Yerim stopped next to him. "What's wrong, Hunter Sung? Is there something behind us?"

Jinwoo didn't answer. His heart was pumping so furiously that he couldn't be bothered.

Is this……?

His gaze, focused beyond the gate, seemed apprehensive.

Yerim finally realized something wasn't right. "Hunter Sung?"

Jinwoo's expression darkened.

* * *

"Arrrgh!"

"Aieeeee!"

Anguished screams echoed throughout the school. Less than half the student body had successfully escaped the building. Those remaining were either already corpses lying on the ground or running for their lives from the orcs. However, their efforts were futile—the orcs had begun their hunt from the bottom floor and gradually moved upward, killing everyone in sight.

"Ahhhhh!"

The trapped students hid in their classrooms and covered their ears to block out the screams coming from below. The twelfth-grade classrooms were on the top floor of the school. Jinah was among those who hadn't had a chance to escape. The only thing standing between the orcs and the students were the doors they'd barricaded with whatever they'd had on hand.

"Ohhh……"

"Crap."

The boys gripped chairs and a mop with trembling hands, but none of them was reliable. Their only chance of survival would be if the hunters found them before the orcs did.

Blam!

The dented door was blown out of its frame.

"Ahhhhhh!"

"Gyaaah!"

Students screamed in terrified wails as two orcs drenched in the blood of countless victims entered the classroom.

"A-argh!" A boy guarding the entrance threw away his mop and bolted toward the back door, but an orc lying in wait on the other side lodged an ax in his forehead.

Krunk.

The boy tumbled to the floor, his eyes lifeless.

"Aieeee!"

"Argh!"

Both exits were blocked by orcs. The rest of the screaming students pressed themselves up against the windows, fully aware that jumping from the sixth-floor windows or getting captured by the orcs would have the same end result.

Jinwoo! Jinwoo!

Jinah huddled with her classmates who were trying to make themselves as small as possible in a corner of the room. She squeezed her eyes shut, trying to manifest her brother, an S-rank hunter. She felt like Jinwoo would come for her if only she called out to him. He was her last hope.

"Grrr!"

"Grrk?"

The orcs herding the students suddenly froze and growled to each other.

"Sir, I sense a human with magic power."

"Kill it first."

Unlike ordinary humans, those who could wield magic power were a threat, so it was imperative to deal with them first. The orc that received the captain's command scanned the group and found Jinah.

"Ah!"

It grabbed her by the wrist and dragged her to the middle of the classroom.

"Is it this one?"

"Yes, Captain."

The underling was right. A tiny hint of magic power could be sensed on this girl. It didn't matter if it was her own power or emanating from a weapon she carried. The fact remained that this female human needed to be the first to die.

The captain lifted his ax.

"A-ah…!" Jinah watched the weapon rise above her head and shut her eyes tightly.

"Grrrr." The captain took a few deep breaths and swung his ax down with a callous expression on his face.

Shiiing!

Jinwoo!

At that moment…

Voooom.

Black smoke rose from Jinah's shadow and instantly solidified into shape.

Tak!

The captain of the reconnaissance team was flabbergasted as he realized a high orc in black armor had suddenly grabbed his wrist.

"Grrk?" Even before the beast could say anything, the high orc slammed its fist on the captain's head, crushing it like a watermelon.

Crack!

* * *

The mouths of the students watching the scene gaped, and their brains struggled to make sense of what was happening.

They'd turned away as one of their classmates was about to be brutally murdered when soldiers clad in black armor appeared out of thin air. Soldiers… Could they even be called soldiers? These creatures resembled the orcs but somehow seemed even more orc-like than their victims. They also had red skin and were much larger. Next to them, the invading monsters were like kids who hadn't hit their growth spurt.

The students' reactions were understandable. The soldiers Jinwoo had hidden in Jinah's shadow used to be high orc bodyguards assigned to protect Fang, the shaman boss of a high-rank dungeon. Even among high orcs, they were the cream of the crop.

Regular orcs versus great high orc warriors? The victor was already decided. One of the high orcs slammed its fist down as if to demonstrate the extreme power gap.

Pow!

An orc's head cracked open with that single blow, and its body flopped to the floor of the classroom.

The students were horrified.

Whoa!

The monstrous beast that had endangered their lives had just been crushed by an even more monstrous beast. The high schoolers shut down at the overwhelming shock and fear they were experiencing—that is, all but one.

Tears welled in Jinah's eyes because she knew what that black armor meant.

Jinwoo? Is Jinwoo......?

Jinah could sense her brother's presence from the three high orcs that had formed a circle around her as if trying to protect her.

"Krrrr......"

The high orc behind Jinah didn't even have to move an inch. The two remaining invaders attempted to run away, but the high orc that had crushed the head of the captain grabbed them by the backs of their necks.

"Grrrr!"

"Grah!"

The dangling orcs flailed desperately to escape, but they stopped resisting as soon as their heads were bashed together.

Bam!

Their foreheads burst, and soon two corpses hit the floor.

Thud.

Thud.

The three orcs assaulting the classroom were dispatched in the blink of an eye. It was over. The high orcs stood in place, silently guarding Jinah.

How many seconds had passed? The other students gradually calmed their racing hearts and exchanged glances.

Wh-what the…?

Did those monsters save us?

Are they protecting us?

The one thing that was clear was that the black-armored orcs weren't going to harm them.

"What about my brother? Where is he?" Jinah asked, sniffling, but the high orcs didn't answer. "Jinwoo?"

Instead, they stopped Jinah from leaving their side.

"……?"

When she cautiously peered up at one of them, the high orc shook its head. Jinah's safety was their top priority. They couldn't let her wander around a building infested with enemies.

And sure enough, the sound of footsteps coming up the stairs echoed outside the classroom.

Stomp, stomp, stomp.

Stomp, stomp, stomp.

The high orc soldiers drew the weapons attached to their waists.

While the footsteps had the nervous students holding their collective breath, many couldn't help but feel a little anticipation at the sight of the high orcs calmly preparing for battle. The kids finally had a fighting chance and were relieved to have such reliable allies on their side.

However, some were also sobbing out of terror, anxiety, worry, and grief.

"Ngh…… Hic……!"

They hugged their crying friends tightly and held their breath.

The footsteps grew closer.

Stomp, stomp, stomp.

All the orcs scattered throughout the school had heard the cries of their brothers and were now gathered in front of the twelfth-grade classroom.

* * *

Jinwoo was picking up on strong signals from the high orc warriors assigned to Jinah.

Has something happened in her area?

"Hunter Sung?" Concerned, Yerim continued calling his name.

"......" Jinwoo pursed his lips and strode past her.

She raised an eyebrow.

What's up with him?

Jinwoo had been completely at ease until just moments before. Looking at his expression now, she thought he was like a different person altogether.

Wait a minute......

Jinwoo was an S-rank hunter who had reacted strangely after looking over his shoulder. Had he detected something they'd missed? Yerim started getting inexplicably nervous.

Hmm? Yoontae glanced back as he sensed someone approaching and noted, "Hunter Sung is coming this way."

"What?" Jongsu stopped walking, and the entire strike squad followed suit.

Why is Hunter Sung suddenly...?

Jongsu casually turned around and swallowed a shocked gasp when he saw Jinwoo's eyes.

Ack!

Jinwoo's mood had totally shifted.

What's going on? Jongsu wondered if he had inadvertently done something to upset their backup, but try as he might, he couldn't come up with anything. *So then......*

Why did Jinwoo look like he was on the warpath? Jongsu swallowed hard at the thought of dealing with such a powerful person in a bad mood. They were in a dungeon, and what happens in a dungeon...

Jongsu decided to tread carefully. "Hunter Sung, is something bothering you?"

Jinwoo was in a rush, so he got straight to the point. "Something urgent's come up, so I have to go."

What?!

Jongsu was floored. The situation was worse than he'd feared. Everything had been going smoothly so far—so smoothly, in fact, that one could question the need for Jinwoo on this raid at all. But Jongsu was no amateur; he'd been working as a hunter since their inception. He knew very well that accidents happened when people lowered their guard.

We must be even more careful, since everything's been going well.

Not knowing what dangers lay ahead, losing their strongest member would be a major liability.

Jongsu's expression darkened. "If you leave, you potentially endanger the rest of us. You understand that, right?" He tried to persuade Jinwoo as gently as he could, as he could tell that it'd be more dangerous to aggravate Jinwoo any further than to face this dungeon without him.

That's how unnerving the S-rank hunter's expression looked.

……

Jongsu felt like he was walking a tightrope as he studied Jinwoo. His mouth had gone very dry by the time Jinwoo finally answered.

"Let's do this, then."

"Right, yes." Jongsu nodded even before hearing what was being suggested.

"I'll summon someone as reliable as I am. He'll take it from here."

Jongsu was keen on the idea. Another hunter—and one endorsed by none other than Jinwoo Sung!

Who could it be? Jongin Choi? Or maybe Haein Cha?

Jongsu recalled spying a document with Haein's profile in Jinwoo's office.

Hunter Cha would be perfect.

Although he couldn't stop Jinwoo from leaving, the tank's expression softened. He'd welcome anyone besides Dongwook Ma from the Fame Guild.

"That would work for me." Jongsu's eyes twinkled.

How powerful would the hunter have to be to replace the one and only Jinwoo? Anxiety began giving way to anticipation. And it wasn't just Jongsu—listening in on the conversation, the rest of the party was staring at Jinwoo with mixed feelings of excitement and doubt.

Without further delay, Jinwoo summoned the most powerful soldier in his shadow army.

Beru.

The Ant King, shrouded by black smoke, answered his master's call.

My king......

Beru emerged from the shadow and, head bowed, knelt on one knee before Jinwoo.

"H-huh?"

"Ah!"

The hunters scurried back, startled by the frightening levels of mana that Beru didn't bother to hide.

"Is that......?"

"How can that be?!"

The hunters immediately recognized Beru as the monstrous ant who had toyed with the S-rank hunters on Jeju Island.

Shocked, Jongsu stammered, "H-Hunter Sung, isn't that the monster ant from Jeju Island?"

Jinwoo nodded. He appreciated not having to provide an explanation as the high-rank hunters instantly grasped Beru's identity. The entire country had witnessed his might.

"He'll be taking over for me."

"What?" Jongsu asked, incredulous.

Jinwoo knew what Jongsu wanted to ask, but he didn't have time to answer every single question. He ignored the panicking guild master and issued Beru an order. *Protect the humans.*

Understood. Beru gave a quick reply and then raised his head. *What shall I do with the nonhumans, my king?*

Jinwoo glanced toward the depths of the cave before giving another command.

Do whatever you like.

The desire to kill that Beru had been suppressing now transformed into a glee that immediately spread throughout his entire body.

SKRRRAAAAA!

Beru stood and roared. His screech rang throughout the cave, making the hunters tremble regardless of whether it was directed at them.

W-we're supposed to finish the raid with this beast......? Jongsu's back was drenched in cold sweat.

Ignoring the other hunters' reactions, Jinwoo then summoned twenty ant shadows to assist Beru.

Skrreeee!

Skrraa!

The shadow beasts cried out at breathing in fresh air for the first time in a while. Needless to say, the hunters were rooted to their spots in fear.

"H-hold on, please!" Yerim's plea stopped Jinwoo in his tracks. "You're leaving? After letting these beasts loose?"

"If you want, I can call back my minions. However..." The icy look Jinwoo gave Yerim sent shivers down her spine. "...if I do, whatever happens to the Knights Guild is on you, not me."

Jinwoo had promised to protect the members of the Knights Guild, but he had no obligation to take responsibility if they rejected his help.

"......"

Jinwoo's firm statement rendered the rest of the strike squad, including Yerim, speechless. In the blink of an eye, he turned and disappeared from the view of the party.

How long do I have left until the cooling-off period is over?

With enough distance between the Knights Guild and him, Jinwoo called up his skills window.

* * *

[SKILL: SHADOW EXCHANGE, LV.1]
Job-exclusive...
...may use the skill after 01:02:16.

Dammit......
Jinwoo bit his lower lip. He had to wait over an hour if he wanted to use the Shadow Exchange skill. He hadn't stopped receiving signals from his soldiers. Jinwoo had an ominous feeling.
I can't wait an hour.
First things first: He needed to get out of the dungeon.
But just as he decided that... One by one, the undead the strike squad had dispatched rose up.
......
Jinwoo glared, his eyes filled with rage. His anger toward these measly beasts blocking his path was immeasurable. But before he could take a step...
......?
The undead magic beasts dropped to their knees before Jinwoo.
Whump.
Whump.
Without exception, all the revived undead bowed to him.
Why are they...? Jinwoo blinked in surprise. Had the undead magic beasts tried to run away from the strike squad because of him? *Is it because I'm a necromancer with an advanced job class with the power to control the undead?*
It was an odd situation, but there was no time to analyze it. After sending the dagger in his hand back into inventory, Jinwoo sprinted for the exit.
The crowd waiting outside the gate gawked at Jinwoo. What was Hunter Sung doing emerging by himself? He paid no attention to their questioning gazes.
Kaisel!
The winged dragon covered in black steam appeared.

Kreeeee!

The spectators recognized the winged dragon from his handful of appearances in the media.

"Wow!"

"Look at that!"

"That's Jinwoo Sung!"

Jinwoo swung himself onto Kaisel's back as the crowd cheered.

To my sister, as fast as you can!

Jinwoo didn't care if Kaisel smashed through anything that appeared in their way. Kaisel roared joyfully at being able to fly unfettered.

Kreeee!

Soon, the dragon flapped his huge wings and was off.

* * *

The final peril was unleashed. Now free to leave its lair, the master of the dungeon lumbered out of the gate.

Chieftain Groctar. Black tattoos covered nearly every inch of its body.

For orcs, tattoos served as records of their victories, providing a count of how many enemies they had killed in battle.

"Groctar!"

"Groctar!"

The other orcs had been waiting for its arrival outside the gate. They chanted its name as they bowed their heads. Groctar's own head stood tall, nearly scraping the ceiling.

……

There was a loud commotion coming from an upper floor. The reconnaissance team had led their warriors on a mission to occupy the humans' castle a while ago, yet the battle was not over. A nervous orc hurried to explain the situation to the displeased chieftain.

"High orc warriors are aiding the humans."

"High orcs?"

Ordinary orcs were no match for high orcs. It was time for the master to step in.

"How many?"

"Three."

Even if they were fighting high orcs, how could tens of warriors from the great orc tribe be struggling against just three opponents?

"How pathetic......," Groctar spat, its face twisting in irritation.

The other orcs shuddered at their chieftain's ire. Five great orcs—Groctar's personal guard—also exited the gate huffing and puffing, unable to keep pace with the chieftain's stride. After confirming they were present, Groctar pointed its chin at the orc that had relayed the information.

"Lead the way."

The orc bowed and started off, the chieftain and bodyguards following close behind.

Groctar's eyes glittered.

Those arrogant upstarts......

It was time for the high orcs to pay the price for disrupting their hunt.

* * *

Jongsu couldn't believe they'd been abruptly abandoned alongside magic beast ants.

"Bos......"

"Hang on, I need to think."

Skkrraa!

Kreee!

Grah!

As he observed the twenty-plus magic beasts—or, well, minions—Jongsu was struck with a burning desire to quit the raid. And that one, the abnormally large one with wings on its back... Wasn't that the monster ant who'd toyed with the S-rank hunters on Jeju Island? The amount of magic power it held sent chills up his spine.

If it directs any hostility toward us......

Jongsu was marveling at the S-rank hunters who had taken on this terrible beast when a thought struck him.

Wait a minute......

Doubts began creeping in. Who in the world was Jinwoo Sung to command such a beast as a minion?

Hunter Sung single-handedly defeated this beast, too, right?

His heart started racing as he got lost in his thoughts.

No, I'm overthinking this.

He shook his head to clear it. Never mind Jinwoo Sung's true identity and how powerful he was. Jongsu needed to focus on whether they should continue this raid with these beasts.

Okay...... Let's say we give up on the raid.

How would he explain that to the reporters waiting outside the gate? Should he say they couldn't continue due to Hunter Sung's unexpected departure? Or that they had to give up because they were too scared of the minions Hunter Sung had summoned for their benefit?

How embarrassing would that be......?

Either explanation would make the guild a laughingstock.

Jongsu gritted his teeth.

Then we keep going.

Minions couldn't be that scary. After all, they were just Jinwoo's lackeys, right? Changing his perspective helped Jongsu relax.

They're just Hunter Sung's minions, so what could go wrong?

As Jongsu looked around with newfound confidence, Beru approached him.

Yikes......

The tank's confidence went up in smoke, and he was barely able to force out a polite "Sh-shall we go, then?"

However, Beru showed no reaction whatsoever to the hunter's voice. He just stood there staring at Jongsu, who wondered if he wasn't being polite enough. With that in mind, he strove to speak even more deferentially. "Sh-shall we be off, then, sir?"

Beru still didn't budge. The longer Jongsu kept his eyes trained on the King Ant's, the more he felt like he was losing his mind from the intense mana those black orbs were radiating.

At that moment, Yoontae approached from behind. "Are we going to press on with these guys?"

Seizing on the vice president's prodding, Jongsu vented his stress on his subordinate. "I said, be quiet!" He barely bit back the words, *Why don't you lead the squad and tell everyone we're giving up!*

He leveled a glare at poor Yoontae for a while, then turned back to Beru and swallowed nervously. He wanted to break free of this awkward situation as soon as he could.

Is it not moving because it doesn't understand me?

Jongsu decided to change his approach and forced his facial muscles into a smile, then pointed to a passageway leading farther into the dungeon. "Front, front."

Then...

Pew!

With the sound of a gunshot through a silencer, the monstrous ant suddenly vanished.

Huh?

Where did the beast go? Beru returned even before Jongsu could start looking for him.

Tak.

Beru raised whatever it was he was holding.

Wh-what's that?

Upon closer inspection, Jongsu realized it was the head of a magic beast—and not just any magic beast. It was a head of a death knight, one of the highest-rank undead magic beasts. The beast's head had been ripped off its body, helmet and all.

"A-argh!" Jongsu fell to the floor, horrified.

The startled strike squad gathered around him. Beru cast an eye over the band of hunters and then shouted at the other ants, throwing the death knight's head away without a care.

"SKRRAAA!"

The army of ants began advancing in perfect unison.

......

Beru gazed down at Jongsu without a word before slowly turning and following the other ants.

The hunters checked on their leader.

"Boss!"

"President Park, are you okay?"

"Are you all right?"

Jongsu looked like he'd had all the energy sucked out of him. "Yeah, yeah. I'm fine."

Physically, he was fine, but his heart ached for some reason. He felt like he'd been mocked by the minion.

It's not possible, but...

There was no way the minion was intelligent enough for that.

In any case, Jongsu couldn't quit the raid after enduring such humiliation. He stood up and dusted himself off. "We need to get moving, too."

The other hunters stared at him in disbelief.

"Pardon?"

"You want us to follow those guys?"

"How do you expect us to do a raid with those monsters? I'm out."

"Me too."

Jongsu sighed in annoyance. Did he really have to spell it out for them? He found the severed head the ant had tossed aside and held it up.

"Whoa!"

"Is that a head of a death knight?"

"A death knight?"

The veteran hunters correctly identified the helmet and audibly gasped.

Jongsu calmly explained. "You all know how valuable essence stones from the top-rank magic beasts are, right?"

The other hunters swallowed hard.

"All we have to do is follow them and pick up the essence stones."

As Jongsu predicted, smiles began blossoming across the strike squad's faces.

He asked them one final question. "Anyone still want out?"

The hunters moved in even more perfect unison than the army of ants.

"What're you waiting for, sir?"

"Hurry up, sir. You'll get left behind."

"Don't just stand there, boss!"

Jongsu tutted. "These people…… Honestly!"

And thus, the Knights Guild's raid resumed.

* * *

Jinwoo kept his gaze trained below. People, roads, cars, buildings, rivers, trees, a mountain, a mountain, a mountain, another mountain… The scenery changed rapidly.

He's fast.

When he wasn't being held back, Kaisel could fly at incredible speeds. Had Jinwoo been an ordinary person and not a high-rank hunter, the side effects of going at such a velocity would have killed him.

Even so, Jinwoo was desperate. The signals from his soldiers were growing weaker. In addition to that…

Stats.

[MP: 8,619/8,770]

Somewhere along the way, his mana level had begun to decrease. This was worse than he thought. It meant the high orc shadow soldiers were being destroyed and having to regenerate.

An enemy powerful enough to kill shadow soldiers is threatening Jinah.

Jinwoo's visage grew grim. Even if the enemy didn't touch a hair on Jinah's head, he was still determined to make mincemeat out of it. His eyes were like daggers.

Faster.

Kreeee! Kaisel roared at the command and sped up.

* * *

The high orc warriors were strong, but they were no match for Groctar, the chieftain of the orc tribe. Groctar waved its subjects aside and stepped forward. It easily avoided the attacks of the high orcs and pulled out the curved blade strapped to its waist.

"Is that all you've got?!"

The classroom was littered with roughly fifty orc corpses. Fifty of its warriors had been killed by these three high orcs.

"Entertain me some more, O high orc warriors!"

The chieftain channeled its rage into its merciless sword swings. Groctar's blade moved fluidly through the air and began slicing through the high orcs' armor.

"Ahhh!"

"Gyahhh!"

The screams came not from its victims but from the humans behind them. Groctar frowned. *Noisy pests.*

They were next after the high orcs. Groctar sliced off a high orc's arm and slit its throat in quick succession, as if bored of this fight.

Shhhk!

The orcs that had been forced to retreat outside the classroom by their enemies cheered.

"Groctar!"

"Groctar!"

However... Groctar's eyes twitched as the headless high orc transformed into black smoke and then rematerialized in its original form.

Is this a magic spell?

The same thing happened multiple times.

"Graaagh!" Groctar let out a furious yell. It'd cut down the high orcs over and over, but the cockroaches kept coming back to life.

I can easily kill them a hundred or even a thousand times.

But the battle would never end. And throughout, the voice in its head continued urging it to kill humans.

Throb, throb.

Groctar had a headache from the incessant nagging. However, it couldn't exactly ignore the high orcs to kill the humans, either.

......I must finish this.

It mulled things over. If the high orcs were soldiers conjured by a spell, there had to be someone controlling them. Over the many battles in its lifetime, Groctar had faced all kinds of magic spells, so it knew very well how to end this dirty trick.

Her!

The female human standing a ways behind the high orcs and holding her breath had a connection, albeit a weak one, to them.

Groctar's eyes blazed.

Is it you?

The beast shifted the target of its ire. Jinah made brief eye contact with Groctar and trembled. She definitely knew something. Groctar went with its hunch and pointed at Jinah while calling over its shoulder.

"Kill the girl!"

Even before Groctar completed its command, its bodyguards sprang into action from where they'd been watching the fight. As they did, the high orcs ignored Groctar and immediately moved to block the guards.

I knew it. Groctar's guess was right. It approached Jinah while the high orcs were preoccupied. "So it *was* you." Groctar grabbed Jinah by the neck with one hand.

"Ah......" Jinah couldn't even scream with the pressure on her throat.

Groctar tilted its head. The woman's neck was so thin, it could snap it with a finger. Could this human really cast high-level spells that made warriors immortal?

There was only one way to find out.

Guess I'll have my answer when I kill her.

Just as Groctar was about to squeeze and break the girl's neck...

SKRRRAAAAA!

...the roar of a winged dragon resonated from the distance.

2
TO THE RESCUE

2

TO THE RESCUE

At that moment, Groctar felt its hair stand on end.

What?

Anxiety seemed to slow down time as honed warrior instincts rang alarm bells in its head.

Ba-dump!

Blood roared in its ears. It would die if it didn't get out of there. Groctar's warrior senses had been sharpened so well that they were like a blade and sometimes acted as precognitive powers—like now!

......!

Groctar let go of the girl and sprang back toward the exit with animallike reflexes.

KABOOM!

There was an ear-piercing bang, and shards of glass exploded everywhere. The orcs guarding the door stumbled back as their chieftain suddenly appeared in front of them.

......

Groctar took cautious, measured breaths as he silently observed the scene in front of him.

The creature sensed an extraordinary energy from a human male Groctar had never seen before, who now stood where the human female had been.

Groctar's gaze shifted to the opposite corner with the windows. The entire wall was now gone, as if it had been struck by a catapult.

Did he enter by breaking the window?

Despite its enhanced vision, Groctar had been unable to follow Jinwoo's movements.

......

The unexpected appearance of such a powerful enemy made it swallow hard. A bead of sweat rolled down its temple.

SKRREEEE!

Groctar looked up in the direction of the roar. It came from beyond the ceiling. Another powerful enemy was circling overhead like a hawk zeroing in its prey.

This could be a difficult battle.

Groctar was feeling uncharacteristically restless, but the enemy ignored the chieftain and its subordinates and moved to check on the female's status.

Groctar addressed its new adversary. "I am Groctar of the Red Blade Tribe!" This was a courtesy afforded only to opponents who could possibly endanger its life. Having introduced itself, Groctar then asked, "Who are you?"

Jinwoo looked up and spoke quietly. "Shut up and wait right there."

The human could speak the language of the orcs? But its surprise was fleeting. None of the orcs, including Groctar, dared to move a muscle at the force of Jinwoo's words.

* * *

"Cough, cough!"

Rubbing his sister's back, Jinwoo thoroughly examined Jinah for any injuries. Thankfully, nothing caught his eye besides the conspicuous handprint on her neck.

Jinwoo frowned. "Are you okay?"

"Big brother!" As soon as her coughing fit passed, Jinah threw her arms around him with tears in her eyes. He gently stroked her hair the way one would to soothe an upset child.

Big brother?
If he's Jinah's brother......
Oh!

The other students finally realized who the man before them was: Jinwoo Sung, an S-rank hunter. They were saved! Students broke down crying as they recognized him. Unlike before, their tears weren't prompted by despair and fear but rather joy and relief.

"Hic!"

"It's okay. You're okay now." As Jinwoo tried to calm his sobbing sister, he extended his senses through the school, but the seventeen people in this classroom were the only humans he could detect on the entire campus.

......

A shadow passed over his stunned face.

Jinwoo carefully pried his sister off him even as she tried to cling fast, then summoned as many shadow soldiers as there were students.

"Go with my minions, everyone."

When the students nodded, the soldiers picked them up to carry them out. Jinwoo made sure to assign Igris to Jinah.

"Go on ahead. I'll meet you downstairs once I'm done here."

Under normal circumstances, Jinah would've insisted that her brother go with her, S-rank hunter or not, but she couldn't bring herself to do so this time. Something about Jinwoo's grave expression unnerved her, so she nodded in understanding instead.

At Jinwoo's signal, the soldiers leaped down through the shattered windows one by one with the students secure in their arms.

The orcs, who had been so close to finishing their hunt, bristled at the sight of their prey getting away, but Jinwoo looked over his shoulder with a frightening glare.

"I told you to wait."

The monsters all froze in place. The thought of going against that glare didn't even cross their minds.

One of the orcs, its face now pale, cautiously monitored Jinwoo's movements as it murmured to its leader. "Sir......"

"Shush." Groctar agreed with Jinwoo. This was not the time to focus on the weak. A hunter stood before their very eyes. The battle to determine who would be predator and who would be prey was about to unfold.

Still… I can't let them go that easily.

Groctar gave its troops a silent order, and two bodyguards mobilized without a sound.

Jinwoo turned around again after confirming that all the students had been safely escorted from the classroom. He hadn't sent them away because he was concerned they might get injured.

These guys are just orcs……

Jinwoo was confident he could take care of them in a matter of seconds. However, he didn't want his sister or the other kids to see what was going to happen next. With no onlookers, Jinwoo could cut loose.

……

Jinwoo's head whipped in the direction of the stairwell outside the classroom. Two orcs that had hidden their presence as much as they were capable were making their way down the stairs. They were going after the students, but Jinwoo wasn't concerned. Igris was with them, and Kaisel was hovering overhead.

The only thing left to do is to get rid of these things.

He softly exhaled, his breath thick with magic power.

Groctar asked again, "Who are you? How do you speak our language?"

Jinwoo ignored the questions and slowly advanced on the orcs.

Groctar bared his fangs, realizing that Jinwoo had no intention of answering. "Attack!"

At the chieftain's order, the fierce orc warriors all leaped at Jinwoo.

"Grrr!"

"Graah!"

From the hunter's perspective, the orcs moved so slowly that it felt like time was standing still. Jinwoo casually weaved through them, crushing them all. He didn't even need to draw a weapon, opting to use his finger. When the tip of his finger made contact with an orc, the creature's head, shoulder, arm, or stomach burst.

He felled more than twenty in the blink of an eye, coming to a stop in front of Groctar.

The orc chieftain could only follow the blur of afterimages Jinwoo left in his wake. Its voice quivered. "Wh-what the…?"

Before Groctar had a chance to swing its curved blade, Jinwoo grasped the monster's jaw in his left hand. The orc chieftain let out a short gasp. "Guh!"

Jinwoo casually strode forward and slammed the beast's head against the wall.

WHAM! The sound echoed loudly in the empty hall.

Jinwoo scanned the area from end to end. The hallway was littered with dead students. It was a gruesome sight, but instead of turning away, Jinwoo took stock of every single corpse. This was to make sure the one responsible for this would pay for its sin.

The hunter's gaze returned to Groctar. "Why?" Jinwoo's voice was infinitely cold. "Why is your kind so keen on killing humans?"

Groctar had already lost any will to resist. Trembling, it replied, "A voice in our heads…… It tells us to kill humans……"

Jinwoo furrowed his brow.

Kill humans?

He had heard something similar before, but at the time, he'd interpreted "humans" to mean "hunters." It was now clear the word had to be taken at face value.

"Then what about me?" Jinwoo posed another question. "Does the voice tell you to kill me, too?"

Jinwoo leaned his face closer to Groctar's so the orc had no choice but to look into his eyes. Whatever it saw in there caused it to recoil violently. "F-for…give…me."

Then something unthinkable happened. The great warrior of the mighty orc tribe began crying like a baby. Jinwoo's simmering rage cooled as he watched the petrified magic beast.

I see……

This creature didn't recognize him as a human, either.

Well, it doesn't matter.

Jinwoo didn't care what magic beasts thought of him. He simply destroyed them because they were a threat to humanity.

Groctar sobbed uncontrollably, shoulders quivering as terror consumed it. "Please...forgive..."

"I'll forgive you," replied Jinwoo. He then summoned the Demon Monarch's Dagger to his right hand. "But don't think the path to forgiveness will be a walk in the park."

* * *

The strike squad from the Knights Guild couldn't help but gasp as they watched the magic beasts battle.

"Ah!"

"How in the world...?"

Could this really be called a raid? The ants easily overwhelmed the undead magic beasts and began gobbling them down.

Chomp! Chomp!

The hunters' eyes popped out of their heads at the horrific scene.

"But will there be anything left if they eat them like that?"

"Right? They're consuming the essence stones, too......"

The hunters were devastated to see such top-tier essence stones ending up in the stomachs of the minions.

Yerim couldn't watch it any longer and sprang into action. "Hey, that's worth a fortune!"

When she tried to retrieve a corpse of a vampire, though, an enraged ant took a swipe at her.

"Argh!"

The soldier's claw slashed Yerim's arm, sending her flying backward.

Whump!

"Ow." She rubbed her sore buttocks and made to stand, but as she did...

"Krrrr!"

...she looked up to see the same ant standing over her. The beast opened its grotesque mandibles as if to bite her head off.

Yerim was petrified. "Ahhh... Ah..."

Just then, Beru appeared and spun the ant around. Exactly as its subordinate had done to Yerim, Beru shoved his face into the ant soldier's, opening his mandibles wide.

"SKRAAAHHH!" A roar erupted from Beru, leaving the ant soldier trembling and unable to meet the eyes of a creature so much more powerful than it.

"Keee..."

As soon as Beru let go of its shoulder, the ant rushed off. Beru then approached the dazed Yerim and extended an arm.

Huh......?

As a matter of reflex, Yerim took Beru's hand, and the ant hauled her to her feet. "Th-thank y—" The words died on her tongue as she spotted a faint-blue light encompassing the tip of Beru's fingers.

"Healing magic?"

Yerim's eyes went wide. The wound on her arm instantly healed when the blue light touched it. Once Beru confirmed the wound was healed, he turned to scream at the other ants.

"Skkrraaaa!"

They stopped their feasting and began moving deeper inside the dungeon.

Yerim quietly mumbled to herself as she watched Beru walk off. "How does a minion cast a better healing spell than I do......?"

* * *

Hunters arrived at the school and followed a mana compass to an upper floor. An incredible amount of magic power was being detected from the sixth-floor hallway.

The leader of the group looked back at the others. "Be careful."

His teammates nodded.

At the top of the stairs on the sixth floor, they discovered the source. "Ah!"

A man holding a bloody dagger stood before an orc he had cut into countless bits.

Is that......?

The leader of the strike squad suddenly found it hard to breathe as he made eye contact with Jinwoo's bone-chilling gaze, but he eventually composed himself and picked up his walkie-talkie.

"Yes. Hunter Jinwoo Sung is here." His eyes swept the scene, and he reported, "All clear."

* * *

Due to the nature of the incident, a lot of people had swarmed around the vicinity of the school.

"My son is in there!"

"Please let me through!"

"I need to see what happened with my own eyes!"

"Oh my God... I can't believe this is happening!"

Had the police and the Hunter's Association not been there for crowd control, the place would've already been overrun.

News reporters who had hurried to the scene once the news broke were busy recording footage.

"Huh? It's Jinwoo Sung!"

"Get a shot of him!"

Jinwoo evaded the reporters and quietly approached someone who looked like association personnel. The staff member tensed at Jinwoo's dark expression. "Hunter Sung......"

"Do you know where my sister is?"

"Miss Sung was transferred to Seoul Ilshin Hospital with the other students."

"......" With a somber look, Jinwoo nodded and walked away.

The staff member let out a breath they'd been unconsciously holding.

When the medics arrived on the scene, the first thing they did was check on Jinah's status as per the association's instructions. Luckily, she was fine. Apart from the abrasions around her neck and wrists, Jinah hadn't sustained any other injuries. Jinwoo most likely already knew all this, as he was the one who'd saved her.

And yet, he's still in such a mood......

Jinah was okay because Jinwoo had arrived on time, but what if he hadn't? The staff member shuddered at the thought. It was truly a relief that she was fine.

On the other hand, Jinwoo pulled out his cell phone with a heavy heart.

Mom will probably hear about this.

Many students had been slain by magic beasts, so of course his mother would be devastated by the news.

I need to let her know Jinah's fine before she hears about what happened.

However, an unexpected voice interjected from behind him before he could dial. "We've sent an employee to your mother, Hunter Sung. She's most likely being escorted by car to the hospital right now."

Jinwoo turned around. "Sir."

President Gunhee Go stood there with a grave expression that matched Jinwoo's. Even if this wasn't his fault per se, it was clear that the head of the Hunter's Association felt personally responsible for this tragedy they'd been unable to prevent.

Jinwoo expressed his appreciation for the elder man's consideration of his family even under these circumstances, but President Go shook his head.

"We are the ones who need to thank you."

Seventeen students. Thanks to Jinwoo, there were seventeen more survivors than there would have been otherwise.

"We continue to owe you a great debt of gratitude."

Jinwoo's smile was bittersweet. Regrets still lingered about how he might have saved more students had he been able to use Shadow Exchange.

President Go's expression conveyed that he had a vague understanding of what Jinwoo was feeling. Nonetheless, he shook his head.

Now isn't the time to get lost in our emotions.

He had a job to do. President Go looked up. "Are you going to the hospital?"

Jinwoo briefly considered Gwangalli Beach but quickly abandoned that thought. His mana levels hadn't changed, which meant things were going smoothly with Beru and the ants.

Not surprising...... It's Beru, after all.

So there was no need to concern himself with the raid.

"Yes."

"Then why don't I give you a ride?"

"That's okay, sir."

"Let's go together. I have something I'd like to tell you."

Jinwoo had initially declined because he'd assumed the offer was a mere courtesy, but he decided to accept President Go's earnest request. "Okay. Thank you."

Jinwoo followed the president to his car, and they both climbed in the rear. Despite the spacious interior, the back seat of the large sedan seemed cramped due to President Go's huge frame and Jinwoo's wide shoulders.

The driver, Jinchul Woo, and Jinwoo exchanged nonverbal greetings via the rearview mirror.

As the wheels of the car slowly began to move, the president of the association started speaking somewhat hesitantly, his expression dark.

"......We might have foreseen this incident."

Jinwoo was puzzled.

Did the association let this happen even though they could've stopped it?

Before Jinwoo's confusion gave way to indignation, President Go took out his phone to share something on the screen. It was a chart of some kind.

"This shows an increase in gates spawning in Seoul over the last six months."

The steady line showed a sharp increase toward the end.

"The statistics are the same all over the world."

The second chart looked almost identical to the first. Jinwoo would've thought they were the same chart if President Go hadn't clarified.

"Gates are increasing exponentially across the globe." He frowned. "However, that's not the only strange phenomenon." He tucked his cell back into the inner pocket of his jacket and continued. "Lately, there have been long lines of people at the association waiting to confirm their ranks as reawakened beings."

The increase in the number of gates and magic beasts paired with a similar increase in the number of hunters to defend those gates… It was as if they were balancing each other out.

Seeing that Jinwoo's curiosity had been piqued, President Go continued, perplexed. "There is a change in the air……"

This was all still his own conjecture, so he ended by emphasizing that point. "But this is just my opinion."

Jinwoo nodded. It was certainly interesting information. No matter who looked at it, it was evident something was going on.

However, there was nothing either Jinwoo or President Go could do about it right this second. Furthermore, this could've been explained over the phone. There had to be another reason the perpetually busy President Go had taken time out of his schedule like this.

"So what is it you wanted to talk to me about?"

The president retrieved some documents from a briefcase on the floor next to his feet, as if he'd been waiting for Jinwoo's cue. "Japan, the United States, China, Russia, France, England, Germany, and even the Middle East…" In other words, global superpowers. "These documents are official requests from countries that want to contact you, Hunter Sung. You've probably already been approached through unofficial channels as well."

Jinwoo recalled his encounter with the American agents from the Hunter Command Center but didn't mention it.

"Truthfully, the Hunter's Association has no right to stop them. We're just protecting your privacy as per your request."

Jinwoo listened to President Go without a word.

"The decision is yours, but…I get the feeling that Korea will have difficulty filling your spot if you do decide to leave."

Instead of responding, Jinwoo looked out the window. While he was deep in thought, the hospital where Jinah had been admitted came into view.

"We will provide everything you need that's within our means."

Nervousness settled across President Go's face as he put away the documents and made his request.

"So will you please stay in Korea?"

* * *

The Knights Guild strike squad followed the army of ants to the entrance of the boss's lair.

Yoontae watched with wide eyes as the ants marched into the lair. "Shouldn't we stop them, boss?"

"……You think that's possible?" Jongsu didn't think he could even attempt to persuade the creatures to pause the raid here to let his team harvest magic beast parts or magic stones. He let out a deep sigh.

Let's just give up on those.

He'd had a change of heart. Their original objective in entering this gate had been to prove to the public that the Knights Guild was still going strong. It would be more than enough to clear a high A-rank dungeon without anyone getting killed or injured.

And without Hunter Sung's help, either.

What happens in the dungeon stays in the dungeon, right? Even if they gave the ants credit for taking out the boss, people would still associate this success with the Knights Guild, not the minions Jinwoo had summoned before his departure. In any event, there would be no way to verify this once the boss was killed and the gate was closed, and Jinwoo didn't seem the type to blab, either.

Having reached this conclusion, Jongsu managed a smile.

It's a blessing in disguise.

But just then… There was a commotion among the hunters in the back of the group.

"President Park, I think something's coming from behind us."

"Yes, I hear them, too."

"Huh?"

Jongsu headed to the rear with a befuddled look on his face. He could also hear several footsteps swiftly approaching.

Did the collection team already come in?

But the experienced Knights Guild collection team wouldn't typically enter a dungeon without orders.

"Oh!" Jongsu's train of thought was interrupted by the sight of a horde of undead magic beasts that hadn't been devoured by the ants.

Could they have......?

He wondered briefly if this was why the ants had been feasting on the undead, but this speculation was quickly forgotten when he realized the beasts' numbers were far greater than his team could handle.

Jongsu urgently yelled, "Everyone, get inside the boss's lair!"

Their only hope resided in the soldiers Jinwoo had left them. The strike squad fled into the lair without bothering to check what sort of horror awaited within.

Once he confirmed that all his subordinates were accounted for, Jongsu barked out, "Block the entrance!"

Yerim threw up a barrier using her skill, Holy Wall.

Bang!

Bang!

The death knights at the forefront of the horde crashed into the invisible barrier.

Sweat beaded on Yerim's forehead as she looked back at Jongsu. "Sir, it won't last even five minutes."

"I know."

The strike squad was already preparing for the inevitable battle they would face once the wall came down, but looking at the swarm of undead magic beasts buzzing around on the other side, they weren't too sure of their chances.

"We'll just have to hope the minions manage to defeat the boss first and then clean up this crowd for us." He frantically turned back to the shadow ants who were facing off against the boss, hoping against hope that it would be easy enough to deal with.

Oh no...

He couldn't help but stare. He knew very well which magic beast the shadow ants were up against; he'd heard its name uttered many times. It was a mage with a pale face and a tattered robe: an Arch Lich, the most infamous undead magic beast that lorded over the other undead.

Just our luck...

Jongsu's face turned grim. He still held out hope that the minions would kill the boss quickly and come to their aid, but their opponent was an Arch Lich. The more likely scenario was that the hunters would finish off the undead first and then join the minions in their fight.

At that moment, Beru approached the Arch Lich. As he did, the undead magic beast summoned over a dozen death knights to surround the ants.

"Skkrrraaa!" Beru bared his mandibles and extended his claws.

......?

The Arch Lich recognized the black steam coming off Beru's body. If it had eyes, they would have widened in surprise.

"The shadow army?" The Arch Lich spoke the language of magic beasts.

Beru retracted his claws as communication was established.

The Arch Lich eyed the ants behind Beru and asked bemusedly, "Why is the king's army attacking us?"

Hee-hee!

Beru let out a sound that seemed to mock the Arch Lich and pointed at himself. "We were chosen by the king." He then pointed at the Arch Lich. "You weren't."

The Arch Lich raised its voice in indignation and disbelief. "Nonsense! I will ask the king myself, so......!"

But before it could complete its sentence, Beru appeared directly in front of its face.

......!

The Arch Lich flinched.

Beru was an apex magic beast created using the life force of an S-rank dungeon boss. Although his abilities had decreased slightly when he was transformed into a shadow soldier, the Arch Lich, the boss of an A-rank dungeon, was still no match for him.

Beru grabbed hold of the pendant around the Arch Lich's neck and thrust both it and his fist into the chest of the stunned boss.

Shhk!

"Argh!"

Beru's hand emerged from the Arch Lich's back with the pendant in hand. Being a former highest-level magic beast himself, Beru was able to detect the location of his enemy's life source—in this case, the pendant.

The Arch Lich shook its head. "No...... NOOO......!"

Beru ignored the screams and squeezed the pendant.

Crack!

"You talk too much for a corpse."

With that, the Arch Lich disintegrated.

Jongsu's mouth hung open. He needed time to process what he had just witnessed with his own eyes.

It only took one blow to defeat the Arch Lich?

One incident in particular had made the Arch Lich so infamous: the annihilation of the Yellow Dragon Guild—a guild that had been quite the powerhouse in China had been completely wiped out by an Arch Lich.

However, their deaths might have been inevitable. An Arch Lich could summon countless death knights, powerful undead magic beasts that also required several A-rank hunters to defeat. Underestimating a boss that at first glance seemed to not have bodyguards could lead to one's demise.

In the end, the Yellow Dragon Guild had failed to close the gate, and a dungeon break had occurred. The timely arrival of Zhigang Liu, the Chinese national-level hunter, had prevented the incident from becoming a full-blown tragedy. Now the story served as a warning to hunters about the dangers of the Arch Lich.

And yet......

That monstrous ant had killed an Arch Lich with a single strike. It was a sight to behold.

Yoontae shared the same sentiment as Jongsu as he stood beside his commander with his jaw on the floor. "Oh my goodness......" Yoontae asked Jongsu in disbelief, "Boss, isn't that an Arch Lich?"

"Yeah, like the one from the Yellow Dragon Guild dungeon break."

"And that ant just killed it......" Yoontae's expression conveyed his amazement.

The other hunters were stunned as they listened to Jongsu and Yoontae's conversation.

"Arch Lich?"

"That's an Arch Lich?"

"And with one punch?"

"Wow..."

Everyone in the Knights Guild was left starry-eyed by Jinwoo's minion and its ability to kill the boss of an A-rank dungeon in the blink of an eye. That is, everyone except the talented healer Yerim, who had been left alone to contend with a clamorous horde of undead beasts. The preoccupied healer was dying to know what was going on behind her.

"What is it? What happened?" Her curiosity didn't last long, as something else shocking transpired before her very eyes. "Huh?"

The undead magic beasts that had been seconds away from bursting through the Holy Wall unceremoniously fell to the ground like marionettes whose strings had been cut.

Whump! Thud!

They remained motionless.

"P-President Park?" Yerim looked at him, taken aback by the sudden turn of events.

Jongsu nodded to reassure her that everything was okay.

Were the fallen undead beasts revived by the Arch Lich's power?

The future had seemed bleak upon seeing the black cloud of magic beasts coming after them, but he could finally rest easy.

"Phew!" Jongsu exhaled as elated grins spread across the faces of the strike squad. They were overjoyed that everyone was going to leave the dungeon unharmed.

"Good job, boss!"

"What did I do? They did all the work."

Yoontae turned to see what Jongsu was gesturing at. The minions silently stared at the hunters as if to ask, *So what next?*

They're kind of cute when they stand quietly like this......

One of the ants suddenly roared at the ceiling for some reason other than out of apparent boredom. "Skrrraaa!"

Yoontae's budding fondness for them evaporated just like that. Instead, he turned to Jongsu. "So, boss, isn't this the same as Hunter Sung clearing this dungeon by himself?"

"Pretty much."

Jongsu agreed with Yoontae's assessment. All the strike squad had done was trail after the ants into the deepest part of an extremely dangerous dungeon. The ants were Jinwoo's personal minions, so it was basically no different than Jinwoo clearing the dungeon solo.

What frightening power......

Jinwoo's abilities were truly as amazing as the Jeju Island broadcast had demonstrated. Jinwoo's minions were stronger than he could have imagined, and the man who could control them as he wished was astonishing in his own right.

"Then Hunter Sung can clear a gate by simply sending those guys in, huh?"

It was a casual observation on Yoontae's part, but the implications gave Jongsu goose bumps.

Wait a minute......

Jinwoo had summoned over two hundred minions on Jeju Island, but that only included the ones caught on camera, making the actual count unfathomable. If Jinwoo stayed outside the dungeon and only sent in his minions...

He'd need mana to summon and control them, so he wouldn't be able to use them all at once, but......

If he could use half or even a quarter of his minions, it would be so much more efficient than any of the top guilds.

Daaamn.

Had Jinwoo's guild been a corporation, Jongsu would've invested his life savings.

"Boss, I recommend we seriously consider joining Hunter Sung's guild."

"Haah… You…" Jongsu glared at the innocent Yoontae. "The proper term is M&A. 'Knights Guild Merges with New Guild Founded by Korea's Best Hunter.' Wouldn't that be quite the headline?"

Yoontae choked a little. "Are you seriously going to push for it?"

"Think about it. With Hunter Sung's abilities and our guild's expertise combined, even the Hunters Guild couldn't hold a candle to us, right?"

There had to be a compelling reason Haein Cha, the vice president of the Hunters Guild, had left the guild to join forces with Hunter Sung, right?

Yoontae brightened and nodded but then pursed his lips and tapped his chin with a finger. "But do you honestly think Hunter Sung needs us, boss?"

Tsk, tsk. Jongsu raised an eyebrow. "Do you think Hunter Sung's guild can operate outside the law?"

"Excuse me?"

"Even if his minions can clear a dungeon for him, he still has to have the minimum number of strike squad members."

Oh.

Yoontae's face lit up as it all became clear. "You've got a point, boss."

"We'd help Hunter Sung reach the minimum head count, and he'd be helping us out."

It was a win-win situation, a surefire way to shorten the time it took to perform a raid while maximizing efficiency. If they couldn't recruit the S-rank hunter to their guild, they just needed to join his.

Yoontae smiled at the rosy future Jongsu had described. "That'd be great, boss…… But wouldn't we be riding Hunter Sung's coattails a little too heavily?"

"What do you mean, 'riding his coattails'?"

Sheesh. Jongsu chided Yoontae before continuing with a grin. "Let's just say we're getting in on the ground floor."

"Whatever you say, boss."

As the two exchanged smiles, they felt tremors roiling the ground beneath them.

Rrrumble......

"Uh-oh."

With the dungeon boss eliminated, the gate was beginning to close.

"Let's discuss this outside."

"You got it, boss."

Jongsu called out to the rest of the strike squad, who were patiently waiting for him. "Okay, team. Let's move out before the gate closes!"

* * *

"You'll provide me with everything I need?"

"Yes, that's right," President Go confirmed.

There were ten Korean S-rank hunters officially on record. The association had lost three of them: Two had fallen to magic beasts, and one had defected to the United States. President Go and the Hunter's Association of Korea couldn't afford to lose another. They would do anything to keep their remaining S ranks.

If it was another S-rank hunter, we might not go this far, but......

Hunter Sung was the one person President Go couldn't lose. His eyes blazed with determination. During his tenure as the president of the Hunter's Association, he had met countless hunters, including his fair share of powerful ones, but none had made his heart race the way Jinwoo did. His desire to keep this man in Korea was as much for his own sake as the country's.

"We will provide you everything you need that's within our means."

That single statement made it clear how high President Go's evaluation of Jinwoo was and showed the veteran hunter's fierce resolution to hold on to him.

"Then......" Jinwoo mulled things over for a bit before asking, "Can you make it so I can enter a high-rank gate on my own?"

"Pardon?" The totally unexpected request caught the president by surprise. "You want us to get rid of the minimum hunter requirement for a raid?"

Jinwoo nodded.

"Hmm......"

The minimum quota for hunters for a raid was a standard safety protocol. The policy was meant to prevent hunters from entering dungeons willy-nilly and endangering their lives. However, did Jinwoo, a man who could defend against S-rank magic beasts with his army of minions, really require such a limitation?

President Go recalled the events of the ant cave and haltingly asked, "Does this mean......you plan to raid all the gates your guild receives permits for all by yourself?"

"Yes."

President Go didn't know what to say to Jinwoo's firm reply.

Is this why he formed a guild in the first place......?

Was it all because he wanted to clear high-rank dungeons alone? There were many strong hunters out there, but none ever considered doing raids quite like this. President Go shuddered as he reconciled the Jinwoo with whom he was sharing a polite conversation and the Jinwoo who'd pushed back the swarm of ants with his minions in the ant cave.

A one-man strike squad......

Those were very attractive words to President Go, as his biggest concern recently had been the large guilds gaining too much influence.

Ba-dump, ba-dump!

President Go's heart sped up again. As he settled a hand on his chest to calm the pangs, he smiled ruefully as he took in the paragon of health seated next to him.

"Am I asking the impossible?"

President Go shook his head. "It's not impossible."

He figured it would be difficult but not impossible, at least not for Gunhee Go, president of the Hunter's Association, S-rank hunter, and congressman. Since it was the one and only Jinwoo Sung making the request, there was nothing President Go wouldn't do to make it happen, no matter how complicated, if it meant the younger hunter would stay.

"I'll take care of it."

Jinwoo smiled at the confidence in the president's voice.

Nice.

That was one thorn in his side sorted.

"Thank you very much."

President Go returned the appreciative smile. "I say this every time, but I'm the one who should be thanking you."

Skrrrt.

The car stopped far from the hospital entrance.

"Until next time, Hunter Sung."

"Yes, sir."

Jinwoo got out of the sedan after a quick exchange of good-byes.

A throng of reporters had gathered in front of the hospital after receiving word that the victims had been transferred here. Taking that into consideration, Jinchul had stopped before reaching the entrance. It would've caused a stir if people spotted Jinwoo getting out of the president of the Hunter's Association's car.

Fame can be so inconvenient sometimes.

Jinwoo shook his head and cloaked himself using Stealth.

* * *

In the chairman's office at Yoojin Construction, Chairman Yoo had fallen asleep at his spacious desk. He slowly sat up, observing the sunlight streaming through the windows. He'd felt his eyelids getting heavy right before nodding off.

Secretary Kim, Chairman Yoo's right-hand man, was sitting upright on the couch facing the desk.

The chairman rubbed the last remnants of sleep from his eyes. "I guess I dozed off. How long was I out?"

Secretary Kim looked down at his watch and answered, "You were asleep for twenty-three hours and forty-six minutes, sir."

......

Chairman Yoo's hands paused while rubbing his face.

"As per your instructions, I was waiting with the intention of taking you to the hospital if you didn't wake up in twenty-four hours."

Was this because of that disease again? Chairman Yoo dropped his hands, stunned.

The Eternal Sleep Disease—those with the illness fell asleep anytime and anywhere but had trouble waking up. It slowly but surely led to their death.

Secretary Kim stood and approached his boss. "There are two matters at hand."

"And those are?"

The chairman wiped away any signs of concern, demonstrating why he'd earned his nickname, Poker Face. His secretary picked up the newspaper lying on the edge of the desk and politely placed it in front of the chairman.

......?

Chairman Yoo quickly and curiously scanned the paper. The front-page story was about a gate that had opened at a school in Seoul, resulting in the deaths of hundreds of students.

Oh dear.

The chairman frowned at the gruesome details of the article. "How terrible. Make sure the company donates money to the school and the victims' families."

"Understood, sir. However..."

His secretary turned the newspaper to the next page, which featured a large photograph.

"I wanted to draw your attention to this." He pointed to a middle-aged woman in the shot. "This woman...... Do you remember her?"

The photo was of the hospital where the surviving students had been admitted. Secretary Kim singled out a woman who appeared to be rushing into the building—a woman Chairman Yoo happened to recognize. "How......?"

He never forgot a face, and he had seen this woman before. She was Hunter Jinwoo Sung's mother.

"Hunter Sung's mother is supposed to have the Eternal Sleep Disease."

Chairman Yoo knew Jinwoo's profile inside out, and as far as he knew, Jinwoo's mother was supposed to be lying in a hospital bed on life support. Yet there she was, seemingly healthy as a horse and walking around freely.

It finally hit Chairman Yoo what Secretary Kim had wanted to share with him. His trembling hands clutched the newspaper.

"Could you please look into this?"

"Yes, sir."

"……Thank you."

Secretary Kim bowed to acknowledge Chairman Yoo's gratitude.

The chairman set down the paper and softly continued. "You said there were two matters of importance?"

"I did, sir."

"What's the other one?"

Chairman Yoo raised his head high and made eye contact. Secretary Kim looked rather uneasy. The man had a habit of opening with good news first and ending with the bad.

He dithered before resignedly admitting, "Miss Yoo returned to Korea yesterday."

And as if on cue…

Slam!

The door to the office burst open, and a beauty with an intelligent spark in her eye entered. Jinhee Yoo gazed upon the gaunt figure of her father with tears welling in her eyes.

"How long have you been like this?"

* * *

A camera flashed continuously as a slim woman with silky-smooth black hair struck various poses.

"Good, very good." The pleased grin never left the photographer's face.

Ka-shak!

He looked up after one last camera flash. "That's a wrap. You were great today."

Suhyun Yoo, Jinho's elder cousin and a good acquaintance of the photographer, bowed with a bright laugh. "It's been a pleasure!"

"Right back at you, Suhyun."

Due to Suhyun's amiable personality, her photo shoots always had a fun and friendly vibe. Photographers initially put off by her spoiled rich-girl image always sought her out again once they gave her a chance.

"Good work today! Thank you!" Suhyun exchanged farewells with not only the photographer but also each of his staff members before making her way over to her stylist, who doubled as her manager. "Did Jinhee call?"

The stylist shook her head worriedly. They'd already tried unsuccessfully to get in contact four separate times. Suhyun pouted at the negative response.

Why is it so hard to reach a girl who got back to Korea yesterday?

Suhyun had been made aware the previous morning that her cousin Jinhee, who was studying abroad, was planning to drop by. Who knew missing one phone call would cause so much trouble? She'd been dead asleep after a nighttime photo shoot when her cousin had tried to contact her, and Jinhee had been unreachable ever since.

Did something happen to her?

No, that wasn't possible. Suhyun dismissed the thought. Jinhee was the eldest daughter of Myunghan Yoo, the chairman of the largest corporation in Korea. The likelihood of something happening to her was about the same as an S-rank hunter meeting an untimely death in a dungeon.

"Can you hand me my phone?" Suhyun decided to try one more time. To her happy surprise, the phone rang at the same moment.

Is it Jinhee?

She frowned in disappointment at the caller ID.

* * *

The Fool

......

Suhyun hit the Talk button and answered, clearly annoyed. "What?"

"Hey, Sis!"

It was Jinho Yoo. Suhyun let out a quiet sigh, knowing full well that Jinho only called her Sis when he wanted to ask for a favor.

"Do you know where Jinhee is?"

"My sister? Why do you ask? Is she back?"

"......" Suhyun recalled hearing that Jinho had been kicked out of the house for defying his father's orders to head up the Yoojin Guild. He really was quite useless to her.

"No, never mind. What's up?"

She figured Jinho wasn't calling at this hour to invite her out for drinks.

His animated voice came over the receiver.

"Sis, how would you like to join our guild?"

What gibberish was Jinho spouting this time? A deep wrinkle appeared on Suhyun's normally smooth forehead.

"Your guild?" she repeated, nonplussed. Jinho's pitch was even more preposterous than his request.

"Wouldn't it be better for you to simply add your name to our guild and have the freedom to do whatever instead of being dragged into my dad's guild to work as some kind of mascot?"

Suspicious, Suhyun lowered her voice. "Why do you need my name?"

"We're short one person for the founding members."

"You're asking me to join a guild that hasn't even been established yet?"

"Yup!"

Jinho answered cheerfully. Suhyun could feel a headache forming from her cousin's unwarranted positivity and confidence.

More importantly...... Who's the third founder?

Forgetting the fool and his ridiculous request, she was more concerned about who would want to form a guild with said fool.

"You sure you're not getting scammed?"

Who else would think to establish a guild with an inexperienced D-rank hunter except a con man?

Jinho's response caught Suhyun off guard.

"Ha!"

She could hear the smirk forming on his face by how relaxed his voice sounded.

"You're not ready to hear who it is."

"Why, who is it??"

"Ha!"

"I'm hanging up."

"No, wait, wait!"

Jinho's frantic plea paused her finger as it navigated toward the End Call button. She brought the cell to her ear again with a grin.

"I'll count down from three. Three, two—"

"It's Jinwoo Sung!"

Jinwoo Sung?

Suhyun's jaw dropped at the unexpected name. "*The* Jinwoo Sung?"

"Ha!"

"The S-rank hunter who vanished without a trace after completely ruining Minsung Lee's press conference?"

"......That's where you remember him from?"

"So it's really him?"

No matter what Jinho thought, to Suhyun, Jinwoo was the S-rank hunter who had put the pest Minsung Lee in his place. It had been extremely gratifying to watch.

"Heh-heh!"

If what Jinho was saying was true, Suhyun understood where his boundless confidence was coming from.

Jinho likes to show off, but he's not the type of guy to lie.

Suhyun pondered her decision for a moment. "Can we discuss this in person?"

"Sure! Do you want to come to our office, Sis? Boss said he'd also drop by later."

"Where is it?" Suhyun, who excitedly jotted down the address on a sticky note she acquired, calmed herself before telling Jinho, "I'm on my way."

"See you soon, Sis!"

Beep!

The call ended, and Suhyun's stylist, who happened to overhear the conversation, discreetly asked, "Are you heading out? You're skipping the staff dinner?"

Suhyun nodded as she rushed to change her clothes and gather her stuff. "There's someone I want to meet."

"Who......?"

"I'll explain later."

The stylist urgently stopped her at the evasive answer. "C'mon, tell me who it is! You know I have to report it to the chairman!"

Suhyun's father was the chairman of a pharmaceutical company. Her father had permitted her career in the entertainment industry under one condition: She had to be accompanied by a chaperone. The stylist was her father's employee, and her duties included being Suhyun's stylist, manager, and aforementioned chaperone.

Suhyun belatedly realized that her confidant would be in hot water with her father if she left without a word, so she turned around and beamed. "Jinwoo Sung!"

The apprehensive stylist could only watch as Suhyun quickly receded into the distance. "The chairman's gonna throw a fit when he finds out Suhyun's meeting a man without his permission."

She sighed and thought back on what Suhyun had just said.

Wait a minute...... Who did she say she was going to meet?

The name sounded familiar. She racked her brain for a minute...then whipped around to gawk at the door through which Suhyun had made her exit.

"She's meeting *who*?!"

* * *

Nope...... Nothing.

Jinho chewed on his nails as he stared at the computer monitor.

Nothing...here and...nothing there, either.

All the posts bad-mouthing Jinwoo were gone, which made sense. The boss had saved the S-rank hunters on Jeju Island, ended a traffic jam by closing a B-rank gate on a highway, and rescued the group of students yesterday. In fact, it would've been odd for anyone to be saying anything bad about him.

It looked like even the most tenacious Jinwoo haters were gone thanks to Jinho's efforts and accomplishments. Not to mention Jinwoo's stellar accomplishments. The rare negative comments on articles about Jinwoo were quickly shouted down after a barrage of replies. This was good. Heck, this was great!

But why......?

Why did Jinho feel so empty inside? It felt like he was slowly losing ways to contribute to the guild.

Tak, tak.

As he despondently clicked his computer's mouse, the office door quietly opened. Jinwoo entered, and Jinho jumped to his feet and bowed with a bright smile.

"Welcome back, boss!"

"Yeah."

Jinwoo looked exhausted, but that was to be expected. He'd stayed up all night at the hospital for Jinah's peace of mind and had headed straight to the office after washing up at home. Just in case an A-rank gate happened to spawn at the hospital, he had hidden Beru in Jinah's shadow.

"How's your sister doing, boss?" Jinho worriedly asked.

"Fine." Jinwoo's reply was short.

His sister had tried feigning being okay, but as her elder brother, he still worried. Her doctor had also warned him that her mental shock would've been tremendous and that they needed to monitor her carefully.

I hope she can brush it off soon......

She was normally such a lively girl. The only thing Jinwoo could do now was cheer her on spiritually.

At that moment... "Whoa, you weren't kidding!" A woman's surprised voice caught him off guard.

Jinwoo turned to see Suhyun openly staring at him. The S-rank hunter raised an eyebrow at Jinho. *So that's her?*

Jinho fretfully nodded.

That's right, boss.

He'd already briefed Jinwoo on the situation.

"I know someone who meets your conditions exactly! Would you like to meet her?"

Someone with a hunter's license but no interest in guild activities who they could still trust.

Plus, she's an A-rank hunter......

Not that her rank was important. In any case, Suhyun's clear eyes and bright smile gave a good first impression right off the bat as they exchanged greetings.

"Um..." Jinwoo had a question for Suhyun before they jumped into discussions regarding a potential contract. "Joining our guild could put you in hot water with your uncle. Are you okay with that?"

"This is much more preferable than having to deal with Jinsung."

"Jinsung?"

Jinho rubbed the back of his head in embarrassment. "She's talking about my elder brother, boss."

Ah yes, his mean elder brother.

Right, the plan was for either Jinho or Jinsung Yoo to take charge of the Yoojin Guild.

Jinwoo nodded. Had Jinho obediently taken over the Yoojin Guild, none of the family drama would've happened. Suhyun was a victim of Jinho's choices in a way.

The rascal's stirred up an awful lot of trouble for multiple people, huh?

Jinho gave Jinwoo a sunny smile, oblivious to why the boss was staring at him.

......

Suhyun inched closer to Jinwoo while he was busy heaving an internal sigh.

"Um......"

"Yes?"

She blushed slightly and had trouble meeting his eyes, as if she had something significant to tell him.

Jinwoo's demeanor turned serious as well. "Is there something you want to say to me......?"

Suhyun faltered, then summoned her courage, her eyes sparkling. "Can you take a selfie with me for my socials?"

* * *

Inside the executive office of a certain pharmaceutical company, Chairman Seokho Yoo, younger brother of Myunghan Yoo, was looking more solemn and serious than usual.

"Are you certain?"

"Yes." The stylist timidly nodded.

"My daughter is meeting with Hunter Jinwoo Sung?"

"Yes, sir."

"And it's not just a different guy with the same name?"

"I had doubts at first, too, but then......" The stylist rooted through her pockets for her cell phone and cautiously handed it to Seokho. One of Suhyun's social media accounts was on the screen.

The chairman gaped at the recently uploaded photo. It was definitely the same face he had often seen on the news.

No way......

Seokho stared intensely at the screen before bringing a hand to his forehead and letting out a loud exhale. "Huh."

"Are you all right, sir?"

"......You can go now."

"Pardon?"

"Go on."

Seokho returned the young woman's phone and waved her out of the room. As soon as he was alone, he turned on his computer to search for articles about Jinwoo.

What Is Hunter Jinwoo Sung's Net Worth?
The Most Coveted Hunter Internationally.
Hunter Jinwoo Sung's Choice Is...?
President Jongsu Park of the Knights Guild Claims Hunter Jinwoo Sung's Power Is "Immeasurable."
A Secret Proposal from the United States for Hunter Jinwoo Sung?
Experts Declare Hunter Jinwoo Sung an Investment on Legs......

The number of posts about Jinwoo Sung reflected the public's exponential increase in interest about him after the Jeju Island raid. Seokho marveled at every article he read.

"Whoa...... I see......!"

After about two hours of focused reading, he leaned back in his chair to rest his strained eyes. His forehead had gotten sweaty from intense concentration, so he dabbed at it with a handkerchief. Just as he was about to light up a cigarette, he paused, put down the cigarette, and picked up his cell phone instead.

Riiing, riiing!

Click.

"Honey?"

A middle-aged woman answered.

"You never call me at this hour."

"Ha-ha! Darling, do you know who our daughter is seeing these days?"

"Excuse me?"

"I think I've raised our daughter well."

"What are you talking about?"

Chairman Seokho Yoo was absolutely certain about this. After all, his Suhyun was pretty, came from an excellent family, and had received a prestigious education. There wasn't a single aspect of her that was lacking. So even if Suhyun and Jinwoo were only acquaintances now, it was just a matter of time before they became close.

"Well, well, look at you."

The voice over the phone sounded baffled.

"Are you sure you're the same person who used to go to her school every year to make sure she wasn't seated next to a boy? You insisted she have only female seatmates until she graduated high school!"

"Ha-ha! Did I really?"

"Who could she possibly be seeing to make you react like this? Stop beating around the bush and just tell me."

Seokho chortled. "You'll be just as shocked as I was when I tell you. Ha-ha-ha-ha!"

3
JINCHUL WOO'S POINT OF VIEW

3

JINCHUL WOO'S POINT OF VIEW

"You want minions to be recognized as members of strike squads? Do you hear yourself?" Junwook Nam bellowed. Congressman Nam had previously been a chief prosecutor, and he was unparalleled when it came to digging up and shredding fallacies.

President Go sat wordlessly across from him. Congressman Nam mentally sneered as he noted the president's silence.

He knows he doesn't have a leg to stand on.

Congressman Nam's victory was secure. No matter how he looked at it, President Go had gone too far this time. The president's lack of retaliation made it clear the old man knew it, too.

However......

Congressman Nam had no intention of letting up. He wasn't one to drive his opponents to the edge of a cliff and not push them off.

He loudly addressed the officials and reporters gathered in meeting room 3. "This ridiculous policy was drawn up as soon as Hunter Jinwoo Sung formed a guild. If that isn't preferential treatment, then what is?"

There was a rumor going around that the Hunter's Association, which was supposed to be unbiased, was acting in Hunter Sung's interests. It was inevitable, then, that this new policy with its impeccable timing would be a strong point of contention. The purpose of this hearing was to weigh President Go's reasoning, but he had yet to say a word.

Excellent.

The congressman could feel victory within his grasp.

President Go's popularity had soared due to the success of the Jeju Island raid, but the recent dungeon break tragedy and the controversy over his special treatment of Hunter Sung had been two consecutive hits to his reputation.

Politics was a battlefield, after all. If Congressman Nam could bring down President Go, the biggest opponent of his political career, he would gain the equivalent of whatever President Go lost. He stared at his rival with a cockiness in his eyes as he imagined himself on the front page of tomorrow's newspapers.

"Please say something, President Go!"

Woooom.

President Go turned on his microphone for the first time that day, tapped the top to verify it was working, and stationed it close to his mouth. "What answers would you like to hear?"

Congressman Nam's eyes narrowed.

Shameless old bastard......

He'd expected an apology, but President Go didn't seem down for the count just yet.

Congressman Nam forcefully demanded, "The new policy you're proposing! Was it established as a special favor for Hunter Jinwoo Sung or not?"

How would President Go weasel out of this one...? Rather than offer some cowardly excuse, though, President Go decided to rain on Congressman Nam's parade.

"Yes, it is indeed a special favor."

It was a short answer, but its impact was massive, causing an uproar among the spectators, reporters, and fellow congressmen.

Congressman Nam was the most surprised of all.

Has the old man gone senile?

President Go should've either denied it to the bitter end or begged for forgiveness, not haughtily confessed his sins. And the veteran politician looked too placid for someone whose slip of the tongue might have just cost him his career and reputation. President Go's calm and shameless attitude was making his interrogator just a tad anxious.

Congressman Nam swallowed hard.

Sure enough, President Go spoke up again. "I will ask everyone one simple question."

He had a commanding presence that was unmatched. As soon as President Go opened his mouth, everyone quieted down and turned to him in unison, as if they'd rehearsed it.

"A strike squad consisting of twenty A-rank hunters versus a strike squad with only Hunter Sung." President Go slowly rose from his seat and locked eyes with those in the room. "If you had to pick between those two during a dungeon break, which would you choose?"

No one could bring themselves to answer out loud, but the choice was clear.

"……"

"……"

With everyone else avoiding eye contact with President Go, he turned his attention to Congressman Nam.

"……" The man also had no rebuttal.

President Go smiled, satisfied with their reactions. "Do you still think that preferential treatment for Hunter Jinwoo Sung is unreasonable?"

Hunter Sung could outperform an elite strike squad from a large guild by himself. He was asking them whether they would chain such a man down with pointless rules and restrictions.

Congressman Nam appeared to have something to say, but President Go didn't give him an opening. "Twenty-one countries including the United States of America, Japan, and China have requested information regarding Hunter Jinwoo Sung from the association."

He held up a thick stack of official documents and waved them in the air. "All these nations have set their sights on Hunter Sung." President

Go's gaze shifted from the reports to Congressman Nam once more. "Do you think Hunter Sung would want to stay in a country that's so inflexible that they wouldn't grant this small a favor?"

"......" The congressman looked rather uneasy. The tables had obviously turned against him. However, President Go had no intention of letting him off that easily.

"I'm asking you if you wish a repeat of the Dongsoo Hwang affair?"

Ugh.

Congressman Nam bit his lower lip as President Go put the documents down, his expression that of someone at ease. The congressman knew what that meant: It was the face of a winner—one a congressman wore when victory was assured.

He gritted his teeth and tried to object. "Still, we must consider fairness—"

"Ah, yes, speaking of..." President Go cut him off. "Congressman Nam, you recently moved to a condominium near the headquarters of the Hunters Guild, did you not?"

Congressman Nam's face turned visibly red.

"Why did you move there despite it being much more expensive than the other accommodations in the area?"

"......"

The congressman was turning very nearly purple, and he looked as if he would've punched the president in the face had the latter not been an S-rank hunter. However, President Go knew better than Congressman Nam how to deal with a cornered opponent.

"I hope you all think carefully about who exactly will keep you safe when another S-rank gate appears on this land." President Go ended his argument with one final statement. "You may be able to buy an expensive condo worth a million or tens of millions, but you cannot buy a life."

* * *

It was Jinho's first time seeing an A-rank gate. He leaned his head back to take in the view up to the top of the portal.

"Whoa......"

The gate was so tall, it was impossible to take it all in at once when they were this close. Jinho's mouth had been agape for some twenty minutes already. Compared to that, Jinwoo's reaction to laying eyes on an A-rank gate for the first time had been anticlimactic.

"Your jaw's about to fall off, Jinho."

"Huh? Oh, sorry, boss. I've just never seen a gate this big before."

How would've he reacted to the gate at Gwangalli Beach? Jinwoo chuckled at the thought.

Jinho rubbed the back of his neck, embarrassed by his obvious amazement. "Boss, are you sure we'll be okay without a collection or excavation team?"

"We'll be fine." Jinwoo summoned thirty elite shadow soldiers who had been with him the longest. "These guys will take care of it."

Jinho started at the soldiers' sudden appearance but quickly caught on to what Jinwoo was saying. "Aha, gotcha, boss."

With their black armor eyes, Jinwoo's minions always had an intimidating aura about them.

At that moment, employees of the association approached the pair. Among them was a familiar face.

"Hunter Sung."

"Manager Woo."

Jinchul, the manager of the Hunter's Association Surveillance Team, accepted a mana meter that resembled a radar speedgun from one of his subordinates. "May I start the inspection?"

"Please go ahead."

Jinwoo stepped aside, and the shadow soldiers moved forward. Jinchul measured each soldier's magic power levels.

Oh my God......

Jinchul's eyes widened at the results. He was thankful his sunglasses prevented others from noticing his shock.

All his minions are at least B rank if not A!

Jinwoo and his soldiers easily passed the safety conditions for an

A-rank gate permit. More importantly, Jinwoo had many more minions at his disposal. If they also possessed similar levels of magic power......

Jinchul's lip turned up on one side.

People who argue whether this is preferential treatment of Hunter Sung don't know what they're talking about.

Jinchul smiled lightly and shook his head before looking up and nodding at Jinwoo. "I'm done. No problems here."

Jinwoo returned the nod and smile. He was ready to start the raid... but had one last order of business.

"Hunter Sung, please look this way!"

"Could you please tell us how you feel as you embark on the Ahjin Guild's first raid?"

"What's the story behind the name Ahjin?"

"What's your relationship with Suhyun Yoo, the third founding member?"

Reporters shouted out questions from the other side of the police line. It was the first raid of Jinwoo Sung's newly established Ahjin Guild, so reporters had been camping out since early in the morning to capture this historical moment on camera. Normally, employees of the guild on the raid would work crowd control, but in this case, the job had been assigned to association employees.

Jinwoo gestured at the masses. "I thought my information was supposed to be classified?"

"We can protect your personal information, but we can't hide the location of a gate," Jinchul answered with a grin. "We'll deal with the reporters, so please feel free to ignore them and focus on the raid."

"......"

As he watched the association staff struggle to keep the reporters at bay, Jinwoo knew who was behind all this. "Please tell the president that I really appreciate his help."

"I'll let him know." Jinchul bowed his head in acknowledgment, then turned and walked away, leaving Jinwoo and Jinho by themselves in front of the gate.

"You sure you'll be fine?"

"Yes, boss." Jinho squared his shoulders with a look of grim determination. "I would follow you into hell."

Jinwoo chuckled at how dramatic Jinho sounded. "I appreciate it."

Jinho was a D-rank hunter, which meant setting foot in an A-rank gate was practically a suicide mission. Jinwoo had tried to stop him several times, but Jinho had insisted on being the porter. The S-rank hunter eventually dropped it.

If it's one person, I can easily keep him safe anyway......

Jinwoo figured Jinho would give up these missions after experiencing what it was like inside an A-rank dungeon. Besides, it'd be nice to have someone to talk to.

"Shall we?"

"Yes, boss."

"Let's go."

Jinwoo and Jinho turned at the third voice behind them. There stood Jinchul decked out in armor instead of his usual pressed suit.

"I thought you left," said Jinwoo.

"President Go has asked me to monitor your raid to make sure it's truly safe, Hunter Sung."

President Go wanted Jinchul to act as a witness in the event there were more objections to Jinwoo's solo raids.

"Are you planning to come with us?"

It was hard to tell whether Jinchul was blushing because he found the armor uncomfortable or if he was embarrassed by the circumstances. "......If that's okay with you?"

The man was just trying to do his job, so why not?

"As long as you don't touch any magic beasts."

"I'm a member of the surveillance team, am I not? I'll only be quietly observing."

"Works for me."

Jinchul bowed in thanks. "I really appreciate this, Hunter Sung."

"All right, then...... Let's go."

With that, Jinho and Jinchul ventured inside the gate, and Jinwoo brought up the rear. As he did, the familiar chime and message from the system welcomed him.

Ping!

[You have entered the dungeon.]

* * *

The raid should have started by now.

President Gunhee Go looked at his wristwatch with a smile.

Had it been possible, he would've liked to witness Hunter Sung's raid for himself, but his health didn't allow it. Consequently, he'd sent his most trusted employee in his stead. He couldn't wait to hear Manager Woo recount his experience.

Oh, but I don't have time for this.

Gunhee cleared his mind of meandering thoughts. There was a veritable tower of documents on his desk. No matter how focused on paperwork he'd been following the dungeon break at the school, the stack hadn't decreased. In fact, it had grown.

Despite his busy schedule, his interest in Jinwoo hadn't waned, either. Maybe someday he'd eventually get to tag along with Jinwoo…

I'm being silly.

Smiling ruefully, he shook his head and began focusing on the task at hand. He remained absorbed in work until three hours later, when a knock at his office door caught his attention.

Knock, knock.

"Sir, it's me, Jinchul."

He had been waiting with bated breath for this report.

Gunhee cheerfully called, "Come in."

Creak.

When Jinchul carefully entered the room, Gunhee stared at him, astonished.

What?

He'd expected Jinchul to return no worse for wear, but the man looked haggard.

Manager Woo was with Hunter Sung of all people, so why is he in such a state......?

Jinchul's sincere plea snapped him out of his thoughts.

"I apologize, sir, but may I sit down?"

Gunhee gestured toward the couch. "Of course, go ahead." Gunhee rose from behind his desk and took a seat on the opposite couch.

Whomp.

Jinchul collapsed on the sofa. Exhaustion took hold as he rubbed his face with both hands.

What in the world had transpired inside that dungeon?

Gunhee couldn't help himself and asked, "What happened? Why do you look...?"

"Sir? Is there something on my face?"

"You just look very tired, like someone who hasn't slept for several days."

"Oh......" Jinchul gave a few nods in agreement. "That is most likely because I am in a state of shock, Mr. President."

"Shock, you say...... Tell me everything. Didn't you get to observe Hunter Sung's raid?"

Jinchul cast his eyes down and slowly shook his head. "That wasn't a raid......"

"...Then...?"

Jinchul looked up with a mix of fear and incredulity in his eyes.

"It was a massacre." Jinchul, the courageous and charismatic manager of the surveillance team, made the proclamation with a trembling voice.

"A massacre......?" Gunhee gulped.

Jinchul replied firmly, "Yes, sir."

Massacre was the only word to describe what he'd witnessed.

Upon the president's request, Jinchul recounted the events without leaving out a single detail. "The dungeon happened to be a naga nest."

Gunhee's eyes narrowed as he recalled details of the beast.

Nagas are......

A cross between a human and a sea serpent, nagas are creatures that prefer wet environments and are skilled in both magic and physical combat. Hunters typically have difficulty dealing with them; not only are they high-rank magic beasts, but they stay in groups. However...

That shouldn't be much of an obstacle for a hunter like Jinwoo, no?

Jinchul confirmed Gunhee's analysis. "......I almost felt bad for the nagas."

"......!"

When over thirty nagas had blocked their path, Jinchul had forgotten who he was with and briefly worried at the appearance of such troublesome beasts. But then...

"Our surroundings grew dark."

To be precise, the shadow beneath Jinwoo's feet had spread out. Jinchul's hair had stood on end as the soldiers in black emerged from the ground. This had been the start of the battle—or rather, the slaughter.

"Hsss!"

"Shaaa!"

"Hiiiissss!"

Jinwoo's minions had jumped out and started mercilessly tearing the nagas apart.

"At least the humanoid minions in black armor and the high orcs showed some restraint......"

The minions shaped like bears and ants had been brutally savage, just like wild animals.

"Some of the ants were feasting on the dead bodies of the magic beasts, but Hunter Sung punished them for it."

A shiver ran up Jinchul's spine as he remembered how a shadow ant had slammed against a wall after a swift kick from Jinwoo for trying to swallow a dead naga's head whole. He couldn't tell if the shivers had been for the gruesome minion or because of the merciless disregard with which Jinwoo had sent it flying.

Jinchul's agitation made Gunhee himself feel restless. "Were the minions powerful?"

"Yes, they were."

They were without a doubt. Whether they resembled humans, orcs, bears, or ants, there was not a weak soldier among them. But one stood above the others.

"There was a minion in a black helmet with a red mane." Jinchul lifted his head and looked President Go directly in the eyes. "Would you believe that lightning struck from its sword with every swing?"

"Oh my……" Gunhee was astonished.

Lightning had the combined destructive power of fire magic and the speed of light magic. For that reason, only highly skilled mage hunters were able to wield it, and even then, it was difficult to use consecutively. Hearing that lightning struck every time the minion swung its sword was……

Gunhee shook his head. He would've found this news hard to swallow had it not come from his most trusted employee. But that wasn't the only incredible piece of news.

"From what I've seen, the minion seemed to be far above an A rank."

"Is that true?" Gunhee's voice rose sharply.

It was unthinkable that a mere minion would be almost as powerful as an S rank.

But Jinchul, who was himself among the top A-rank hunters, declared, "I…highly doubt I could defeat that minion in a one-on-one battle."

If the self-assured Jinchul had reached such a conclusion, then it was safe to assume the minion was an S rank.

"Hmm……" Gunhee leaned back on the couch.

He was aware how extraordinary Hunter Sung was, but he had no idea his minions also held such amazing abilities. It was a pity he was unable to witness any of this with his own eyes. This was a lot to process for someone sitting comfortably on a couch, so how difficult must it have been for Jinchul to witness everything firsthand? No wonder the

A-rank hunter was in such a state. It must have been shock after unrelenting shock for him.

"But then something even more surprising happened." Jinchul wasn't done with his tale. "The ants......went to work."

He blinked rapidly as he recounted this part.

The vice president from the Ahjin Guild had distributed the pickaxes he'd brought along to the ants. They'd busied themselves with excavating magic stones from the cave walls and transporting those and magic beast corpses outside. Jinchul had been mesmerized, marveling at how the ants moved in such organized fashion. They were labor workers incarnate.

"He isn't merely a one-man strike squad."

Jinwoo could attack a dungeon, collect the dead bodies of beasts, and excavate gems, so Jinchul was adamant that it was disrespectful to Hunter Sung to call him a "one-man strike squad."

"Hunter Sung is a walking guild."

The Ahjin Guild vice president had technically been there as well, but his absence would have had no impact on the raid. It was therefore fair to call Hunter Sung a one-man guild.

Gunhee excitedly slapped his knee.

I was right about him.

He couldn't stop smiling. Jinwoo would bring a new balance of power to the world of hunters in Korea and might even make waves on a global level.

"After that, we arrived at the boss's lair."

There was more? Gunhee refocused his attention on Jinchul.

The younger hunter explained that while nagas were normally two to three times bigger than humans, the one in the lair was four times more massive than a regular naga and absolutely intimidating.

"I'm assuming the minions also defeated the magic beast boss in a flash?"

Jinchul shook his head. "He actually dismissed all of them except the worker ants."

"What, why?" The president was dumbfounded.

Jinchul responded. "I was curious, too, so I asked Hunter Sung why he pulled back his minions right before the battle with the boss."

Gunhee unconsciously leaned forward, keen to hear Jinwoo's answer. "What did he say?"

"He said…" Jinchul took his time, as if calling up the memory. "'If I rely on the minions too much…'"

* * *

"…I'll lose my touch."

Jinwoo took a step and summoned the Demon Monarch's Daggers to both hands. There was no need to use his soldiers. All that remained of the beasts were the boss and its four bodyguards.

Jinwoo slammed a foot into the ground and rushed forward.

Flash.

He instantly closed the gap between himself and the boss before the bodyguards could react.

Mutilation!

Dozens of pinpricks of light shot out of the lower half of the boss's body.

Shk-shk-shk-shk!

"SHAAAA!" As the boss screamed and struggled, its bodyguards leaped at Jinwoo, who used one of their heads as a springboard.

Tak!

Jinwoo made eye contact with the extremely tall boss in midair and swung his daggers.

Shhhk!

"Shaaa!"

An alert sounded as his target's head slid off its neck.

Ping!

[You have defeated the master of the dungeon.]
[You have leveled up!]

* * *

Jinwoo was delighted at this notification.

Yes!

A quick spin as soon as he landed took care of the lackeys. Messages continued pouring in.

Ping, ping, ping…!

The chime wouldn't stop ringing.

What's going on?

His confusion didn't last long.

[You have reached level IOI.]
[Your job-exclusive skills have leveled up.]
[Skill: Shadow Extraction has leveled up.]
[Skill: Shadow Storage has leveled up.]
[Skill: Monarch's Domain has leveled up.]
[Skill: Shadow Exchange has leveled up.]

Jinwoo's eyes widened at the stream of notifications.

* * *

Ooh…!

The job-exclusive skills had shown no signs of upgrade despite frequent use, and now they'd leveled up all at once.

Ba-dump, ba-dump!

His heart hadn't raced this fast in a while.

Jinho and Jinchul were the only other humans in the boss's lair, and neither was inclined to question Jinwoo's actions, so he called up the status window without a second thought.

Status window.

Ping!

The chime was accompanied by a complete overview of Jinwoo, from his current level down to his equipped items. He paused at the list of the job-exclusive skills.

* * *

【Job-Exclusive Skills】
Active skill: Shadow Extraction Lv.2, Shadow Storage Lv.2,
Monarch's Domain Lv.2, Shadow Exchange Lv.2

It really happened.
Seeing was believing. Jinwoo was especially overjoyed at Shadow Exchange leveling up.
Finally!
It was an extremely useful skill, but the lengthy cooldown period had been frustrating to deal with.
The waiting period is supposed to change depending on the skill level, right?
Now both the cooldown and his frustration would be reduced. This was the biggest gain from today's raid. Jinwoo was happier about this than leveling up for the first time in a long while.
Let's see how big the time difference is.
He slowly opened the information window for the Shadow Exchange skill as if he were opening a gift.
Ping!

[SKILL: SHADOW EXCHANGE LV.2]
Job-exclusive skill...
...Once used, you may activate it again only after a two-hour cooldown period. Wait times can vary depending on skill level.

......!
A full hour less! Leveling up once had cut down a third of the wait time. Jinwoo couldn't hide his excitement.
One level shaved off one hour.
Assuming this was the general rule, the possibility that the waiting period would decrease to a single hour at the next level was quite high. And if the skill went up yet another level...

Mom and Jinah would be safe no matter where I am......

He was almost vibrating with excitement at the idea, as their safety was of his highest priority.

Jinho smiled at Jinwoo's obvious glee. "Did something good happen, boss?"

"What?" Jinwoo realized with a start that Jinho was standing next to him.

I guess I was busy looking through the stats window......

He spotted Jinchul walking toward them over Jinho's shoulder. Jinwoo laughed to himself as he closed the status window. Although they wouldn't have said anything, there was no reason to make them think he was out of his mind.

"Yeah, something like that."

"I see." Working with Jinwoo had taught Jinho how to read the room, so he didn't ask any more questions. He shifted his attention to the creature inside the room. "Wow..."

This was the first time Jinho had seen an A-rank magic beast boss with his own eyes. It resembled a human from the waist up, but its lower body was that of a sea serpent. It looked huge even from a distance, but up close, it was much bigger and much creepier. Jinho was understandably awestruck.

Now that I think about it, Boss has been through several high-rank dungeons already......

Had he defeated terrifying beasts like this each time?

Gulp.

Jinwoo seemed even more impressive than before, and Jinho was proud to be the one person with the privilege of standing beside the hunter like this. "Boss!"

"Hmm?"

"I truly respect you, boss."

"Huh?"

"Never mind." Jinho turned away, mortified, when Jinwoo stared at him.

Jinchul also appeared quite thunderstruck.

I knew Hunter Sung was powerful, but......

He hadn't expected Jinwoo to deal with a boss-level naga so easily. Any other strike squad would need a slew of tanks, damage dealers, and healers on top of their game to narrowly defeat such a threat. If another squad had witnessed this, they'd hang their heads in shame.

......

Jinchul walked over to the naga's remains and tapped the beast's scales. They felt hard as steel to him. Well-known for their durability, naga scales were often used to craft defensive gear such as armor and shields.

But against Hunter Sung......

Some of the scales on the lower half of the beast's body were crumpled or torn as if they were made of paper. This was the direct result of the Mutilation skill.

I can't believe he had this much destructive power using two daggers.

Jinchul broke into a cold sweat as he inspected the carcass. It was a relief that Jinwoo was his ally.

Just then, Jinwoo's voice came from behind him. "......Could you step aside, please?"

Jinchul was startled out of his thoughts and turned around, flustered. "Pardon?"

"I'd like to turn that naga into a minion, but you're standing a little too close, Manager Woo."

"Oh."

Jinho, who already knew the drill, waved Jinchul over from where he was standing a short distance away.

"S-sorry." Jinchul offered a short apology and hurriedly stepped back, watching with anticipation all the while. He'd seen Jinwoo create minions earlier on their way to the lair, but this would be his first time witnessing the process for a magic beast boss.

Will that gigantic monster transform into a minion of the same size?

Jinho's eyes twinkled as he, too, awaited the result.

Arise.

The shadow answered his new master's call.

Shaaaa!

Black hands shot out of the beast's shadow and eventually pulled its body above the dark ground. However, the minion was much smaller than Jinchul had expected. The new shadow soldier was actually similar in size or perhaps slightly bigger than a minion born of an ordinary naga.

Ha-ha......

Jinchul couldn't help but let out a laugh as tension left his body, his sweaty palms an indication of just how nervous he'd been. In a way, this was to be expected. How could a minion created with power borrowed from a dead body compare to the actual creature? The reduced strength and size of the minion made sense. Jinchul felt somewhat relieved at the sight.

Maybe this is the limit of Hunter Sung's abilities?

Not that this meant he thought any less of the S-rank hunter; Jinwoo's combat power still surpassed Jinchul's imagination. And contrary to Jinchul's opinion, Jinwoo himself was delighted with the results.

[The voice of the monarch has awakened the dead's fighting spirit.]
[Shadow Enhancement successful.]
[The shadow will start with a base level of 13.]

Yes!

This was the first notification Jinwoo had received about Shadow Enhancement since he'd recruited Igris. Was this because Shadow Extraction had leveled up? Jinwoo rushed to check the new soldier's information.

[?? LV.13]
Elite Knight Rank

* * *

Since this was the boss of an A-rank dungeon, it made sense the new shadow soldier was an elite knight rank just like Fang. But level 13? Jinwoo couldn't stop smiling at the number.

He's about as strong as he was when he was alive. Maybe because of his level?

Unlike other soldiers, Jinwoo couldn't detect a difference between the soldier's abilities in its current form versus the original. The small frame hid a powerful amount of mana. He found it strange that there was such a big change in physical size, but he had a theory.

Maybe this is his original form?

Indeed, how could there be such a huge size discrepancy between the regular nagas and the boss? Everything made sense if it had been using a magic spell to augment its size just as Fang often did. Jinwoo's theory was supported by the fact that this naga also wielded magic, though it wasn't as strong as Fang.

At that moment…

[Please choose a name.]

Jinwoo received the usual message asking him to name his new soldier. Jinwoo didn't think too hard and chose Jima.

[Would you like to use "Jima"?]

Yes.

With that, a powerful mage and his infantry of naga became the newest additions to Jinwoo's shadow army. The hunter absorbed Jima into his shadow once the extraction process was complete.

Right on cue, the masterless dungeon sent them a preliminary warning.

Rrrumble…

There was a small tremor, signaling that the gate would close in the next hour.

Jinho rushed over to Jinwoo. "We have to leave, boss."

"Okay."

Jinho took one last look around the lair and smacked his lips in disappointment. "It kind of feels like a waste." Jinho's eyes were fixed on the carcass of the magic beast boss. "We could make so much money if we could take this with us."

With the gate closing soon, they would be taking a huge risk transporting the boss's corpse out of the dungeon. One mistake, and they would be lost inside it forever. It was near impossible to carry such a huge carcass anyhow, but it was harder seeing it get left behind. Talk about leaving money on the table...

But Jinwoo didn't see the problem. "We can just take it with us, you know."

"Huh?" Jinho blinked at him. "Isn't it too big to carry, boss?"

Jinwoo laughed. "It's not a problem."

Jinwoo wasn't sure he had the muscle for the job, but he did know someone for whom it wouldn't be an issue in terms of sheer size.

Come out.

The robed shadow soldier who appeared was the former shaman of the high orcs.

Vwooooom.

Fang gave a bow to Jinwoo, who pointed to the cadaver with his chin.

Begin.

Fang enlarged his body to twice the size of the naga boss's in no time and began dragging it across the floor of the lair.

"Whoa!" Jinchul was close to losing his mind at the unbelievable sight.

Isn't that......?

That was definitely the high orc shaman he had watched Jinwoo defeat during the raid with the Hunters Guild. He was currently twice as big as when Jinchul had last seen him, but physical size wasn't the only difference. Jinchul had sensed a wave of mana from the minion when he cast the enlargement spell, and he was appalled to realize that the beast seemed to have gotten stronger compared to their last encounter.

What the...? Isn't a magic beast supposed to get weaker when it's summoned as a minion?

But if so, how to explain the mana levels of the high orc shaman? Not only could Jinwoo turn a master of an A-rank dungeon into a minion, but he could boost their power as well?

None of this makes any sense......

"Manager Woo, are you coming?" Jinwoo's voice snapped the dazed Jinchul out of his thoughts.

"Oh......"

If shock shortened one's life span, Jinchul's had been cut in half. He had a mountain of questions he wanted to ask Jinwoo but refrained from doing so for fear of the answers he might receive.

Jinchul wavered a moment before he tiredly replied, "......I'm coming."

* * *

The reporters were about to break for lunch when Jinwoo emerged from the gate.

"What? Is he already done?"

"No way..."

Did Hunter Sung really clear the A-rank dungeon in a mere three hours? A fire was lit under the reporters.

This is a huge scoop!

Every reporter with a camera dashed over to the gate so as not miss Jinwoo, but hunters from the surveillance team blocked their path.

"Hey! Move aside! I'm not gonna interview him!"

"Let me take just one picture! I'll hold you personally responsible if I get fired for not getting a picture of Hunter Sung!"

"Give me a break! It's just one picture!"

As the struggle between the reporters and the surveillance team became heated...

Boom!

The sound of something heavy slamming onto the ground rang out.

"Oh......" One of the reporters dropped their camera.

Crack.

He pointed at the gate, paying no attention to the other reporters stepping on his camera. "Th-there......" He was pointing at the enormous beast emerging from the gate.

"R-run! No, take pictures! Hurry!"

"You're getting this, right?"

"Yes, sir!"

The reporters stopped fighting with the surveillance team and quickly started taking photos. Despite the fear of being attacked by this beast, they kept snapping pictures as if possessed by a higher power.

Ka-shak-shak-shak-shak-shak-shak!

Fang was working hard to drag the naga carcass out of the gate. He felt countless gazes prickling at his back and slowly turned around.

......?

Reporters, the police, association personnel, and even pedestrians passing by had all paused whatever they were doing to gawk at the giant.

Fang bashfully rubbed the back of his neck, embarrassed at the attention.

4

OMEN OF
DESTRUCTION

4

OMEN OF DESTRUCTION

A man sneaked into the large hospital. He was on high alert due to the oil canister he was holding. His eyes, usually lackluster, burned with passion.

How dare they look down on me?

He was prepared to die. After wandering around for a while, he found the perfect spot: a hallway with very little foot traffic. He began methodically dousing the area with the oil he had brought.

You think I'd go down alone?

A week earlier, he had been stumbling down the street completely wasted and picked a meaningless fight with a stranger. He'd been beaten up badly and carted off to the hospital. When he regained consciousness, he'd insisted that the doctor stop treating him because he lacked funds.

It was at that moment. He saw the way the doctor had looked at him as if he was utterly pathetic. That bastard doctor... The details of his face had grown fuzzy over the past week, but the man would never forget that look.

He had resolved to get his revenge, which was why he had returned to the hospital. Reaching old age had never been part of his life plan anyway.

After meticulously covering every corner, he poured whatever fuel remained over his own head.

"I'm taking you with me," he spat.

Of course, he wouldn't be able to burn down the entire hospital given its size, but he could at least take a few people with him. If the doctor was one of them, that'd be the icing on the cake, but he wasn't too hung up about it. Gambling debts had ruined his life, but he had no intention of fading into the shadows like others in his situation.

He threw the empty canister away and pulled out a lighter. One flick, one spark, and this tedious life would be over.

"......"

Expressionless, he braced his thumb—and paused as he felt a cold breeze.

A breeze?

He sensed something was off and checked his surroundings. How could wind be blowing in a windowless corridor?

What's going on?

His hand was suddenly gripping the air. He looked down to see that the lighter had vanished.

......!

How bizarre... He searched the floor in case he'd accidentally dropped it, but his search was in vain.

Where the heck did it go......?

He furrowed his brow and looked up from the floor. He caught sight of something huge and black standing in front of him. It was an insect with hands and feet. The man's eyes were about to pop out of his head.

The insect stretched out its hand and covered the man's mouth before he could let loose a scream.

"Mmph!"

Keh-heh-heh!

The insect raised its other hand and pressed its index finger to its lips. "Shhh."

The soldier couldn't let this man cause a fuss, as the young woman his king had asked him to protect was sleeping in a room nearby.

The would-be arsonist put up a fight, but the insect didn't even flinch.

"Ngh, mmmmph!"

The image of Beru's mandibles reflected on the widened pupils of his victim.

* * *

Why level 101? Jinwoo mulled over the sudden upgrade of his skills as he smoothly drove back to the guild office.

It didn't happen at level 100.

He'd been under the impression that any significant changes would happen at level 100, but his job-exclusive skills had gone up a level at 101 instead. He ran through multiples theories and landed on two that struck him as most likely.

The first was about the significance of the number 1. 1 symbolized beginnings, so maybe a limitation on his skill level had been lifted once Jinwoo's overall level had reached 101?

Otherwise……

Jinwoo's expression hardened. Personally, he really hoped this wasn't the case.

Maybe it's because my job changed at level 51……

Which meant his skills had possibly been upgraded after gaining exactly 50 levels. If this theory was correct, his next upgrade wouldn't be until he reached level 151.

……That would suck.

Considering the speed at which he'd been leveling up lately, he was pinning his hopes on the former.

The building where the guild office was located came into view, and he drove into the underground parking lot. Jinwoo was the only one in Boonggo, the Ahjin Guild's beloved van.

Jinho had volunteered to stay behind at the gate to wrap things up. The raid may have been finished, but there was still the matter of handing over the loot they acquired to the brokers. As the one who'd contacted them in the first place, Jinho had wanted to see it through to the end.

* * *

"Leave it to me, boss!"

Jinwoo could practically hear Jinho's voice overflowing with confidence.

I wonder if he's doing a good job.

It was great that the vice president was eager to get things done, but hiring experienced employees might be in their best interest... Jinwoo made up his mind to do so as he exited the parking lot.

Huh?

The hunter spotted a familiar face approaching the building. She in turn noticed Jinwoo as well.

"Oh......" Haein Cha stopped in her tracks, seemingly surprised to see him. She backed away slowly, then turned and fled.

Huh?

The whole situation was absurd. Never mind why she was running away...

Does she really think she can outrun me?

Who did she think he was? Jinwoo's competitive nature flared, and he sprinted at full speed using Flash. Time seemed to slow, but his surroundings zipped by as he darted past. He caught up with Haein in the blink of an eye.

If I grab her from behind or bump into her, she could get hurt.

Jinwoo took a flying leap and whirled around to face Haein in midair. He landed directly in front of her.

......!

Her escape route blocked, Haein faltered. Jinwoo grabbed her by both shoulders.

"Ahhh!"

The chase between the two S-rank hunters ended just like that. Haein couldn't look Jinwoo in the eyes.

Puzzled, he softly asked, "Why did you run away as soon as you saw me?"

"......"

And if she was going to run away... "Why did you bother coming here?"

If Haein wanted to avoid seeing Jinwoo that badly, she shouldn't have come in the first place.

Haein's voice came out as a whisper. "My car is...in the parking lot..."

Jinwoo recalled noticing an unfamiliar car parked there. The day she had visited the office after applying to join Jinwoo's guild, he had teleported them directly to the Hunter's Association gymnasium, and she'd never returned to pick up her car.

I guess she heard we had a raid today and assumed we'd be out.

Unfortunately, she couldn't have predicted they'd complete an A-rank raid in just a couple of hours. As a result, they'd run into each other and ended up here.

......

Haein wilted under Jinwoo's wordless gaze, so he gently sighed and let her go.

"There's no need to run away from me," he told her, smiling. "People change their minds all the time. It happens."

People's hearts were fickle in that they could lose interest in something just as fast as it had been sparked. There was no reason to go out of one's way to avoid others like that.

"......" Despite Jinwoo's reassurance, Haein wouldn't respond or raise her head.

Maybe she doesn't feel like talking to me?

Her mood might have soured after he accosted her.

"Okay, well..."

With that, he made to leave—but Haein hurriedly grabbed the end of his sleeve before he could turn away from her.

"Um......"

"......?"

Haein could almost see question marks floating above the dashing

hunter as he waited for her. After some hesitation and with a great deal
of difficulty, Haein finally managed to speak.

"Could you spare me some of your time?"

The woman who'd fled from him wanted to talk?

Sensing his confusion, Haein hurriedly continued. "Hunter Byunggu
Min really wanted me to relay something to you."

Jinwoo's expression shifted at the unexpected name. "To me?"

Haein's head bobbed. "He had something to tell you regarding your
abilities......"

There was no way. Jinwoo had never met Hunter Min when he was
alive. The first and last time he'd ever interacted with him was when
he had briefly made Hunter Min one of his shadow soldiers. Hunter
Min had bravely fulfilled his duty, and Haein had been saved from the
brink of death in the process. It was thanks to him that she and Jinwoo
could be here talking to each other in this moment.

But when had Hunter Min had a chance to leave a message with
her? Jinwoo had never displayed his power in front of the man; he'd
already passed by the time Jinwoo arrived as backup. This didn't make
any sense.

Seeing the doubt in his eyes, Haein slowly continued. "Hunter Sung,
your power is—"

"Hold on, please."

Whether she was telling the truth or not, it wasn't something they
should be discussing in the middle of the street.

Jinwoo glanced at their surroundings. "Let's find somewhere quiet to
talk."

* * *

Chairman Yoo took the documents handed to him by his secretary.
"These are...?"

"Information from the investigation at Seoul Ilshin Hospital."

That was where Jinwoo's mother had been hospitalized. Chairman
Yoo's gaze sharpened as he started scanning through the pages.

A nurse entered her room in the morning to discover she'd woken up? And Hunter Sung was by her side?

And another point of interest: The hospital had recommended a thorough evaluation of her condition, but Hunter Sung had insisted on having her discharged.

Chairman Yoo found himself shaking his head.

That doesn't sound like him......

Hunter Sung was a filial son who had risked his own life doing raids to pay his mother's medical bills. Yet he wanted her discharged without having her checked out first?

It should've been the other way around.

That meant Hunter Sung had already been certain about his mother's recovery. But how?

The frown lines on Chairman Yoo's face multiplied as he continued to read. Everything written about Hunter Sung was perplexing.

The double dungeon incident, his sudden second awakening, his mother's recovery, and his unidentified ability that allows him to make countless minions......

Too many coincidences meant that nothing was a coincidence. Everything about this was bothering Chairman Yoo, and so he came to a decision.

"I need to meet with Hunter Sung."

"I will send someone for him today."

"No need."

Surprised, Secretary Kim asked, "Are you going to visit him yourself, sir?"

"Think carefully about who the other party is."

"......" Secretary Kim had nothing to say to that.

Vmmm...

Secretary Kim's cell phone vibrated as Chairman Yoo turned back to the documents. "Go ahead."

With his boss's permission, Secretary Kim checked his cell to see a text message relaying some breaking news.

"Sir."

Chairman Yoo looked up.

"There seems to be a broadcast out of Japan. Would you like to see?"

Secretary Kim wasn't one to make a fuss over pointless matters, so if he brought it up, it was a matter worthy of attention. At Chairman Yoo's nod, Secretary Kim turned on the large TV mounted on the wall.

"This is special correspondent Sungwoo Park. As you can see......"

The screen changed to show live footage of Japan's busiest neighborhood.

* * *

Shinjuku, Tokyo, Japan—the liveliest area within the heart of Japan was cloaked in shadows. Everything on the street, from cars, bicycles, and even people, had come to a halt. The only movement was people getting out of their cars one by one. Despite the piling traffic, no one honked or yelled at fellow drivers.

It was as if the neighborhood had become possessed by something. Their gazes were fixed on one thing.

"Oh, shit......"

"My God......"

An enormous gate hanging in the air was blocking out the sky. People couldn't hide their horror at the sheer size, its height rivaling that of a skyscraper.

"......"

"......"

The usual hustle and bustle of the street was replaced by an uncomfortable, almost nauseating silence.

* * *

The atmosphere at the prime minister's residence was suffocating.

Krak!

Unable to keep his temper in check, the prime minister threw the remote at the TV playing the news, cracking the screen.

"P-Prime Minister!"

His aides jumped to their feet but then docilely sat back down under his glare.

"What does the Hunter's Association have to say about this?"

Shigeo Matsumoto, the president of the Hunter's Association of Japan, helplessly hung his head. Since his return from Korea, he had become quite haggard.

The prime minister's face darkened. "Dammit......!"

A terrifying gate had appeared in the center of the capital city, but the association wasn't rising to the task!

"What do you mean, the association has no countermeasure for an S-rank gate appearing smack-dab in the middle of Tokyo?!" demanded the leader of the nation.

Instead of answering his outburst, the others gathered there pressed their lips together and remained silent. Eventually, the prime minister flopped back into his seat, his expression pained like he was carrying the weight of the world on his shoulders.

"Be honest with me, President Matsumoto." His finger pointed at the cracked TV screen. "What happens if it explodes?"

"......It'll all be over."

Just as the prime minister had suspected. He wrapped his hands around his head and mumbled, "I see...... So Tokyo is doomed because of a single gate."

"That's not what I meant, sir."

"......?" The prime minister looked up.

President Matsumoto's voice was stripped of emotion. "I meant, it's over for Japan."

* * *

"Somewhere......quiet?"

But as they scanned their surroundings, both Haein and Jinwoo grew flustered.

Why are all these buildings......?

They were surrounded by establishments where a man and a woman entering together would raise some eyebrows.

Jinwoo ended the awkward tension. "Since you have to pick up your car, should we go back to the office?"

"Oh, that sounds good."

Haein's blush as she slowly nodded struck Jinwoo as cute for a second. He turned in the direction of his office. "Shall we?"

"Sure."

The walk back served as a reminder that Haein was an S-rank hunter in her own right.

We ran so far.

Their brief chase had covered a distance that would take the average person ten minutes to walk.

They reached the third-floor office, and Jinwoo used his thumbprint to unlock the door. He headed toward the meeting room, but Haein lingered in the entryway.

"......?" He shot her a questioning look.

"Isn't it too dark in here?"

Only then did Jinwoo notice how poorly illuminated the office was. This had been happening occasionally because darkness didn't affect Jinwoo's vision up to a certain point. Haein, however, didn't have that advantage.

Click. Jinwoo flicked on the light switch.

His guest looked around the bright office and carefully asked, "Is nobody else here?"

"Our vice president is still at the raid site."

"Are there only two people in your guild—?" Haein noticed Jinwoo's indignant expression. "Never mind."

She was quickly learning that common sense didn't apply to the man in front of her.

Wait a minute. Haein froze. *So we're the only two people in the building?*

She realized she hadn't felt nervous like this in a long while.

It might be the first time since I became an awakened being......

Haein was a cut above most S ranks, so how many men could make her restless? Her heart had begun palpitating ever since the proposal to go somewhere quiet. She let out a small laugh at feeling like a normal woman again instead of an S-rank hunter.

Hee-hee!

Jinwoo watched Haein attempt to stifle a laugh.

Is it that funny that there are only two people in the guild?

He supposed that the situation might seem a bit silly to a member of the Hunters Guild, the number one guild in Korea. Jinwoo shrugged it off and entered the meeting room, offering her a chair close to the door and sitting down across from her.

Jinwoo waited until Haein had acclimated herself before getting back to the topic at hand.

"So what happened?"

The mood changed at his question.

"How could Hunter Min possibly leave you a message for me?"

Jinwoo's expression was sincere. He didn't know much about Hunter Cha, but she didn't strike him as the type of person who would lie to get some attention. Consequently, he was ready to take her words seriously.

"……"

Whether she was trying to dredge up the memory or figure out where to start, it took Haein a while to begin her tale.

"That day……" Haein lifted her head and met his gaze.

Tears welled in her kind eyes, and Jinwoo instantly realized where her story began.

Haein softly continued. "I heard a voice."

* * *

As Haein sank into the abyss, Byunggu's hand shot down from above and grabbed her.

"Hunter……Min?"

Byunggu slowly nodded. Haein had to check several times that it was him, as he was clad in strange black armor from head to toe. If his face hadn't been uncovered, she wouldn't have recognized him.

Haein asked, "Where......where are we?"

"I'm not sure, either, but I do know what will happen if you let go."

Haein was about to look down, but Byunggu quickly stopped her. "No, don't!"

"Pardon?" Surprised, Haein looked back up at him.

Byunggu gravely explained. "If you look down, you may not be able to come back up."

Haein sensed a longing exuding from him.

Could it be......?

Her memories from before she lost consciousness came flooding back. The Jeju Island raid, the queen ant, and the unforeseen appearance of the terrifying monster ant. She'd felt something rapidly approaching her and then...darkness.

"Did I...die?"

Byunggu shook his head. "Not yet."

"Then what about you, Hunter Min?"

Byunggu didn't answer. "We're running out of time, so let's skip the pleasantries."

This was likely his last chance. If Byunggu missed this opportunity, his message would be lost forever.

He urgently told her, "Please relay this to Hunter Sung."

Hunter Sung......?

Haein was bewildered by the change in topic.

"He must be careful of the power he possesses."

"What do you mean by that?"

"I'm sure you realized by now that I was dead once. I fell to the bottom of the pit. But someone pulled me up from the endless darkness."

"And that person was......?"

"Yes, it was Hunter Sung."

Haein didn't know how to process this information. Jinwoo might be a powerful hunter, but how could he revive a dead person?

Byunggu steadily recounted his experience. "But I wasn't myself. I was conscious, my identity restored, but it felt like I would do anything for him...... Like I had become a loyal servant whose sole purpose was living for him."

She swallowed hard as she took it all in. It was clear who Byunggu was talking about.

"It was frightening just how deliriously happy I was by that prospect."

Byunggu looked bitter. "Please let Hunter Sung know." His expression was grave. "His power is greater and more menacing than he knows. He must be made aware."

Byunggu recalled the eerie sight he'd been greeted by when he first transformed into a shadow soldier. He'd laid eyes on tens of thousands—perhaps even millions—of black-armored soldiers lined up behind him, wordlessly awaiting orders from their king.

Just when Byunggu met the gaze of the general positioned at the front of the army, he lost consciousness and opened his eyes to see Haein before him. He'd known then what was required of him—and that he needed to inform Jinwoo about the dreadful power he held. In the short time they'd been mentally connected, Byunggu had seen the true nature of Jinwoo's ability and army.

Byunggu sensed he was out of time, so he yelled, "Please remember that Hunter Sung's army is—"

A light shining from above engulfed Haein.

Byunggu's face hardened. "His true army is—!"

Alas, his cry echoed through the emptiness and faded away.

* * *

"......"

That was the end of Haein's memories, and even those had only recently returned to her in a dreamlike blur.

Jinwoo's expression had grown heavy as he listened.

A soul close to death met a soul of the deceased?

It was hard to believe. Perhaps this was a false memory of some kind created by post-traumatic stress due to coming so close to death?

Jinwoo shared his theory. "I also considered that possibility."

That's why she had waited a few days to mull it over before sharing it with Jinwoo.

Jinwoo nodded in understanding, then handed her his cell. "Would you like to exchange numbers? I'd appreciate it if you could let me know right away if you recall anything else."

Haein nodded. "Sure, I can do that." Her face looked a smidgen brighter than before.

* * *

Japan immediately requested help from the international community. This was inevitable, since they had lost more than half of their S-rank combat power. However, the reception it received was cold.

The international community hadn't forgotten that Japan had ignored the crisis in Korea, a neighboring country, and had stepped in to help only when the problem reached their shores. The United States never sent their S-rank hunters abroad anyway, but even China, the strongest nation of hunters in Asia, turned their backs.

America Washes Hands of Japan.
Will China Merely Watch Japan's Demise?
Second Day of Gate in Tokyo. The Time
Remaining Is......
What Will Korea Do?

The eyes of the world shifted to Japan, and provocative articles were published daily.

Amid the fear and despair, one hunter offered Japan salvation: Yuri Orlov. The Russian S-rank hunter invited them to open negotiations with the Japanese government.

President Matsumoto immediately flew to Russia. Yuri didn't bother meeting the Japanese representatives at the airport, choosing instead to greet them in the living room of his palatial mansion.

"I'm Shigeo Matsumoto."

A haughty middle-aged white male with blond hair introduced himself. "Yuri Orlov. I'm sure you're already aware that I'm the best support-type hunter out there."

They took a seat to begin their discussion. Prior to the meeting, Yuri had requested to be supplied with information about the gate. He started reviewing the documents as soon as they were handed to him.

Time passed, and he nodded as he ran calculations in his head. "Ten billion yen per day, and I'll block the gate as long as you wish."

Ten billion yen a day? The Japanese representatives stirred at the unreasonable fee—except President Matsumoto, who raised his hand to stop them. The Japanese hunters took a seat.

"Looks like you and I can have a civilized conversation." As Yuri laughed, his gold tooth was on full display. "Three trillion and sixty billion a year. That's what it'll take to save your country. It's not like I'm asking for a hundred billion a day, right? What do you say? Pay ten billion yen for your country or give up on your nation because you think that's too much?"

The richest man in the world was officially reported to own a little over one hundred trillion yen, so three trillion yen a year wasn't an affordable price by any means.

But it's a small price to pay for our country.

President Matsumoto reached a decision. "We can pay your fee."

"Good. I'll sign the contract, and you give me the signing bonus."

"Before that......"

Yuri stopped in the middle of telling his employee to bring out the contract and faced President Matsumoto.

"......?"

President Matsumoto politely requested something from the unreserved hunter. "May we please see a demonstration of your abilities?"

When he heard the interpreter's translation, Yuri burst out in loud guffaws. "Bwa-ha-ha-ha-ha!"

With tears in his eyes from laughing so hard, he chortled. "Beggars can't be choosers! You're lucky I'm not asking you to lick my boots."

Two of the Japanese S-rank hunters accompanying President Matsumoto could no longer stand the humiliation and leaped to their feet.

"Gentlemen!" President Matsumoto hastily yelled, but they were already caught up in the heat of the moment.

Bam!

Thud!

The Japanese S-rank hunters were immobilized by an invisible wall boxing them in. They looked like two mice caught in a jar as they exchanged looks of surprise.

Yuri snickered. "Come on out if you can. You won't be able to move one step without my permission when you're in there."

Yuri Orlov was an expert in creating such barriers. The Japanese party was stunned by this display of power.

Yuri sneered and repeated his offer. "I'll block the S-rank gate for ten billion a day, and as a bonus, I'll let these two live. Do we have a deal?"

His gold tooth glimmered under the lights of the room. He had the ability to trap two S-rank hunters without lifting a finger.

I suppose our best option currently is to put our faith in this man......

Matsumoto slowly nodded. "May I make a quick call?"

"Of course."

The next day, Yuri Orlov's name made international headlines.

* * *

Jinwoo called up the stat window as soon as he got back home.

Stats.

His eyes scrolled down past his level, job, titles, and stopped at the list of skills.

* * *

[Skills]
Passive skill: (Unknown) Lv.Max, Willpower Lv.I, Dagger
Master Lv.Max
Active skill: Flash Lv.Max, Murderous Intent Lv.2, Mutilation
Lv.Max, Dagger Barrage Lv.Max, Stealth Lv.2, Ruler's Hand
Lv.Max

Many of those on display had either upgraded or were about to upgrade to their ultimate versions. The maximum level for a skill was 3, and once it was reached, the level would change to "Max." If the proficiency of a maxed-out skill kept increasing, it would eventually get upgraded to its final version. The difference in efficiency between the basic and final versions was huge.

The skill Dash had become Flash, Fatal Strike had become Mutilation, and Dagger Throw had become Dagger Barrage. Advanced Dagger Wielding, a passive skill that had helped Jinwoo handle a dagger skillfully, was now Dagger Master.

Jinwoo summoned a Demon Monarch's Dagger, spun it on his index finger, and let it slide down his hand and into his palm, where he smoothly gripped it. It was almost as if he was performing a stunt.

Tak!

He was having fun tossing the dagger above his head and grabbing it with a snap of his wrist.

It's too bad I don't have an audience.

Thanks to the Dagger Master skill, the weapon felt like an extension of his own hand. Jinwoo looked back at the skill window as he repeatedly threw and caught the dagger.

I guess the only skills I can focus on are Murderous Intent and Stealth?

Unfortunately, Willpower remained at level 1 and was unlikely to ever increase.

* * *

[SKILL: WILLPOWER LV.1]
Passive skill.
No mana required.
You have endless willpower. When your stamina falls below
30 percent, Willpower will activate, and you will receive 50
percent less damage.

Willpower activated only when Jinwoo's stamina dipped to 30, but he couldn't put his life at risk to increase one skill. Besides, he'd dealt with his fair share of dangerous situations even after acquiring Willpower, but the skill had stayed at level 1, which meant developing it wouldn't be an easy task.

The other problem was that Jinwoo had become too strong. Could he even find a formidable-enough enemy? And so Jinwoo skipped over Willpower.

He decided to increase the proficiency of Murderous Intent and Stealth, which had stayed at level 2, since he'd had little opportunity to use them. Murderous Intent wasn't the type of skill he could whip out on the regular, but he could use Stealth in his daily life.

Jinwoo's gaze fixated on the top of the skill window.

What the heck is this?

He was referring to the Unknown designation in the passive skill section. He'd had this since he first became a Player, yet no information about it had been revealed.

I thought I'd unlock it after a certain amount of time passed, but......

Was there a prerequisite? Jinwoo had high expectations, since it had been set at the Max level when he received it. No matter how much time passed, his curiosity about it never waned.

......

After staring at the Unknown skill for some time, Jinwoo shook his head and continued down the window to what he really wanted to check. Right below the regular skills were the job-exclusive skills that had increased one level today.

〖Job-Exclusive Skills〗
Active skill: Shadow Extraction Lv.2, Shadow Storage Lv.2, Monarch's Domain Lv.2, Shadow Exchange Lv.2

I wonder how much has changed...
Jinwoo clicked through all except Shadow Exchange, which he'd already looked at.

[SKILL: SHADOW EXTRACTION LV.2]
Job-exclusive skill.
No mana required.
Extracts mana from a body whose life has come to an end and transforms it into a shadow soldier. Odds of extraction failure rise depending on the target's stats and the amount of time between death and extraction.
Active Shadow Extraction: 590/1,300
Lv.2 Buff: Augmentation: The possibility of Shadow Enhancement has increased.

The Shadow Extraction limit had jumped a lot due to the level increase.
I can summon 1,300 of them now!
If there were enough extractable shadows around, Jinwoo could more than double his army. Additionally, the special Augmentation buff increased the chances for a shadow soldier's level to go up instantly following an extraction.
Like I thought......

It hadn't been a coincidence that Jima, a boss-level magic beast, had spawned at level 13.

What if Enhancement had kicked in when I summoned Beru?

He would've been even more terrifying than he was now.

They do say that there's no end to humans' greed.

Jinwoo smiled as he checked Shadow Storage and Monarch's Domain. The performance of each had increased greatly, and buffs had been added.

Awesome.

Jinwoo closed the stat window, satisfied. His growth as a hunter was slowing down, but the fact that he could still go farther gave him a rush. He wanted to climb higher.

I don't know where the top of the mountain is, but......

He felt elated every time he improved.

Ba-dump, ba-dump!

Jinwoo sent his dagger to the inventory and put his right hand on his chest.

Ba-dump, ba-dump!

He found the sound of his beating heart pleasing.

......But why did Hunter Min refer to this as terrifying?

Jinwoo recalled what Haein had told him a few hours ago. Hunter Min had warned him to be careful, as he possessed a frightening power.

Was he talking about the system?

Jinwoo had also initially feared what was happening to him and the system generating the abnormalities, but the feeling had quickly faded as he got used to the system and started considering it a useful tool. Though it was concerning that there were still so many mysteries.

......

He looked up at the empty space. "What in the world are you?"

There was no reply.

"Isn't it about time you answered me?"

Jinwoo waited for an answer that didn't come.

Inventory.

He took out a shining black key.

[ITEM: CARTENON TEMPLE'S KEY]
Acquisition Difficulty...
...revealed after the allotted time passes.
Remaining Time: 249:25:07

This was an invitation from the system. A week had flown by, and fewer than 250 hours now remained.

What kind of answer will I find here?

Jinwoo was an equal mixture of anticipation and curiosity. As his heart started pounding again, the hunter dropped his hand from his chest.

He resolved to make thorough preparations until the time was up. He grabbed the phone and quickly made a call.

"What's up, boss?"

Jinho answered cheerfully.

Jinwoo got straight to the point. "Hey, Jinho?"

"Yes, boss?"

"Can you book all the high-rank dungeons in the area starting tomorrow?"

"You mean like the time we did those C-rank dungeon raids, boss?"

"Yeah, exactly."

Jinho considered this for a moment before replying enthusiastically.

"Will do, boss!"

* * *

Yuri Orlov, the S-rank hunter from Russia, was met with a huge crowd at the airport when he landed in Japan. He smirked, as the sight reminded him of a swarm of ants.

Personnel from the Hunter's Association of Japan approached him with their heads bowed, as if they were ashamed that they needed to rely on foreign help to prevent a disaster in their home country. Up until a few weeks ago, Japan had criticized Korea for that exact shortcoming, but here was Japan, forced to do the same.

None of the representatives of the association, including President Matsumoto, could bring themselves to raise their heads as they reflected on their past attitudes.

If we hadn't lost those hunters on Jeju Island……

President Matsumoto bit his lower lip.

"Yuri Orlov!"

"It's Yuri!"

Reporters from all over the world started snapping pictures as soon as they spotted the Russian.

Ka-shak-shak-shak-shak-shak!

Yuri smiled widely to show off his gold tooth.

The entry papers were processed at lightning speed, and the first job the Japanese government requested of their recruit was to reassure the citizens of Japan.

Yuri readily agreed. People called him Savior due to the large number of gates he'd blocked to prevent dungeon breaks. He didn't mind the nickname because of the money and fame that accompanied it.

"Are you ready, Mr. Orlov?"

"Of course."

That same evening, they whisked him to a TV station. Everyone in Japan was glued to their sets to watch his interview.

The host asked Yuri, "How are you planning to block the gate?"

"My usual way," he replied, completely at ease. He used both hands to draw a big circle in the air. "I'm going to put a huge divination circle, like this, around the gate."

The broadcast switched to a shot of the Shinjuku gate, then showed it with a 3-D image of a divination circle superimposed.

"And once I pour my mana into it, that'll be it. Whatever's inside won't be able to escape."

However, his explanation wasn't enough to put the Japanese people at ease.

The host tilted his head. "Excuse me, but...are you sure that's possible?"

Yuri's eyebrows twitched. "What do you mean?"

The host took care not to offend Yuri as he elaborated. "I mean...... It's a little hard to believe that only one S-rank hunter can block the S-rank gate."

Yuri smirked. The host was relieved that the seemingly hotheaded hunter was laughing, but the host was still anxious that he'd gotten on the Russian's nerves.

However, Yuri's grin didn't slip. "If I was maintaining it solely with my mana, then yes, it would be an impossible feat."

Impossible? The host swallowed hard. Since the Japanese S-rank hunters had given up on the raid, if Yuri also threw in the towel, that would be the end of the line for Japan.

Yuri reveled in how his interviewer stiffened before continuing. "However, my ability is that my divination circles are powered by absorbing the magic around them."

"......!" The host's expression immediately softened. "So when you say you only need to use your mana at first......?"

"It's like starting a car engine. Once the divination circle is activated, it's fueled by the mana around it, and the circle becomes like a huge, sturdy castle wall."

The faces of the host and the show's crew lit up as Yuri explained how it worked. The Russian's voice was filled with confidence and reassurance. Those listening to him felt their anxiety melting away.

If what he said was true, his barrier would grow stronger as the magic power around the barrier increased! An incredible amount of magic power emanated from the S-rank gate, and with Yuri's barrier encompassing it, the threat would be trapped by its own power. It was like being struck down by its own sword. This barrier would be the strongest ever recorded in history.

Yuri stabbed his finger toward the camera and viewers as he proclaimed, "I will save you! So you just remember who's rescuing you from doom!"

Beep!
The TV shut off, and President Go of the Hunter's Association of Korea put down the remote control, his expression displeased.

Jinchul sat beside him. "What do you think, sir?"

"I don't know." President Go was worried as he leaned back on the couch.

Unlike a certain Japanese man, President Go would never laugh at his neighbor's misery. Of course, he also had no intention of helping this neighbor at the risk of his own country, either.

"I'm not sure whether Yuri Orlov can block the gate." President Go's gaze was shrewd. "But I know what will happen if he fails."

"......I'm glad, though."

"......?" President Go looked at Jinchul.

The A-rank hunter realized how his words could have been perceived and hastily waved his hand. "I didn't mean I was glad this happened to Japan." After a short pause, he continued. "I meant I'm relieved that we at least have a reliable hunter."

President Go vehemently nodded in agreement. No need to name the hunter to which Jinchul was referring; his presence alone was extremely reassuring.

"Oh right, how's he doing nowadays?"

Jinchul handed his superior a printout listing the high-rank gates that had recently appeared in Seoul and the surrounding area of Gyeonggi-do.

"Why are you suddenly giving me this......?"

"Do you see everything circled in red?"

"It looks like about half of the listed dungeons."

Jinchul wiped the sweat off his forehead. "The Ahjin Guild has requested permits for all those gates."

President Go was taken aback. "All...these?"

"Yes, sir."

Jinchul was an elite A-rank hunter and the top dog of the surveillance team, a man whose power was unrivaled in the association except by President Go himself. Seeing as how such a hunter had been shocked by how powerful Jinwoo's minions were, this tight schedule might not be a problem for Jinwoo and his hundreds of soldiers. But why was he in such a rush?

Hmm...

President Go's brow furrowed. Had it been any other hunter, he would have tried to stop them, even if he had to go in person.

I can't imagine Hunter Sung getting injured inside an A- or B-rank dungeon.

Jinchul had said he'd felt bad for those magic beasts, hadn't he?

President Go nodded with a chuckle. "If there are no issues, give Hunter Sung what he wants."

The Hunter's Association was thankful there was a hunter taking the initiative to deal with magic beasts, provided, of course, that there was little need to worry about him getting hurt.

"I think there might be a problem," interjected Jinchul.

"You're talking about the fact that the gates are under the large guilds' jurisdiction?"

"That's right, sir."

There were a total of three large guilds operating in metropolitan Seoul: White Tiger, the Hunters, and the Reapers. Each had a designated territory and took care of gates that spawned therein, but if the Ahjin Guild suddenly started encroaching on their turf, they would have something to say about the new driving out the old.

Conflict should be expected.

The two men came to the same conclusion. However, a smile graced the president's features.

I thought President Go was on Hunter Sung's side?

Jinchul curiously asked, "......What's made you so happy, sir?"

"Well, if you think about it, Jinwoo's new guild has only three members, and just one of them is a fighter. Even so, they're as good as any of the large guilds and disregarding their territorial claims. I find that amusing."

"Ah......," Jinchul agreed. "I feel the same."

"Did the Ahjin Guild tell you what they were up to?"

"They've asked to be allowed to handle the gates around Seoul for one week."

"One week......"

Jinwoo had saved the lives of the guild masters on Jeju Island, so it shouldn't be difficult for those large guilds to make an exception for a week.

The unusual thing is......

It might not seem that way to Jinwoo, but the schedule he'd set was extremely tight for the average person.

It can't be about money......

Had that been Jinwoo's goal, there were better ways. He could've made an astronomical sum had he chosen to work for the United States or China. Even in Korea, Jinwoo could have joined an established guild.

Then why......?

President Go's gaze fell on Jinchul. "Why do you think Hunter Sung wants to do so many raids?"

Jinchul briefly thought about it before responding. "I have one theory."

President Go hadn't been expecting an actual answer, so his subordinate had his attention.

"What is it?"

"Hunter Sung looked very happy while hunting magic beasts."

"He looked happy?"

"Yes, sir."

Jinchul recalled the Hunters Guild raid with the high orcs. Hunter Sung had looked like he was having fun at the time.

"He seemed especially delighted when he killed the boss-level magic beast."

"He finds joy in defeating a powerful magic beast......" Something Jinwoo had mentioned before came back to Go:

"I want to hunt magic beasts."

And that's exactly what he was doing.
What an interesting young man.
And what a great person he was.
At that moment, the landline of the president's office rang.
"Sir."
It was President Go's secretary.
"What is it?"
"There's a call from the Hunter Command Center in the US."
"The US?"
And the Hunter Command Center to boot? President Go frowned.
Why is the Hunter Command Center calling the president of the Hunter's Association?
A superpower such as the United States wouldn't call Korea for assistance, so what could it be?
"Patch them through."
Two seconds later, another person's voice came over the phone.
"This is Adam White from the Hunter Command Center."
"This is President Gunhee Go of the Hunter's Association of Korea."
Speaking English was one of the basic skills required of any good businessman. President Go spoke fluent English, and he was much better at it than Japanese, which he'd used only briefly when he was younger.
"What kind of business does the Hunter Command Center have with us?"
Adam got straight to the point.
"The Hunter Command Center is planning an event early next month and will invite the best hunters from all over the world."
"......Yes, and?"

"We would like to invite Hunter Sung as the Korean representative."

* * *

Before starting the raids in earnest, Jinwoo searched for another guild that could handle selling the different kinds of loot from high-rank dungeons.

We could handle it ourselves if we only did a raid once every few days, but......

In order to stick to their tight schedule, Jinho the rookie vice president needed help, and it would benefit the Ahjin Guild to partner with another guild instead of finding a middleman.

The problem is which to choose.

He considered the White Tiger Guild, with which he'd had plenty of past interactions, or Haein's Hunters Guild, but he ultimately chose the Knights Guild. He'd already worked with them before, and since the Knights were stationed in Busan, their activities wouldn't overlap with Ahjin's.

Jinwoo called them early in the evening.

Jongsu, the president of the Knights Guild, was lying on the couch and laughing at some TV show.

Vmmmm.

He picked up his vibrating phone from the armrest without much thought.

Huh?

Jinwoo Sung (Hunter)

Jongsu's eyes widened at the caller ID, and he quickly sat up and accepted the call. "Yes?"

"This is Jinwoo Sung from the Ahjin Guild."

"Oh yes. This is Jongsu Park of the Knights Guild."

"Do you have time to talk right now?"

"Of course." Jongsu's smile grew wider and wider as he listened to Jinwoo's proposition.

Jongsu had been feeling disappointed that his plan to develop a closer relationship with Jinwoo had been ruined by the new regulations. His idea to combine the Knights Guild's prior experience and Hunter Sung's abilities had gone down the drain. Vice President Yoontae had also been upset by the turn of events.

So this abrupt outreach was very welcome.

"Yes, of course. That's not a problem." A grin never left Jongsu's voice. "Please leave it to us."

Managing loot from dungeons would be a simple task for the experienced Knights Guild. After all, this was why they had a separate processing team.

Jongsu beamed. "Then I'll see you tomorrow!"

* * *

The lunch his mom had packed for him was delicious, despite the fact that he was eating it inside a dungeon filled with magic beasts.

Jinho looked around as he chewed. "Eating lunch like this reminds me of the time we spent in those C-rank dungeons, boss."

Jinwoo laughed. "You might want to swallow before you talk."

"Ah. Sorry, boss."

But Jinwoo understood how Jinho felt. There'd been a time when they had booked all the available gates they could find and had spent the day zipping from dungeon to dungeon. The only difference between then and now was that the gates had gone from C rank to B rank or higher.

And if Jinwoo was nitpicking...

......

Igris noticed him staring and politely bowed.

We have a lookout while we eat.

Not that Jinwoo needed someone to watch out for him. Thanks to his high perception stat, Jinwoo could sense movements in the dungeon even if he wasn't paying attention, which meant he could deal with a magic beast nearby with his eyes closed. However, he preferred not having his meal interrupted, and wanting Jinho to feel at ease, he posted guards during mealtimes.

Jinwoo looked in the other direction.

......

Iron met his master's gaze and pounded his chest hard, as if to indicate that he had things under control.

Klung, klung!

The sound of metal hitting metal echoed throughout the cave. Jinwoo shook his head.

That dude's problem is he's too intense.

Jinho glanced toward the source of the commotion and suddenly asked a question. "Boss?"

"Yeah?"

"Your minions can move on their own, right?"

"Yeah, something like that."

Hunter Min had mentioned something about shadow soldiers having their own identities.

I don't know how much of that I should believe, though.

Jinho went on. "So why not let your minions continue the raid while we eat or when you're otherwise preoccupied, boss?"

"No, I can't do that."

Jinwoo earned fewer experience points the farther he was from his soldiers, but as he wasn't about to bother explaining stuff like "experience points" to Jinho, he put on a serious expression.

"Who knows what they'll get up to if I'm not around?"

"Oh!"

Jinwoo could almost hear Jinho's stomach drop as the vice president lost his appetite. But that was enough joking around.

Should I try out this skill now?

Jinwoo finished his lunch and laid down his spoon.

* * *

[SKILL: SHADOW STORAGE LV.2]
Job-exclusive skill.
No mana required.
Shadow soldiers can be stored by absorbing them into the
caster's shadow.
Stored soldiers can be summoned or reabsorbed at any time.
Number of shadows stored: 840/840
Lv. 2 Buff: Sensory Sharing: A stored shadow soldier can share
their senses with the host.

The buff Sensory Sharing had been added to the Shadow Storage skill. It was a unique ability that allowed a soldier to relay its senses to the caster, so it was quite handy for checking on a situation from a distance.

Jinwoo closed his eyes.

Sensory Sharing.

He felt linked to the shadow soldiers outside the dungeon that were located throughout Korea.

I spread out quite a lot of them.

Jinwoo picked one at random. It happened to be the shadow soldier he had placed with Haein.

Ffsshhh.

He heard water hitting the floor.

It's not raining, so what's the water sound......?

His confusion was short-lived, and his eyes shot open as soon as he caught sight of Haein's naked body surrounded by steam.

Jinho flinched at Jinwoo's reaction. "Boss? Did you nod off for a bit?"

"......No, it's nothing." Jinwoo shook his head. He briefly considered taking Haein out for dinner sometime as an apology.

"Oh, hey, boss. Did you hear?"

"About what?"

"You know, the S-rank gate in Shinjuku. People are expecting there to be a dungeon break there tomorrow."

Time had flown by…

Jinwoo nodded.

It's already been six days since we started raiding these high-rank dungeons.

During that time, Jinwoo hadn't been twiddling his thumbs. Slowly but surely, he had gathered experience points, and he'd advanced from 101 to 103 as a result. That was his reward for dropping everything and focusing solely on leveling up.

Jinwoo called up the black key from inventory.

Fshhh.

It appeared in the palm of his hand.

[ITEM: CARTENON TEMPLE'S KEY]
Acquisition Difficulty…
…revealed after the allotted time passes.
Remaining Time: 26:51:49

Just one day left.

Jinwoo gripped the key tightly. His heart fluttered whenever he laid eyes on it.

"Stop."

"Huh?" Jinho, who had kept sneaking peeks at Igris and Iron because of Jinwoo's little prank, jumped in surprise.

"Not you."

The shadow soldiers stopped in their tracks at Jinwoo's command.

"Grrrrr…"

"Grawrrrr."

Fanged beasts carrying weapons, such as sickles and swords, emerged from the other side of the cave. Jinwoo slowly rose to his feet as he stared them down.

Just one more day.

I still have twenty-four hours.

He smirked as he wrapped his hand around a Demon Monarch's Dagger.

* * *

The night before the dungeon break, a huge divination circle encompassed Shinjuku, courtesy of Yuri. No one had ever seen such a massive circle before.

Citizens had already been evacuated from the area, but Yuri had stayed behind to perform final checks on the barrier. The Japanese personnel watched the hunter nervously, paying attention to his every word and action.

Yuri rubbed his chin and frowned. "……This is weird."

The interpreter's eyes widened. "Huh? Was there an error?"

"No, it's not that."

The barrier had been perfectly cast. Yuri was certain this would be the pinnacle of his abilities.

"I can sense someone in the vicinity."

"What?"

Why else would his heart be beating so fast? Yuri scanned the area and yelled at the top of his lungs. "Who are you? Where are you hiding?"

But there was no answer to his voice ringing through the empty streets.

"……"

The staff member wiped the sweat from his forehead and forced a smile. "There shouldn't be anyone left, since the dungeon break is tomorrow, right?"

The Russian sneered at him. "I didn't say it was a human, did I?"

"I beg your pardon?"

Yuri cast a pitying glare at the pale Japanese man before turning away. "Maybe it was just my imagination……?"

But at the same time, a hooded man watched the Russian from atop a tall building in the distance.

He's very perceptive.

Considering where Yuri's power originated, it made sense.

The onlooker's gaze shifted to the more important matter: the S-rank gate. A silent, unpleasant energy encircled it.

......

The man removed his hood, revealing an Asian male in his late thirties. His bushy, unkempt beard gave away his identity. It was Ilhwan Sung.

He regarded the gate with regret before flipping his hood back up.

Finally...it begins.

Everything was progressing as planned.

5

THE ONE TRYING
TO ENTER AND THE
ONES TRYING TO LEAVE

5

THE ONE TRYING
TO ENTER AND THE
ONES TRYING TO LEAVE

Reporters from all over the world flocked to Japan. Most were war correspondents who had experience on the battlefield, proving that covering this story was much like setting foot inside a war zone.

Security around the gate was tight. The reporters aimed their cameras toward the divination circle encompassing the massive gate and the surrounding army. The tension in the air was palpable, and it felt like the peace could get shattered at any moment.

William Bell, a famous English war correspondent, was there with his assistant, who swallowed hard before posing a question. "The most advanced firearms don't work on magic beasts, so why is the military here?"

William took pictures of the soldiers' resolute expressions as he replied, "To buy some time."

"What?"

"They'll draw attention to themselves to buy time for hunters to prepare their attack. They'll also be bait, so people like us and the higher-ups watching can escape."

Ka-shak!

The next picture he took was of Shigeo Matsumoto, president of the Hunter's Association of Japan. He looked grim as he stood near the gate, discussing things with other officials.

Well, I guess there's nothing to smile about here.

Ka-shak!

"You mean......?" The inexperienced assistant looked apprehensive. "They're...human shields?"

"Hey, don't knock it."

"Huh?"

"You're here as my human shield."

"Excuse me?" The assistant was flabbergasted.

William elbowed him in the ribs. "Loosen up. You'll get yourself killed if you're this tense."

He winked, and the young man sighed in relief.

I can't believe Mr. Bell can even joke at a time like this......

The novice reporter was able to center himself after seeing how relaxed his mentor was. However, he also knew that William made light of a situation only during the darkest times.

The young man craned his neck to look up at the gate. "What's going to come out?"

William's finger paused on the shutter button and followed his assistant's gaze.

The gate was huge to the point where it overwhelmed everyone. Ever since gates began appearing, they had become secondary battlefields for war correspondents, which meant that William had covered many at this point. He had even once covered a dungeon break, but......

The one above him was on a different level. Just looking at it made him begin to sweat.

No wonder they didn't bother sending in a reconnaissance team.

None of the high-rank hunters had dared to step foot in the dungeon, even for a short time, so the magic beasts it contained were a mystery.

William eventually murmured, "I don't know what will come out of there, but..." He smiled bitterly. "I hope Yuri Orlov's force field is strong enough to hold it back."

Lastly, his camera focused on Yuri, who was inspecting his barrier.

The Russian was beaming. "Excellent. It's perfect."

Yuri had absolute confidence in his creation; his barrier was impressive.

On top of that, due to fear of public backlash, President Matsumoto had kept it a secret that he was paying the Russian, so the Japanese people were under the impression that Yuri had taken this job out of the goodness of his heart. As a result, the people of Japan had donated a huge sum of money for his sake.

The best part was that he was now a media darling. Dozens of reporters had risked their lives to come to this perilous place and cover Yuri's story.

He'd amassed fame and fortune, everything Yuri loved, from just one job.

He emphasized once more, "It's perfect!"

Today he would go down in history as the first man to block an S-rank gate all by himself.

I would've liked the title of the first man to clear an S-rank gate by himself, but no matter.

Unfortunately, that title had already been claimed by another hunter. He was a brawler, and Yuri was a support-type hunter, making it apples and oranges. Yuri was satisfied with being the best in his field.

That's right!

The cocky Russian pulled a flask out of his inner pocket. A strong whiff of alcohol came from the container.

"M-Mr. Orlov! You can't drink—!" The association employee in charge of handling the star hunter tried to stop him, but Yuri shot him a glare.

"I'm having a celebratory drink! A toast! Relax, you're about to witness the best show ever."

"B-but still……"

"Want a sip? It'll calm your nerves."

President Matsumoto frowned as Yuri slung an arm around the handler's shoulders and nudged the flask at him.

I can't believe the fate of Japan is in the hands of a man like that.

He tutted and turned to his secretary. "How many S-rank hunters are on standby?"

"Three in total, sir."

"Three, huh......?"

Only three S-rank hunters out of more than ten had responded to the association's call. President Matsumoto's wrinkles deepened. His influence among the hunters was at an all-time low following the disaster at Jeju Island. Some even blamed his greed for the deaths of the S-rank hunters.

Most of the remaining S ranks had turned their backs on him, with some even proclaiming that they wouldn't heed the association's orders as long as he remained president.

If only Ryuji were still with me......

President Matsumoto's fists trembled. Ryuji Goto used to be his right-hand man, and his death had been an incredibly painful loss.

But because of what happened......

What happened today would be extremely important. If the S-rank gate could be successfully blocked by the efforts of the Hunter's Association, he would redeem himself.

Gunhee Go...and Jinwoo Sung.

And someday, Matsumoto might be able to return the humiliation he'd faced at the hands of those two.

No matter what it takes......

It had to happen.

President Matsumoto solemnly watched the gate.

His secretary checked the time and whispered to him, "Three minutes before the dungeon break, sir."

"Got it," acknowledged President Matsumoto.

Countless thoughts flew through his mind as he stared at the hole in the sky.

Two minutes, one minute and fifty-nine seconds, fifty-eight seconds...... Time flew by like an arrow shot from a bow, until the black membrane blocking the entrance finally began fading.

The reporters shouted.

"Ah…!"

"The gate is open!"

"H-here they come……!"

* * *

"Jinwoo."

Jinwoo had tried to sneak out, but he obediently sat back down.

"Hmm?"

His mother looked over her shoulder from the TV to him.

The S-rank gate in Japan was all over the news, and most networks were counting down to the dungeon break.

"You're not heading out somewhere, are you?"

Sometimes, a mother's intuition was sharper than a high-rank hunter's perception.

Guilt pricked at him, but Jinwoo answered nonchalantly. "I made plans with someone."

"Plans? On a day like this?"

"I made them a while back. I didn't cancel them, since the gate is in Japan, so it has nothing to do with me."

His mother eyed him suspiciously, but Jinwoo wasn't technically lying.

I kind of made a previous engagement with the system.

Kyunghye stared at him for a moment before asking, "So I don't have to be worried?"

Jinwoo responded firmly. "No, you don't."

He'd been strengthening himself to avoid just that.

Seeing the confidence in her son's eyes, Kyunghye finally cracked a smile. "All right. Stay safe."

Jinwoo returned her smile. "I'm off."

With that, he left the apartment. Their unit was located on the ninth floor, and for the first time, Jinwoo realized how slow the elevator was. He was feeling impatient because he was excited to see what kind of dungeon the black key would open.

Ding!

The elevator doors opened on the first floor, and a middle-aged man whom Jinwoo had never seen before made eye contact with him. Apparently, the man had no idea an S-rank hunter lived in the building, because his eyes widened as he recognized Jinwoo.

"Huh?"

Jinwoo walked past him and put up his hood. His steps quickened, fueled by his eagerness. Once he was outside the apartment complex, he checked his surroundings.

Maybe it's because of the gate in Japan?

The streets were dead, so Jinwoo was able to take his time checking on the black key without worrying about prying eyes.

[ITEM: CARTENON TEMPLE'S KEY]
Acquisition Difficulty: ??
Category: Key
The required conditions have been fulfilled.
This key unlocks the entrance to the Cartenon Temple. You can use it at the designated gate.
The location of the designated gate will be revealed after the allotted time passes.
Remaining Time: 00:01:02

Just over a minute left.

......*It's almost time.*

His heart started fluttering.

Ba-dump, ba-dump!

He spent the final minute listening to his heartbeat. There was no need to check the time. Due to his extreme training, his mental clock was more accurate than any timepiece in the world.

......*3, 2, 1.*

Jinwoo opened his eyes after exactly one minute.

Beep.

* * *

[Remaining Time: 00:00:00]
[The location of the designated gate will be revealed.]

Jinwoo startled.

But that's......?

The location of the gate indicated by the system wasn't far from him. In fact, it was somewhere familiar. Using his hunter-issue phone to access the association's website, he searched it up, and sure enough, there was a recent record of a gate appearing there. Who knew that would be where Jinwoo could use the key?

It felt like someone had pulled the rug out from under him.

I misunderstood the description.

The system hadn't misinformed him. It had said the location of the gate would be revealed, but it never mentioned that a new gate would spawn.

Jinwoo kind of felt like he'd been tricked.

His fingers were a blur over the phone screen. The records indicated that a guild had already started a raid, and measurements indicated it to be a C-rank gate.

It's not high rank, but......

The problem was that no one knew what was hidden inside.

Good thing it's nearby.

The gate was ten minutes away by car, and if he ran at full speed, he could get there in sixty seconds. He turned invisible using Stealth and sprinted to his destination using Flash.

The location was the yard at Jinah's high school. Since the school was temporarily closed subsequent to the orc episode, it was unlikely that any civilians were in harm's way.

But the strike squad is in danger.

Jinwoo recalled the first time he had ventured into the underground temple. It had been one horror after another with multiple near-death experiences.

And yet… The memories were frightening and traumatic to be sure, but they also made Jinwoo's heart race. Ironically, the temple had made Jinwoo feel alive for the first time in his life. In that moment, he hadn't been a useless E-rank hunter but rather a challenger of the impossible.

After weaving his way through a few alleys, Jinwoo spotted the school up ahead. He really had arrived at the school in about a minute.

The entrance to the dungeon floated in a corner of the schoolyard, and there were a few guild and association employees minding it. Everything looked calm, with nothing major to report.

Jinwoo's appearance broke the peace as he deactivated Stealth and approached them.

"H-huh?!"

The guild members belatedly spotted him and rushed to block his path.

"You're not allowed in this area."

Jinwoo pulled down his hood and revealed his face.

There was an audible gasp to one side of him. "You!"

The association employee assigned to the gate recognized Jinwoo. It was the same woman with glasses whom Jinwoo had encountered at the B-rank gate in the middle of the highway.

Jinwoo figured it would be easier to settle things with her, so he ignored the guild members and addressed her. "You need to stop the raid right now."

"Excuse me?" She sounded nonplussed. "But according to the measurements, it's only a C-rank gate……"

Jinwoo shook his head. "If you don't, they'll all die."

"……!"

He turned to look at the gate. Couldn't they sense the bone-chilling, ominous energy emanating from inside?

"How long have they been in there?" Jinwoo hurriedly asked.

The longer they'd been inside, the farther they'd have gotten, so the lower their chances of survival.

In her bewilderment, the association employee responded, "It's been about two hours."

Two hours... It was hard to say if that was a long time or no time at all.

"Who the hell are you? You with the association?"

One of the guild members grabbed Jinwoo by the shoulder and tried to turn him around. He was irritated at this stranger who had appeared out of nowhere, ignored most of the people in the area, and spouted off inflammatory nonsense about their strike squad being in danger. His grip was weak, but Jinwoo went with the flow and faced the man. Revealing his face would be more effective than trying to explain the situation in detail.

"When someone asks you a question—" The guild member paused as he took in the other man's features.

Wait a minute. I've seen him somewhere before......

But where? When the name came to him, he stammered, "H-H-Hunter Jinwoo Sung?"

He never expected to meet an S-rank hunter in front of a C-rank gate. And he'd grabbed his shoulder and yelled at him! The shocked staff member removed his hand and retreated a few steps.

"I'm...I'm sorry, sir."

"......"

The clock was still ticking, so Jinwoo didn't have time to waste on the rude newcomer. He turned to the woman from the association. "I'll bring them back."

The representative was flustered. Here was the man who'd exited a B-rank red gate with a smile, yet he appeared devastated and convinced that the squad inside this C-rank gate was in danger.

"What's going on? If you could just explain it to me—"

"There's no time for that." Jinwoo cut her off.

Truthfully, he could've sneaked inside using Stealth. There were also a handful of ways to draw these people's attention away from the gate.

However, Jinwoo refrained from doing so because he wanted to cover his bases in case of unforeseen complications down the line.

The association employee opened and closed her mouth several times as she debated what to do. Would it be okay to let another hunter go inside without any evidence of danger when a guild with an official permit was already in the middle of the raid?

In theory, it was unacceptable…but she couldn't bring herself to stop Jinwoo, given the look in his eyes.

"……Please go ahead."

"I'll see you later." Jinwoo gave a short nod and quickly ran through the gate.

[You have entered the dungeon.]

Carcasses of magic beasts were scattered throughout the dungeon with their essence stones already extracted. Unlike the dead bodies of magic beasts from high-rank dungeons, which were worth a fortune, those from low-rank dungeons were valuable only for their essence stones. This was a familiar scene to Jinwoo.

He closed his eyes and focused, but for some reason, he couldn't detect the presence of the strike squad.

Could they already be……?

Jinwoo shook his head. The bodies of the recently deceased hunters would release mana, but he couldn't sense that, either.

As Jinwoo inspected his surroundings, he was suddenly hit with a feeling of déjà vu. This place somehow seemed familiar, like he had seen this exact dungeon before.

Oh.

It was a replica of the dungeon where Jinwoo had first received his powers.

That means…

He found the spot where the entrance to the double dungeon had been, and sure enough, there it was.

It's just like that time.

He then realized why he couldn't sense any of the hunters.

This dungeon is......insanely huge.

It had been that way the last time, too. Even if they moved at the speed of low-rank hunters, it would still have taken them almost an hour to reach the strange door. If this dungeon truly did have the same layout, then there was a significant distance between himself and the strike squad. No wonder he couldn't detect the presence of the hunters who possessed such small quantities of mana.

Jinwoo stared into the passageway. There was only one tunnel, and just like back then, the way was pitch-black. However, that didn't bother Jinwoo. His increased perception allowed him to detect the path hidden in the dark. His eyes glowed blue, like those of an animal with night vision.

I can see.

Jinwoo's eyes adjusted to the darkness, allowing him to make out the interior of the tunnel clearly.

Whew...

Jinwoo took a deep breath and then shot off like a bullet. He put quite some distance behind him in the blink of an eye.

I can't believe it used to take me almost an hour......

His speed now was incomparable to what it had been back then.

He suddenly picked up on something. It was the strike squad! They'd come to a stop, and at first, Jinwoo thought that either they were in the middle of a battle or perhaps even dead. However, that wasn't the case.

As he approached, he heard their voices.

"So you just want to turn around even though we're already here?"

Tak.

Jinwoo stopped not far from the hunters and couldn't help but snort at the familiar conversation. He was relieved, though, since the strike squad hadn't yet set foot inside. They wouldn't have been arguing so casually otherwise.

He heard a woman's voice next. "Then what do we do? We couldn't open the door even after throwing all our magic spells at it."

"Isn't it better to turn back and strike a deal with a larger guild?"

"I think that's best, too."

The hunters were arguing in front of the door they couldn't open.

Jinwoo understood their thinking. They probably believed they had struck it rich after discovering the double dungeon and didn't want to make another one-hour trek empty-handed.

He, a survivor of a similar predicament, decided to speak up. "It's a trap."

The hunters hadn't noticed his approach, so his sudden interjection startled them and made them recoil.

"Son of a—!"

"Wh-who are you?"

Jinwoo pointed his chin toward the gigantic steel door from his memories. "I'm a survivor of the double dungeon."

A survivor of a double dungeon? The hunters exchanged looks and whispered among themselves. In the darkness, it took a while for them to recognize Jinwoo.

"Wait......"

"What?"

"Isn't that Hunter Jinwoo Sung?"

"Huh?"

Everyone stared at the hunter who had said Jinwoo's name, then at Jinwoo himself.

"Now that you mention it......"

"It's really him, isn't it?"

"But what brings an S-rank hunter here?"

Jinwoo strode forward, and the hunters near the entry automatically made way for him. He gently placed his hand on the entrance.

"I know what lies beyond these doors."

It felt somewhat different standing in this spot again. But this was not the time to be sentimental. The system itself had invited him here, so he couldn't tolerate gate-crashers, either for their sake or his own.

Jinwoo turned and spoke to them gravely. "This is a horrifically dangerous place. You should turn back. I'll take it from here."

The strike squad's discontented mutters grew louder, but they kept their thoughts to themselves because Jinwoo was a well-known S-rank hunter. But there's always one in every group, and the man who didn't want to go back empty-handed eventually stepped up.

"Excuse me, Hunter Sung." He was the master of the midsize guild managing this raid. "The Bravery Guild acquired the permit to raid this dungeon fair and square. You don't have the right to tell us to leave."

"Yeah! You think you can do whatever just because you're an S rank?"

Jinwoo pursed his lips at their protests.

……

He'd been trying to help them as a gesture of goodwill, but he had no intention of trying harder to persuade them.

I'm not obliged to do anything here.

Jinwoo had done everything that could be expected of him. As someone who knew the price other low-rank hunters, including himself, had paid for the decision made regarding this place, he hadn't wished it upon these hunters. However, he would let them make their own choices.

He went ahead and grabbed the doorknob.

Klung!

Despite his exertions, the door wouldn't open.

Is there a magic spell on it?

Otherwise, there was no way this door would be so immovable. Just then, there came a chime.

[The door to the Cartenon Temple is currently locked.]
[Please use the key.]

Ah, no wonder.

Jinwoo summoned the black key, and the door swung open as soon as he inserted it into the keyhole.

Creaaaak!

The Bravery Guild stared in surprise at the previously impenetrable doors.

Huh?!

What the…?! How did he open it?

Jinwoo ignored their whispers and coldly warned them, "Feel free to enter. I won't stop you. Just know that once you're inside, it won't be easy to come back out alive."

The strike squad froze, unable to take the cautionary words coming from an S-rank hunter lightly. But in true Bravery Guild fashion, the guild master courageously stepped up to the plate.

"I'll go in."

"……" Jinwoo didn't try to stop him.

It was their call, so they'd have to deal with the consequences.

The guild master looked back at his colleagues, but they exchanged looks and didn't move to accompany him. The guild master glared at his squad in disappointment, then stood in front of the door. Jinwoo held it open for him.

Boom!

The heavy door swung inward. Looking quite determined, the guild master briefly made eye contact with Jinwoo and, after wavering slightly, worked up his courage and set one foot inside the room.

As he did, Jinwoo received a few alerts.

Ping, ping, ping!

[A trespasser has entered the temple.]
[Entry is denied.]
[Failure to follow instructions will activate the door-keepers.]

Only Jinwoo saw the system's warning, and so, oblivious to what was waiting, the guild master took another step.

Whoosh!

A hammer fell toward his head.

Kroom!

It crushed the stone tile he was standing on.

"Argh!"

Jinwoo had pulled the man out of harm's way just in time, saving him from losing his head.

"A-ahhhh!" The guild master freaked out as doorkeepers grabbed at him.

Jinwoo threw him outside the room and quickly closed the door. "The entire room is like that." He turned to address the group. "Still want to go inside?"

The guild master vigorously shook his head from his spot on the ground. His colleagues helped him up and carried him away.

After they were out of sight, Jinwoo went through the door alone.

Ping!

[The keeper of the key has entered.]

Thud!

The door closed.

The room was enormous. Statues lined the walls, the largest of which sat looming in the farthest part of the hall. It was all just as he remembered.

I'm......back.

His heart pounded.

One thing had changed, though: Jinwoo himself. The newly evolved Jinwoo could now tell the true nature of the statues.

They're not magic beasts or living beings.

They were mere puppets connected to something else. Only one being in the room possessed magic power, and it hid its mana so well that the only way Jinwoo could single it out was by its strange, sinister aura.

He slowly walked to a specific statue.

"So it was you."

No response.

"That's how you want to play it?"

Jinwoo's lips twitched up, and he swiftly stabbed his dagger into his target's chest.

Crack!

The attack was blocked by a stone slate held by the only statue armed with one.

"Finally." The statue with six wings smiled beatifically. "You've made it."

* * *

Magic beasts began emerging from the humongous gate in Shinjuku.

Stomp!

Stomp!

"Whoa......!"

"Wh-what are—?!"

They were giants, the kind of magic beasts that sometimes appeared as bosses in top-ranking A-rank dungeons.

"Giants!"

"They're giants!"

Everyone watching recoiled in fear, but Yuri took a sip from his flask.

I can handle this, no problem.

These magic beasts instilled chills in others, but Yuri was adamant that his work was flawless.

"Come at me!"

And as he expected...

Bam!

Wham!

The giants struck in vain at the invisible wall blocking them.

Thud! Thud!

The beasts charged and threw their bodies against the force field, but the Russian's divination circle held.

"Ah-ha-ha-ha-ha-ha!" Yuri chortled at the sight.

After struggling for half an hour, the giants retreated as if weary from trying to break down the barrier.

The spectators exclaimed in surprise.

"Oh my God!"

"The magic beasts are going back inside the gate?"

No one had ever seen or even heard of anything like this before, and even the most seasoned journalists snapped pictures as if their lives depended on it at this heretofore undocumented phenomenon.

As the last giant disappeared from view, President Matsumoto rose to his feet and applauded.

Clap, clap, clap, clap!

One clap turned into a succession, which transformed into sighs of relief, and finally cheers.

Whooooooo!

At the enthusiastic reception, Yuri faced the reporters. "This is something only I could do. I blocked this S-rank gate!" he shouted at the top of his lungs. "That other dude only killed a couple ants, but I turned those giants back! Who's the man now?!"

Yuri's face was flushed red from the alcohol, and he grinned to show off his gold tooth.

Stomp!

The ground shook.

Stomp!

The military tanks on standby shook from the force.

......?

Yuri finally realized that the reporters were no longer looking at him but at the gate. He followed their gazes…and dropped his flask of vodka.

Clank!

Oh, hell......

The hunter's eyes popped out of his skull at the behemoth emerging from the gate that dwarfed the other giants.

As it stood up straight, Yuri couldn't wrap his head around its sheer size.

H-how is it so big that it had to duck to come through?

No explanation was needed to know that this was the boss of the dungeon.

The terrifying creature scanned the area and then charged at the invisible wall.

Boooom!

The sound resonated and made the ground quake.

Boooom! Boooom! Boooom!

The divination circle, visible only to Yuri, began showing hairline fractures.

How is this happening......?

The hunter collapsed to his knees.

The boss stopped pushing against the barrier with its shoulder, then purposefully drew back and threw itself at the wall at full speed.

KABOOM!

The light of the divination circle dissipated with an explosive concussion.

"N-nooooo!"

No sooner had Yuri let out a wail than the freed giant snatched up the human responsible for the barrier. The Russian cried out at the pain of feeling his bones snap and struggled to escape the giant's grip.

"Aaaaaargh! Ahhhhhhhhh!"

The hunter's screams were cut off as the behemoth opened its mouth. The smaller giants that had retreated inside the gate now poured out from behind their leader, who had swallowed Yuri whole.

* * *

Kri-kri-krik!

An odd sound came from the statue's joints as it began to move.

Jinwoo eyed it warily. The creature had several differences from the other statues, but its most distinguishable feature was its wings. It was the only depiction of an angel and had six wings attached, standing tall at an imposing three meters.

Fwip!

Jinwoo quickly took a few steps back and lowered his center of gravity, gripping a dagger in each hand. Determined to fight, his mind, body, and senses optimized for battle.

......

Despite sensing Jinwoo's desire to fight, the angel grinned. Its smile was creepy and unnatural, giving Jinwoo goose bumps. It looked down at its damaged stone slate and tossed it aside without a second thought.

Crash!

Naturally, the slate shattered into several pieces upon hitting the ground. The angel statue laughed stiffly at the broken shards. "Ha-ha!"

Jinwoo's eyes narrowed.

Then this whole time......

The commandments on the stone slate had been meaningless from the start.

Otherwise, the statue wouldn't have treated it so carelessly.

So then, what was this place for? And what did it want?

And......

What was the point of the quests, level-ups, keys, and all the strange occurrences that had happened after he left this place? This was Jinwoo's opportunity to get some answers, and the thought excited him.

Ba-dump, ba-dump, ba-dump!

His usually steady heart seemed to be slamming against his ribs like an engine that had been revved.

This thing knows everything.

Without dropping his guard, Jinwoo prompted in a low voice, "Are you the one who called me here?"

What was the relationship between the system and the statue?

"Yes." The angel statue tested the joints of its fingers. "You successfully made your way back."

It then tested its neck, rotating it to the right and left.

Krick-krack!

Krick!

It was stretching, and it wasn't hard to guess why. Normally, Jinwoo wouldn't have missed a chance to get in the first attack, but he held back this time. He had so many things he wanted to ask the angel and didn't want to waste his chance by engaging it in battle.

"Are you a magic beast?"

The magic power radiating from the angel statue was different from that of a magic beast. However, the term *magic beast* was a human construct anyway. If the term encompassed all monsters, then this was a statue that could talk and move, and was there anything more monstrous than that? In other words, Jinwoo wanted to know if the statue and magic beasts were one and the same.

Kri-kri-kri-krick!

Kri-kri-krack!

The angel statue bent to reach its toes and then straightened up again. "You're asking the wrong question."

"……?"

"You should've asked me who you are instead of who I am."

Jinwoo froze, momentarily stunned, but the angel clapped to get his attention.

Clap!

"Now, this will be the final test."

The statue finished warming up, and its smile faded.

"If you're still standing when this test is over, I will tell you everything. That will be…" The angel snapped its fingers, and the eyes of the other statues glowed red. "…your reward from me."

The rest of the stone figures' heads snapped toward Jinwoo.

Stomp!

They stepped off their pedestals and raised their weapons.

Jinwoo looked at each in turn. Even though they were only puppets, they looked powerful and had almost killed him on more than one occasion.

Jinwoo calmly summoned his shadow soldiers.

Come out.
Ping!

[Job-exclusive skills may not be used during the final test.]
[The use of potions and the shop are forbidden. Condition recovery rewards gained through leveling up and quest completion have been disabled.]
[You may not leave until the final test has ended.]

What?

Jinwoo frowned at each message, but he didn't have time to dwell on any of them.

The statues began their attack. They moved quickly and quietly—a sharp contrast from the hundreds of knights that had mobbed him during the job change quest.

So that's how it's gonna be, huh?

The different kinds of potions and quest rewards he'd prepared, just in case, had gone up in flames. The system knew Jinwoo's tricks well by this point.

Fine, I'll pass this test under my own power!

Jinwoo resolutely tightened his grip on the daggers. The fastest way to end the crisis would be to take out the puppeteer, the angel statue. However, Jinwoo wouldn't get what he was here for if he did that. He'd save that as his last resort. First, he'd comply and take its test.

It was all for this moment......

Jinwoo had never stopped bettering himself so he would be able to tackle any given situation without faltering.

Hwoo......

The hunter exhaled a warm puff of air.

In the past, the statues had moved so fast that, to the naked eye, it seemed like they were using teleportation. But now, he was able to follow their movements easily.

Left.

He blocked a spear coming from the left with his dagger.

Klang!

Left again.

Another statue leaped off the shoulders of the attacker with a spear and swung down its ax. Since attempting to block a strike from above wouldn't be efficient, Jinwoo chose to dodge it by twisting his body in a half circle.

Crash!

The ax struck the ground and sent fragments of stone flying everywhere. Jinwoo kicked the statue's face with all his might.

Krak!

Its head exploded into pieces.

Fwish!

Jinwoo bent his torso backward to avoid an arrow, which lodged in the wall behind him. The relentless attacks left no time to celebrate getting rid of one of them.

Right side.

A sword swung toward him.

Shing!

Klang!

Jinwoo pushed away the sword with all his strength using one dagger and brought the other across in a diagonal slash.

Shunk!

He sliced off the statue's arm and sent it stumbling backward, writhing in pain.

Left, right, right, left, front, front, right, left.

I've got this!

The harder Jinwoo focused on the battle, the slower the statues' movements seemed as his own grew faster.

Suddenly, he sensed a chill on the back of his neck.

Behind me!

Jinwoo leaped over a statue approaching from the rear and lopped off its head.

Slash!

Thanks to his perception stat, he was covered on all sides.

Whew!

He let out a heavy sigh. Each nerve in his body was attuned to the statues' every move.

His eyes burned bright as he parried, blocked, and repelled every blow and cut down the number of tenacious statues.

This is the moment I've been waiting for......

He easily sliced through his assailants with the Demon Monarch's Daggers, as if they'd been made to cut through stone. His body, mind, nerves, and daggers had fused to make an unstoppable machine.

The angel statue shivered in delight as it carefully observed Jinwoo.

He's moving well for a human......

A smile returned to the angel's face. It had made the right choice.

However, the test was far from over.

The angel statue turned to gaze upon the colossus seated on a huge throne. Its eyes turned bright red as if it had been awaiting its cue, and it gripped the armrests of the throne and heaved itself to its feet.

Rrrrrumble!

The colossus's size alone was enough to send chills up one's spine.

Boom!

The entire lair shook as it took its first step.

Boom, boom, boom!

Because of its enormous stride, it reached Jinwoo in a few steps. A mound of broken statues surrounded the hunter. The monstrosity stopped in front of the heap and raised its right arm.

Amid his intense battle with the other statues, Jinwoo sensed something strange. He looked up as something cast a shadow over him.

......?

A gigantic hand came into view as the colossus forcefully smacked the ground with no regard for its smaller brethren.

Crash!

Jinwoo flung his body to the side and rolled on the ground a few times before finally getting up, having successfully avoided its palm. Jinwoo's face hardened as he registered his new opponent.

Right. That's a thing.

Out of the frying pan and into the fire. There were at least a hundred statues still alive and charging toward him at full speed. His opponents soon caught up to him.

He changed the direction of a mace speeding toward him by tapping it with his dagger. He then smoothly slid in front of the puppet and severed its neck.

Thud!

As that statue's head hit the ground, the one right behind it took its place. However, that wasn't the real danger.

Jinwoo felt all the hairs on his body stand on end. He flinched and quickly looked up.

......!

An eerie red light was growing in intensity within the colossus's eyes.

Is it too late to avoid it......?

He'd be liquefied by the giant's heat vision if he went the wrong way and found his path blocked by the other statues.

In that case...

He dropped the dagger in his left hand and reached toward the oncoming foot soldiers.

Ruler's Hand!

Five of the statues were smooshed together by Ruler's Hand.

Ping!

[Skill: Ruler's Hand has been upgraded to its ultimate version, Skill: Ruler's Authority.]

Nice!

But there was no time to celebrate. Jinwoo moved his makeshift shield directly in the path of the giant's eyes.

Zzzzap!

As Jinwoo had predicted, a red laser shot forward.

Zzzzzt!

While it took less than a second for his shield to melt from the heat vision, that was enough time for Jinwoo to make his escape. The remains of the statues fell to the ground as he deactivated Ruler's Authority.

Thud!

Jinwoo changed his tactic now that he'd gotten a look at what the colossus could do to its companions.

I knew I should've taken it down first.

His goal set, Jinwoo sprang into action right before the second beam was fired.

Flash!

With his elevated speed, Jinwoo was now moving so quickly that the colossus couldn't track him. He arrived at the behemoth's feet and squatted, focusing all energy on his legs.

He only had one chance. It would be near impossible to dodge the red beam in midair, but if Jinwoo had learned one thing, it was that you missed every shot you didn't take.

So do me a favor.

Determined, Jinwoo launched himself with all his might. His body shot up like a rocket.

Hurry up and die!

6

THE ARCHITECT

6

THE ARCHITECT

At the zenith of his jump, Jinwoo hovered at eye level with the colossus. Time slowed to a point where he watched a drop of sweat glisten as it flung off him in tiny increments.

Jinwoo was in a state of extreme focus, a result of the pressure that one simple mistake could mean the difference between life or death heightening his abilities to their limits.

This is the true power of the agility stat......

Jinwoo was amazed to see the epitome of what he could do with this ability.

But this was no time to enjoy the fruits of his labor. The gaze of the colossus was slowly but surely shifting toward him. Seeing glowing red-hot eyes at this distance gave him goose bumps. It would be the end if the beam so much as grazed him.

The sense of danger simultaneously made him nauseous and gave him clarity.

Stay calm......

Jinwoo stretched out his empty left hand.

Ruler's Authority!

He used the recently upgraded skill to tug at the statue's shoulder. His aim was to drag himself closer to the massive block of stone instead of the other way around.

Vwooom!

The statue did move unexpectedly, though very slightly.

......!

The strength of the skill had doubled with the Ruler's Authority upgrade and acted as a gravitational pull now. Jinwoo landed safely on the statue's shoulder.

Zzzzzing!

The red beam accurately struck where Jinwoo had been a mere moment before.

Okay, good.

He'd bought a couple seconds of safety from the laser now. He ran across the shoulder and streaked toward the colossus's neck at full speed with the Demon Monarch's Dagger tightly gripped in his right hand.

Mutilation!

Numerous pinpricks of silver light shone on its neck.

Shink-shink-shink-shink-shink-shink!

Multiple times, he stabbed where the lights were indicating, but doing so had no effect. None of the strikes proved fatal but mere flesh wounds to the statue.

Daggers don't work on it?

The Demon Monarch's Dagger, which had penetrated the steel-like scales of a boss-level naga, felt useless in this moment.

Just then, Jinwoo spied a gigantic hand coming toward him, so he ran across the back of the neck and onto the other shoulder to avoid being nabbed. En route, he glanced below and realized how dizzyingly high he was.

Jinwoo refocused on the statue's profile. It wasn't the first enemy to thwart his dagger attacks. Been there, done that.

If I can't pierce it, then I need to crush it!

There was a reason he had invested so many points on his strength stat.

Determination shone in Jinwoo's eyes as he jumped lightly and struck his left hand against the statue's temple.

Crack!

His fingers penetrated the surface.

Yes!

Jinwoo made a fist with his left hand and hung off the statue's face like a professional rock climber clinging to the side of a cliff with one hand.

He'd finished his preparations, and now it was the moment of truth. The right side of Jinwoo's back, shoulder, and arm muscles bulged to an impossible degree as he poured an incredible amount of mana into them.

He threw the first punch.

Pow!

Though it had been unaffected by the dagger strikes, the statue's head shook from the impact.

. . . . . . !

The angel statue observed the scene with shock. The mana reverberating from the top of the colossus filled the length of the temple. The puppeteer couldn't hide its overflowing excitement.

The angel hadn't expected Jinwoo to deal with its masterpiece in this fashion, and it looked forward to what would happen next.

Ka-pow!

The hunter punched the giant in the face again, and the colossus briefly wobbled. Jinwoo's attacks were working.

But his opponent wasn't one to sit and take it.

Whoosh!

It raised its gigantic palm as if looking to squash a mosquito.

Bam!

Jinwoo evaded the hand and landed back on the statue's shoulder. He smirked as it smacked its own face. As soon as the hand moved away, Jinwoo climbed back up, and…

Pow! Ka-pow! Bam! Pow! Blam!

The awful sound echoed throughout the lair.

Krik! Craaack!

A fissure on the giant's face began spreading out like a spiderweb. The colossus tried in vain to regain its footing and eventually staggered toward the side of the chamber.

Stomp, stomp, stomp!

The creature's enormous feet hit the ground hard. It appeared as though it was planning to crush Jinwoo by throwing itself against the wall.

But before that happens......

Jinwoo resolved to end his opponent first and began punching its face harder, faster, and mercilessly.

Pow! Pow! Pow! Pow!

Stomp! Stomp! Stomp!

The statue sped up and quickly closed the gap between itself and the wall.

Jinwoo took a peek at the approaching collision to measure the distance and then focused all the power in his right arm for the final blow. His muscles bulged, and his veins throbbed as an unbelievable amount of mana was concentrated in his arm.

......Perfect.

Right before impact, Jinwoo put all the strength of a level 103 Player behind one final swing.

BAM!

CRACK!

The colossus dropped to its knees, accompanied by a sound reminiscent of a watermelon being split.

THUD!

The entire lair shook as the enormous statue crashed lifelessly to the ground.

THUMP!

As the heavy hunk of stone collided with the dry ground, it kicked up a thick cloud of dust from which Jinwoo emerged, unscathed.

"Phew." He slowly exhaled.

Ba-dump, ba-dump, ba-dump!

His ears were filled with the sound of his own blood pumping furiously.

The colossus that had petrified Jinwoo when he'd first laid eyes on it now lay in a heap on the floor.

Nobody had done this for him. This was something he had accomplished on his own.

......I can do it.

He could do anything.

Jinwoo became emotional as he recalled the faces of the hunters who had lost their lives in this very place. But the other statues quickly mobilized, denying him time to dwell in the past. They closed in on him, but before they could attack...

Jinwoo looked up from his hands. "Ruler's Authority."

Slam!

The statues' heads slammed into the ground, at which point they stopped moving. Such was the might of the invisible hand of Ruler's Authority.

Jinwoo looked back down at his two palms.

I've become stronger from this fight.

He opened and then closed his fists. Powerful energy flowed through his hands—no, through his entire body. He could feel the flow of this energy. His heart wouldn't stop fluttering. It felt like something inside him had been awakened during the life-threatening battle.

Clap, clap, clap, clap, clap!

As the slow clap reverberated, Jinwoo looked toward the source.

The angel statue wore the same creepy smile and was now applauding with overly exaggerated movements. "Extraordinary."

Contrary to the manner in which it had greeted Jinwoo, the angel's eyes seemed sinister.

"Didn't you promise me something?" asked the hunter.

The statue had promised him answers if Jinwoo was still standing by the end of the test.

The angel gave a stiff laugh, having no intention of making this easy for him. "Ha-ha."

It took a step toward Jinwoo.

"Your test isn't over yet."

Then one more step.

"After all..."

And another. The angel statue stopped right in front of him.

"I'm still here, aren't I?"

Kriiiiiik, krack!

The wings on the angel's back twisted and tangled until they were transformed into arms, two on its shoulders and six on its back. The stone angel clenched all eight of its fists.

"I am the final test."

Jinwoo frowned. Even before Jinwoo could say anything, the statue cut him off.

"You don't have to worry about my life."

Jinwoo recoiled. It had known exactly what the Player was about to ask: whether killing it would destroy any chance of getting answers.

"Surprised?" The angel pointed at its own head with one of its eight hands. "All the information about you is in here."

Did that mean......? Jinwoo broke out into a cold sweat.

"You do catch on quick."

Ha-ha.

The angel statue laughed mechanically. "But it would be difficult to properly measure your true abilities if you hold back to avoid killing me."

At that moment, the angel statue's lips moved quickly...but the voice came from elsewhere.

[An urgent quest has arrived.]
[If you do not defeat the enemy by the designated time, your heart will stop.]
[Remaining Time: 10:00]

It took Jinwoo one second to read the message.
Tick.

[Remaining Time: 09:59]

Jinwoo stared, thunderstruck, at the angel statue.
"That's right."
[That's right.]

Whenever it spoke, the system said the same thing.

No sooner than Jinwoo's heart had settled down, it now began pounding frantically once more. His breath quickened, and his hands trembled.

As it observed Jinwoo's reaction, the stone angel finally deigned to answer Jinwoo's very first question of "Who are you?"

"I am the architect of the system."

[I am the architect of the system.]

* * *

"Considering the chaos in Japan because of the dungeon break, should you really be here, Mr. Kim?" Jinchul asked tiredly.

Kim, a reporter, scratched his sideburns as he yawned. "There are plenty of reporters at the scene already, so no need for little old me. Better to be here with the surveillance team and wait for a scoop."

"......" Jinchul considered telling the reporter to either scratch his head or yawn, not both. Instead, he just sighed quietly to himself.

Kim was pretty much the only reporter who wrote articles that painted the Hunter's Association in a favorable light while everyone else wrote provocative pieces about corruption within the association or the private lives of hunters.

No need to turn an ally against us......

Which was why Jinchul humored Kim whenever he paid a visit to the surveillance team.

Kim let out a long yawn before continuing. "By the way, should *you* be here while the whole country is in an uproar, Manager Woo?"

Jinchul closed the file he was working on and let out another long-suffering sigh before quietly answering. "All the more need for one person to be at the ready."

Hmm...

Kim perked up and took out a pen and palm-size notebook. "That's a cool quote. Could you repeat it one more time so I can write it down verbatim?"

"Mr. Kim, you really—" Jinchul's sharp reply was interrupted by a phone call.

Huh?

It was the emergency dispatch. A direct call to him instead of the surveillance team meant it was something urgent.

Jinchul hurriedly answered. "This is Manager Jinchul Woo of the surveillance team."

"Manager Woo, we have a report that may require your attention."

Jinchul's eyes narrowed. "What happened?"

"You know the school that was attacked by orcs?"

"Did something else happen......?"

"Not yet, but the report indicates that a double dungeon was discovered in the schoolyard."

A double dungeon?

Jinchul's eyes widened.

"And..."

The emergency dispatcher seemed to have something else to say.

Jinchul pressed them. "And?"

"I was told that Hunter Jinwoo Sung has entered the gate."

* * *

There was no time to be surprised, as the angel statue lunged at Jinwoo. Tightly clenched fists came flying at the hunter quick as lightning. His opponent was too close and too fast to evade.

Jinwoo's brain made a flash decision based on past experiences in battle. He instinctively raised his arms to block. It wasn't a wrong move, but it wasn't the right move, either.

Bam!

The angel sent Jinwoo flying into a wall.

Crack!

Pieces of rubble fell to the ground.

Argh...

Jinwoo choked down a pained groan. The punch hurt him more than he'd expected. However, the angel statue was already right in front of his nose before he could recover.

Pow!

Jinwoo narrowly dodged another punch by tilting his head. The angel's fist left a hole in the wall behind him. But that was only the beginning. With its adversary pinned with his back to the wall, the angel mercilessly threw a barrage of punches. One blow was strong enough to instantly kill a high-rank hunter.

Pow, pow, pow, pow, pow, pow, pow!

The angel's eyes widened.

He's…blocking my punches?

Jinwoo was able to block, divert, and withstand the attacks made with eight fists using his two. The angel could only see afterimages of his hands. The self-proclaimed architect was amazed at the feat.

But the result of this fight had been decided from the start. This was just a part of the process. Giving Jinwoo a final test had nothing to do with the angel's will. The angel figured it would be bored throughout.

This is entertaining.

Little did the angel statue know it would enjoy sparring with a human. Throughout the course of its long life, it never imagined humans could be worthy opponents.

At that moment, a light flickered. No, not a light—the human had thrown a punch.

Ka-pow!

Jinwoo aimed for its face, sending the angel tumbling. It quickly jumped back on its feet, smiling despite the cracks on its face.

[Ha-ha.]

The angel couldn't remember the last time it had had this much fun. It was so delighted that it shook with regret that this time would soon come to an end.

"Phew…" Meanwhile, Jinwoo could only breathe deeply, unable to revel in the fact that he'd landed a solid hit.

It's strong.

It was stronger than any opponent Jinwoo had ever faced.

The architect of the system… That's how it had introduced itself.

For what reason had it created the system? Why had it chosen Jinwoo as a Player? What was going on in the world right now? Jinwoo had a mountain of questions.

But before I can ask them……

He had to defeat it. The hunter clenched his fists tightly. It was then that he felt something warm and wet on his face.

Drip…

It was blood from a cut on his forehead.

I guess I wasn't able to avoid all those attacks.

Jinwoo had thought he'd perfectly evaded the blows, but it seemed he had missed one. To make matters worse, blood was seeping into one of his eyes, and he couldn't see properly. On the other hand, his enemy was doing fine. Either way, things weren't looking good for him.

I'm at a disadvantage in close-quarter battles.

That much was obvious. The angel statue was a few times bigger and had six more arms. It was next to impossible to avoid or block strikes coming in such quick succession from different directions. The wound on his forehead proved it.

Then……

Jinwoo needed to shift the narrative.

As he reached this conclusion, the angel threw another punch toward him like a bullet.

Blam!

The blow struck a wall and brought it crumbling down. The angel turned to see that Jinwoo had already put distance between them before it realized he was gone.

I won't lose to it in speed.

If Jinwoo could keep some space between them as he attacked…… Jinwoo activated Ruler's Authority.

Whud!

The strong force slammed down on the angel statue. It was the same move Jinwoo had used to kill Beru. However……

……?

Jinwoo couldn't believe what he was seeing. The same skill that had moved even the colossus's torso only bent the angel's neck by a fraction.

Jinwoo didn't know with what exactly, but he was certain his opponent was countering with something invisible.

How is it doing that?

He soon found out.

[This is really, really fun.]

At some point, the deep voice of the angel statue and the female voice of the system had synchronized. The unnatural combination grated on Jinwoo.

[I'm truly having so much fun.]

The angel stretched out its eight arms, and the weapons in the hands of the other statues began to quiver.

Is that......?

Jinwoo's jaw dropped.

The weapons floated into the air and flew toward the angel statue. Each of the angel's eight hands gripped a separate weapon.

It's Ruler's Hand.

The angel was able to use Ruler's Hand as well. Despite not having mastered the skill to the degree Jinwoo had, it was now clear how it had blocked him. His opponent was truly unlike anything he'd ever faced.

Tick.

Jinwoo's gaze traveled up.

[Remaining Time: 06:19]

He had about six minutes left.

I need to end this quickly.

Having discovered that long-range attacks were ineffective, Jinwoo switched gears and summoned a Demon Monarch's Dagger. He had lost track of the other dagger after having thrown it somewhere earlier.

Eight weapons against one dagger...

Ba-dump, ba-dump!

His heart pounded as he felt cornered.

Tak.

The angel statue jumped nearly as high as the ceiling and landed in front of him.

Crack!

The stone tiles shattered at the impact, sending pieces of rubble everywhere.

Jinwoo raised his dagger, weathering the fine pieces of debris pelting his ankles.

I can do this.

He would succeed.

Jinwoo regulated his breathing as he looked the angel in the eyes. A chill ran up his spine as eight weapons—including a sword, spear, blade, ax, and hammer—rushed toward him as if they were alive.

Whew...

He exhaled forcefully and opened his eyes wide. Under these interior lights, which were neither bright nor dark, his movements left a trail.

Bang bang bang bang bang bang bang bang bang bang!

If bullets could block bullets, would they sound like this? In an instant, Jinwoo and the stone angel exchanged countless blows, causing a cacophony of noises one would hear in a war zone. In a world where everything else was in slow motion, the two engaged in fierce battle that moved against the flow of time. They were evenly matched with neither inferior nor superior to the other.

I can sense it.

Jinwoo moved his shoulder ever so slightly. The angel's sword missed him by a gap so small, it was unnoticeable to the naked eye.

It didn't matter that he couldn't see out of one eye at the moment. Jinwoo's perception had reached its limit and then gone beyond, allowing him to track the movements of his enemy's weapons even without seeing them. He just barely evaded the angel's attacks and landed counterattacks one after another.

The wounds sustained by his opponent multiplied. It maintained its speed, but Jinwoo sped up.

The angel statue was stunned. "......!"

The architect didn't have to go this far for the test. However, this human compelled it to come out full force. The statue was literally using its full power but finding itself matched. How was this possible?

The angel stared at Jinwoo suspiciously and soon understood.

There's only a trace...but it's in him.

The architect shuddered at the realization. Is this why Jinwoo was able to easily wield such power? Yet, this was something for which the angel had been hoping.

As a smile crept across its face, a severed arm flew through the air. The stone angel looked up. The one that had dropped its weapon was...its right arm.

[Arrrrghhh!]

Although this was not its real body, it felt pain. It stumbled backward.

[To think a mere human would...!]

The eyes of the angel statue turned red, and its true nature awakened, pushing its duty to the back of its mind.

[How dare you!]

At its exclamation, the other statues rose.

Stomp!

Even those with their heads bashed in got up from the ground. Jinwoo took note of their positions and, without panicking, threw himself at the architect once more.

Klang!

The angel used four hands to block his dagger, yet its feet still slid backward. Agility, perception, strength, stamina—all of Jinwoo's stats were beyond its expectations.

[Grah!]

The angel cried out like an animal, mobilizing the other statues. The battle between Jinwoo and the guardians of the temple was underway.

Tick.

[03:02]

* * *

The countdown continued.

Jinwoo's dagger sliced off one of the six arms that were formerly wings.

[Arghhhh!]

Yet, the retaliation of the revived statues was nothing to laugh about, and it was impossible for Jinwoo to avoid so many incoming attacks. He focused on evading any fatal blows, ignoring the rest to keep up his attack on his primary target.

This rapidly depleted his stamina.

Klunk!

A statue slammed a shield down onto Jinwoo's right shoulder.

Ngh!

Jinwoo looked over his shoulder to see the statue holding the shield, preparing to strike again. Jinwoo frowned. Never mind the other lackeys; he had a grudge against this particular one.

Jinwoo separated from the angel statue to slam an elbow into its head.

Crack!

The mana-powered elbow drop turned its head to dust.

In the meantime, other statues quickly surrounded Jinwoo and threw themselves at him, but…

Ruler's Authority!

Bam!

A horde of assailants flew backward as if a bomb had detonated.

"Huff, huff!"

But before Jinwoo could catch his breath, the colossus slammed down its giant fist. Jinwoo evaded the attack with a small jump to the side.

Whoosh!

The gigantic fist took down dozens of statues near Jinwoo. The hunter ran in a large circle in order to shake off the others as he approached the angel.

The architect scowled at Jinwoo, enraged.

Once again, the hunter, the angel, and the other statues tangled together. Jinwoo's sweat and blood splattered everywhere, but this lasted only a moment. As these began to evaporate, red steam rose from his shoulders.

Statues flew backward. The colossus pounded its fist. The angel statue's hands moved at lightning speed. And at the center of it all was Jinwoo.

[Arghhh!]

The architect lost another arm, and Jinwoo finally pressed his dagger against the angel's neck. Above their heads, the colossus had clasped its hands together, preparing to slam them down. Jinwoo calmly put more pressure on the blade at the angel's throat.

It was at that moment that the architect voiced its surrender.

[I've lost.]

Immediately, the rest of the statues froze.

[The test is over.]

Tick.

The timer came to a halt as well.

[Remaining Time: 02:11]

Steam rose from Jinwoo's body. He lowered his gaze to the angel after confirming the timer had stopped.

"I have a question for you."

[I will answer any question within the extent of my knowledge.]

The angel statue was expressionless as it readily agreed to cooperate with Jinwoo.

......

Jinwoo pondered what he should ask. When he had first asked the angel who it was, he'd been met with a laugh and told he'd asked the wrong question. Now that he knew the angel statue's identity, even more questions flooded his mind. So he followed the statue's advice.

"Who am I?"

* * *

The ranks of the surveillance team arrived at the location. There were seven high-rank hunters, the most elite members the association could summon on such short notice. However, Jinchul was fully aware that even this much combat power wouldn't be much help to Hunter Sung.

Still, worst-case scenario……

They could buy time to let Jinwoo escape. They had come here determined to help however they could.

"Is that it, sir?"

"I believe so."

The hunters stepped out of a van and onto the school grounds. The members of the Bravery Guild had been awaiting them since reporting the incident. Their faces brightened at the sight of the surveillance team.

"Over here!" The guild master ran up to greet them.

Jinchul's eyes remained trained on the gate. He sensed an extraordinary energy emanating from it.

He turned to his subordinates. "Let's hurry."

"Yes, sir."

The hunters of the surveillance team picked up the pace. They crossed the field quickly and arrived in front of the gate, but as they did…Jinchul stopped in his tracks.

"Manager Woo?"

"Sir?"

The support team following him stopped as well. Jinchul cautiously took off his sunglasses. The hand holding them trembled slightly.

What the……? What the hell is this……?

A nauseatingly forceful storm of magic power was brewing. The space around the gate looked distorted by the magic power leaking out from it.

Appalled, Jinchul took a step back.

Was this an illusion or an omen of bad luck? It almost seemed like a black curtain was covering the gate, like a shadow of death. It made the hair on the back of his neck stand up.

Jinchul instinctively knew that the fight taking place inside the gate was not one he could join.

One of Jinchul's subordinates was alarmed by his pale face. "Manager Woo, are you okay?"

"......" Jinchul asked a question in return. "Is there...a large guild available nearby?"

The subordinate searched the association's files. "Yes. The Hunters Guild members are on standby in the area."

"What about the two S-rank hunters?"

"Both Hunter Jongin Choi and Hunter Haein Cha are scheduled to participate in the raid."

Jongin Choi and Haein Cha... Those two might be able to do something.

Jinchul looked back toward the gate again. The tremor in his hand was spreading to the rest of his body. He nervously swallowed, barely able to steady his voice enough to give the order. "Tell the Hunters Guild...that it's an emergency."

* * *

Jinwoo posed the question the angel statue had suggested.

His labored breathing soon settled back to normal, like he hadn't been fighting for his life a few seconds ago.

[......]

Jinwoo dug in the blade at the angel's neck to prompt a quicker response. A human would have bled out from that type of open wound. It didn't bleed, as it was a statue, so Jinwoo also didn't have a problem with lopping off its head entirely.

Was the angel aware of this, though?

Eventually, its lips parted.

[Finally.]

The statue's voice was more unsettling up close.

[You asked me a proper question.]

The statue smiled. Despite having lost a few arms and with a dagger sinking into its neck, it showed no fear.

Where is its real body?

Jinwoo scanned the entire area but couldn't locate it even with his heightened senses. If the statue was using a skill to conceal its true form, how incredible would that skill have to be?

The angel statue continued.
[The answer is in you.]
In me?

Jinwoo, on the alert for any trickery, narrowed his eyes. He had spent four years of his life as a low-rank hunter fighting against countless enemies that could have easily killed him. Despite being the weakest of the E rank, he'd managed to survive. Through those experiences, his instincts had been honed to help him make the best possible decisions during the worst possible situations. Those same instincts now warned him of a significant change in the air, and sure enough...

Ping!

The chime was followed by the system, now back to the pleasant woman's voice.

[Retrieving data from storage.]
[Would you like to accept?] (Y/N)

A screen came up as well. Jinwoo looked at the blinking YES and NO awaiting his input.

Huh......?

Was this another trap? Jinwoo's gaze shifted from the screen to the angel.

Its face was blank once more. "The choice is yours."

Unlike earlier, its voice was now separate from that of the system. A stiff, mechanical-sounding male cadence grated at Jinwoo's ears.

Jinwoo pursed his lips.

Data from storage......

Did the system have a save file like in a video game? One Jinwoo could check?

......

Numerous thoughts raced through his head, but he had already made up his mind. This might be his one and only chance to discover the truth, so there was no turning back now. Besides, if this was a trap, the system wouldn't have gone through such a complicated process, as it had the ability to stop Jinwoo's heart at any time.

If this was the final test…then I've earned the right to check the file.

Jinwoo briefly recalled what the angel had said before the fight began.

"If you're still standing when this test is over, I will tell you everything. That will be your reward from me."

His reward was the right to check the data.

Jinwoo made up his mind, and having made his decision, he spoke deliberately. "……Yes."

Darkness surrounded him.

Ping!

And then came the system's voice.

[You have successfully retrieved the data.]

* * *

Jinwoo was traveling through an endless tunnel at warp speed. He soon shot through the darkness and was flung into a blinding light on the other side.

He gasped as his sight adjusted, and he took in the spectacle spreading out below him.

Oh my God……

An infinite army of magic beasts stood in countless rows, as far as the eye could see. There were so many of them that Jinwoo couldn't make out the ground they were standing on. It was truly a horrifying sight. If they escaped through a gate, the entire human race would be doomed.

Jinwoo felt sick to his stomach.

Wait a minute…… Where is this?

It certainly wasn't Earth. The land was brownish red and arid. There wasn't a single plant, and odd-looking, tall, thin rock formations jutted toward the sky. He had never seen such a foreign environment before.

His gaze moved toward the magic beasts. There were little ones, the likes of which were commonly found in low-rank dungeons, as well as more powerful ones such as high orcs, Ice Slayers, and giants. Regardless of their size, rank, or type, they were all looking up and waiting.

What are they looking at?

Jinwoo followed their gazes.

......!

A black lake floated up high in the sky—or no, it wasn't a lake. It was a gate so enormous that it could be easily mistaken for a huge lake. The black hole blocked out a purple sky.

A purple sky......

Given the color, Jinwoo was now absolutely sure this wasn't Earth. Something was about to go down between the magic beasts and that gate in this otherworldly place.

Jinwoo swallowed hard. In the prolonged eerie silence, his nervousness grew.

Vwooooooom.

What would come out of the gate? Jinwoo was expecting an army of humans, armed to the teeth, charging through the gate just like magic beasts did in gates on Earth.

Kraak!

Pouring out of the broken gate were winged soldiers in silver armor. They swarmed out like angry bees whose hive had been disturbed, occupying the heavens the same way the magic beasts covered the land.

It was a grand spectacle that blew Jinwoo's mind.

However, the magic beasts had the opposite reaction, crying out and going berserk at the sight of the soldiers filling their skies.

It was clear what Jinwoo was witnessing. This was war.

Kroom!

The soldiers struck the ground like silver streaks of lightning. More gates opened, and silver soldiers swarmed out. With the magic beasts on the ground and the soldiers overhead, the two hostile groups clashed spectacularly in an epic battle.

GROOAAAAAAR!

Magic beasts roared and shook the earth.

WHOOOOOOM!

The silver soldiers blew horns that sounded majestically.

Weapons clashed, armor was crushed, and yells turned into screams and groans. The land was stained red.

It was immediately obvious who held the upper hand. The silver soldiers easily lopped the heads off magic beasts capable of tearing apart high-rank hunters. There was no question that the monsters were outmatched, and the battle tilted in favor of the soldiers.

Nonetheless, despite their assured victory, soldiers continuously streamed from the gates, and in no time, the silver wave swept over all the beasts below.

Grraaahhh!

Arrrghh!

What began as a battle was now a massacre as the swords and spears of the soldiers were as merciless as Jinwoo had been with his enemies. The numbers of magic beasts dwindled rapidly. Jinwoo couldn't explain why he had mixed feelings as he watched the horrific creatures being so helplessly overwhelmed.

Do I feel bad for them, or am I jealous that humans can't have that kind of power?

His musings didn't last long as something extraordinary happened next. With the complete annihilation of the magic beasts at hand, the soldiers of the sky ceased their onslaught and froze one by one.

What's happening?

Did the soldiers suddenly feel compassion for their enemies? No, that couldn't be it. The invading army maintained a tight grip on their weapons—but their hands were also trembling slightly. Instead of pity, their eyes were full of terror.

Their gazes were trained on something behind Jinwoo. It was clear that whatever lay behind him was about to turn the tide of this battle. Jinwoo looked down instead of over his shoulder.

A shadow was creeping across the brownish-red terrain, quickly spreading to the dead bodies and covering the blood-soaked land below. As the shadow passed beneath the dead, screams originated from places unknown.

Jinwoo couldn't ascertain the source of the cries, but he did know a skill that had the exact same effect.

Monarch's Domain......

Shivers ran up his spine, and Jinwoo slowly looked behind him.

There stood a knight covered from head to toe in black armor. An ominous, dark aura rose from the knight and the horse he rode. Could that be...?

Jinwoo instinctively knew there was only one name befitting this knight.

......Shadow Monarch.

Simply being in his presence made the very air feel heavy and suffocating. Everyone—from the soldiers of the sky to the intelligent and unintelligent magic beasts alike on the ground—held their collective breath and gave the Shadow Monarch their full attention. All eyes on the battlefield were on him.

[......]

Shadow Monarch glared at the flying soldiers and stretched out his hand as if grabbing something. The aerial army flinched and retreated slightly. An eerie silence weighed heavily on everyone's shoulders.

The monarch's dignified voice shattered the quiet.

[Arise.]

Ba-dump!

Jinwoo's heart leaped.

Arise. That single word caused a ripple that spread out at a frightening speed, animating the shadows. The bloodred battlefield turned into rolling black waves.

Grrrargh!

The shadow soldiers turned their dark eyes toward the enemy, their strange cries indistinguishable from angry roars or screams of anguish. There was no more fear of the enemy in those eyes. This scene was cause enough to make the soldiers of the sky tremble, but the monarch didn't stop there.

[ROOOOAR!]

The knight gave a mighty bellow that reverberated in Jinwoo's heart instead of his eardrums. It shook hearts, knees, and the land below. The shadow soldiers raised their weapons high and answered.

ROOOOOOOAR!

With that, the shadow soldiers were transformed. Across the land, the deceased magic beasts were now shadow soldiers ready for battle.

Jinwoo held his breath. He found the roar of the shadow soldiers thrilling.

Ba-dump!

His heart thumped loudly. If this was the peak of the Shadow Monarch's power, then Jinwoo still had a very long way to go.

The hesitant soldiers of the sky were on the move again. They regrouped and then struck the soldiers in black, again reminding Jinwoo of silver bees.

But these reborn magic beasts weren't as easy to defeat. Weapons struck weapons, and soldiers fought soldiers as the silver and black armies clashed and became one giant mass.

The earth shook from the din of the battle. A battle that had almost ended as a one-sided massacre was a full-on war again. The appearance of just one individual, albeit a terrifying individual with incredible power, had turned the tide.

Jinwoo had no idea why the system was showing him this scene, but he couldn't take his eyes off it.

The battle raged. This was a much bloodier and fiercer conflict unfolding than before. While the magic beasts had been no match for soldiers of the sky in life, they were able to stand their ground as shadow soldiers after death.

However, what made them truly terrifying had nothing to do with bravery or combat abilities. The intrepid soldiers of the sky still overpowered their shadow enemies in terms of fighting skills and weapons. Reincarnation hadn't helped the shadow army in that regard, so initially, it did not seem as though the scales of war had changed.

However, as soon as the shadow soldiers were defeated, they immediately regenerated.

Arghhh!

A shadow soldier writhed in pain and cried out as it was stabbed. The silver soldier, certain of its victory, lowered its spear and drew its sword to behead the black creature.

Shhhk!

But as soon as the head flew off…

……!

…the decapitated body and head dissipated into smoke and rematerialized whole a couple of steps away. The silver soldier flinched, and the shadow soldier took the opportunity to return the stab to the chest.

Krrrunk!

The sword pierced the silver armor and came out the other side. The soldier of the sky fell helplessly to the dirt.

Thud!

Its eyes lost focus as the life drained from its body. But then, it heard a majestic voice.

[Arise.]

At some point, the silver soldier realized it was holding a black spear. This was not the end for it but, rather, a new beginning. Its eyes turned solid black as it looked at its former comrades.

Its former brothers-in-arms trembled as they made eye contact. But this new recruit knew its mission…

[Grooooar!]

…and eagerly accepted its new lot in life.

Jinwoo took a wider view of the entire battlefield. The conflict between the silver soldiers emerging from the gates in the sky and the respawning soldiers in black was quite even, the number pouring out of the gate matching the ranks rising from the shadows of the dead.

Is this what war in hell would look like? No human could truly comprehend the atrocities raging in this expansive land.

The delicate balance between the two opposing forces shifted as soon as the Shadow Monarch stopped issuing commands to his army and joined the fray. His black horse charged onto the battlefield. Whenever he swung his sword, he mowed down thousands of enemies in his path, and the dead then rose again as his shadow soldiers. With a mere wave of his hand, soldiers of the sky attempting to flee lost the use of their wings and plummeted to the earth.

Ruler's Authority......

The Shadow Monarch ravaged the land like a storm. For the first time since the battle began, the silver soldiers were pushed back. The millions who had conquered both sky and land were forced back by a single enemy.

Jinwoo let out an impressed hum. The end looked nigh.

However, just as the army of the sky was being driven back, an eerie wind blew, followed by an intense aura that brought goose bumps.

The Shadow Monarch looked back even with the enemy in front of him.

Two more huge gates, as large as the ones floating overhead, appeared behind him, and two distinct types of magic beasts emerged from both. One group consisted of animal-type magic beasts led by an enormous wolf as big as a mountain. The other contained knights and soldiers waving the standards of noble clans as they charged.

Jinwoo's eyes widened at the sight.

Huh......?

Jinwoo recognized all the crests on the standards: Ricardo, Pathos, Lokhan, Ingleias, and even Radar.

......Esil.

They were the crests of the noble clans from the Demon's Castle.

Jinwoo didn't have time to wonder why the demons had appeared. The animal-type beasts and the demons attacked the shadow soldiers in tandem. Those shadow ranks in their path were torn apart by the joint attack.

But that was just the beginning. The mighty soldiers of the sky renewed their onslaught. With the silver soldiers in front of them and the joint animal and demon armies behind, the shadow soldiers were surrounded.

The tides of war had turned once again.

Ba-dump!

Jinwoo grabbed his chest, and it throbbed in pain. The hunter slowly shifted his attention toward the Shadow Monarch standing next to him. He could somehow sense how the knight felt... But how? Just as Jinwoo could sense the emotions of the shadow soldiers, he also picked up on what Shadow Monarch was feeling. Intense anger was boiling inside him. No, it was beyond anger; it was profound rage.

Shadow soldiers were repeatedly dying and regenerating. Though their ability to recover may have appeared endless, Jinwoo knew all too well the limits of this power he likewise possessed.

It only lasts if you have enough mana......

Once one's mana levels were drained, the shadow soldiers would stay down, and the Shadow Monarch would have no soldiers to command. Jinwoo sensed that his vast store of magic power was slowly draining.

The monarch turned his horse around and charged the new arrivals.

The ensuing battle was fierce and resulted in piles of dead bodies and an ocean of blood. The flame of the war lit by countless soldiers was consuming all living things.

However, the end was nigh. Not many creatures remained on the battlefield. The monarch himself had lost his mount during the battle, but that didn't stop him from cutting down two demon knights in his way.

He then stood before one demon leaning against an odd-looking rock formation to catch its breath. Its face was obscured by a helmet, but Shadow Monarch knew whom he faced.

[We could have ended the war today.]

"......"

[Why did you betray me?]

The demon feebly looked up. It had suffered serious wounds and was unlikely to survive. The voice that came from behind the helmet sounded near death.

"What…could have been. We could have exterminated all of you, but……"

Shadow Monarch's voice was cold as ice.

[I asked why you betrayed me?]

Hee-hee!

The demon laughed heartily and replied.

"#$%#^#%#%@$."

Jinwoo couldn't make out what it said. Had he misheard? No.

"@$^$##."

Though Jinwoo couldn't understand, the monarch apparently did. He reached out and grabbed the demon by its neck to pull it closer.

The demon gurgled in pain. "Urrk."

Krunk!

The part of its armor that protected its neck was bent out of shape by Shadow Monarch's grip. Yet, the demon made sure to relay everything it intended.

"……%^&*$@%^&."

Shlick.

The monarch's thumb plunged into the demon's neck.

Kaff.

The demon coughed blood.

At that moment, Jinwoo made eye contact with the demon from under its helmet. Stunned, the hunter released its neck.

Whump!

The demon hit the ground, lifeless.

No way.

Jinwoo had seen those eyes before, but that couldn't be.

Ba-dump!

Jinwoo's heart pounded hard. He shook his head a few times and then cautiously removed the demon's helmet. They were definitely the same eyes. How could Jinwoo forget them?

The helmet fell from Jinwoo's hands.

Clang!

The demon's eyes were still open and filled with burning hatred. Jinwoo had seen these eyes on the top floor of the Demon's Castle.

"Balan...the Demon Monarch?"

As Jinwoo realized who the demon was, he had another startling revelation. His hands...and his feet, legs, and chest were all covered in black armor. At some point, Jinwoo had taken control of the body of the Shadow Monarch.

Ba-dump, ba-dump, ba-dump!

Jinwoo's heart began pounding loudly in his ears. He placed his hand on his chest.

Ba-dump, ba-dump, ba-dump!

His eyes widened.

How......? Why didn't I realize until now?

He had grown more conscious of his heartbeat after the double dungeon, yet he had failed to notice earlier. Jinwoo's trembling hand moved to the right side of his chest.

He felt the heartbeat—one from the left and another from the right.

Ba-dump!

Two hearts were beating as one.

As he stared at the ground in complete shock, four shadows approached from above, slowly growing larger. He quickly looked to the skies.

Four angels, each with six wings, slowly descended toward him.

That was the end of the memory.

Ping!

At the chime, he was once again surrounded by darkness. As he drifted into unconsciousness, he heard the clear voice of the system.

[Data retrieval is complete.]

7
UNINVITED GUESTS

7

UNINVITED GUESTS

As the master of the top guild in Korea, Jongin Choi was initially unhappy about the request from Jinchul to go to a C-rank gate. He even considered sending a strike squad with some high-rank hunters in his place.

However, once he heard the details, he couldn't resist.

Hunter Sung entered a double dungeon?

A double dungeon was intriguing enough, but Hunter Sung was also involved. How many hunters, much less guild masters, wouldn't be excited?

Jongin postponed the raid he'd been preparing for and immediately summoned his elite hunters, as Jinchul had emphasized this was an urgent matter.

"The association has asked for our cooperation. It seems we'll need to intervene."

The hunters murmured in hushed tones. The association had summoned them just as they were about to embark on an A-rank raid, so the gravity of the situation wasn't lost on them.

They had also just heard the breaking news about what was happening in Japan, so they were feeling even more agitated.

"What happened?" The question came from the second-most-influential member of the guild.

Jongin turned to the vice guild master. "I'm told a double dungeon was discovered in a C-rank gate."

A double dungeon?

Haein blinked. A dungeon within a dungeon was certainly uncommon, but it didn't make much sense for the association to call on the Hunters Guild for a mere C-rank gate.

Seeing her puzzlement, Jongin explained further. "It looks like Hunter Jinwoo Sung is fighting something in there alone. For Manager Woo to not act himself and call on us— What's the matter, Hunter Cha?"

Her expression had transformed. "Nothing."

"……Okay, then. Hunter Sung should be fine on his own, but let's get going just in case."

Haein nodded, and the others hurriedly packed their bags. Their only luggage was their weapons, but they still needed to be stowed with the utmost care.

"Hmm, we're missing some—"

Another hunter tapped the shoulder of the colleague doing the head count and pointed toward a corner of the room where a man was slumped on the ground in abject despair.

"Suzuki?"

"Leave him be."

"Oh, right……" The hunter understood right away.

Suzuki was a Japanese hunter who had been recruited by Korea not too long ago. His eyes were glued to the news broadcast on his cell phone.

"Let's go do our part."

"Got it."

The two hunters left Suzuki at the offices and got in one of the guild vans. One by one, the vehicles carrying the elite strike squad sped off to their destination.

* * *

"Yikes! Hot, hot!" The cigarette had fallen out of the startled Kim's hand. It landed on the sand, so there was no need to put it out. The way he aggressively stomped on the butt, though, spoke to his emotional state. Still, this was no time to vent one's frustrations on some stupid cigarette.

Kim's gaze turned back to the parked vans. He'd been so busy noting that every person emerging from the vehicles was an elite member of the Hunters Guild that he hadn't initially felt the cigarette ashes falling on his fingers.

Jongin Choi, Haein Cha, and Jeongho Yeun? Even Kihoon Son?

The top dogs of the Hunters Guild had gathered in this location. To think he'd stumbled on this galaxy of stars after following Jinchul on a whim.

Strangely, the gate in question was only a C rank. Kim's mouth went dry. He couldn't even begin to imagine what was going on inside.

Manager Woo was usually forthcoming about these matters, but as even he was keeping tight-lipped, Kim had been unable to do much except chain-smoke to calm his nerves. All the butts he'd discarded had formed a small mound at his feet.

Jinchul paid no attention to the yearning gaze of the reporter and hurriedly approached Jongin. Like Jinchul earlier, the latter couldn't tear his eyes away from the gate.

"Holy shit......! What the fuck......? What *is* that thing?" Jongin couldn't stem the tide of the curses from spilling unconsciously from his mouth.

Jinchul possessed exceptionally sharp senses for a brawler, but Jongin was Korea's most powerful mage. When it came to detecting the flow of magic energy, he was only behind Yoonho Baek with his Eyes of a Beast and Jinwoo Sung's supernatural level of perception.

"Can you handle it?" That's how Jinchul framed his question, but Jongin heard the unspoken, *I cannot.*

He replied grimly, "You said Hunter Sung was inside?"

"Affirmative."

Jongin nodded slowly. Who else would be? Better yet, who else would be capable of taking on an enemy emitting this much mana?

"Is he trying to single-handedly save the planet or something?" Jongin blurted out.

Jinchul sympathized with a tired nod. It sounded quite plausible to him.

"Whether we can handle it or not, we still need to go in there. We owe it to Hunter Sung."

If the combined might of Jinwoo Sung and the Hunters Guild couldn't tackle this, then no one else in Korea could. In other words, if they couldn't stop the beasts here, the country was screwed.

What was that? Did they say Hunter Sung? Kim, who was doing his best to eavesdrop from a distance, picked up Jinwoo's name, and his eyes became as wide as a rabbit's. *Hunter Sung is in there?*

Kim stared at the gate before he hastily scanned the area. Besides two S-rank hunters, there were a sizable number of A ranks, in addition to Hunter Sung already inside.

My...my notepad! Where's my notepad?

Smelling a huge scoop, he rushed to find his notebook. From this point on, he couldn't afford to miss a single word uttered or the smallest event transpiring here. Everyone else was preoccupied with what was going on in Japan. This opportunity was like mana from heaven, a once-in-a-lifetime exclusive involving three S-rank hunters and the Hunter's Association.

Is that why Manager Woo wouldn't give me a quote earlier?

Hunter Sung's information was classified, so he was a VIP under special supervision by the Hunter's Association. No wonder Manager Woo had stayed mum.

The elite strike squad finished their preparations as Jinchul and Jongin ended their conversation. The tanks picked up their defensive gear, the damage dealers grabbed their weapons, and the healers equipped themselves with magic tools charged with mana. They were ready as quickly and efficiently as one would expect from the top guild in the country.

Jongin exchanged looks with Haein and nodded. Haein nodded back to let him know that her inspection of the squad was done. They were good to go.

The elite members of the surveillance team had completed their preparations earlier. Jinchul reviewed some information from a subordinate and then turned to face the others with a solemn expression.

"Let's move out."

* * *

They had a long way to go. The hunters sped down the tunnel, but they didn't run. Although they were all high rank, not everyone could move at the same speed.

Haein was especially fast, but when she tried to dash ahead, Jongin grabbed her by the wrist. "What are you going to do alone, Hunter Cha?"

"……"

Jongin understood her desire to rescue Jinwoo, but haste would endanger everyone.

"Some of us can't keep up with you, and we'll be at a disadvantage if we try to push ourselves."

With a sullen expression, Haein moved to the rear of the group.

Seeing her reaction, Jinchul mumbled under his breath, "So the rumor is true, then."

"Excuse me?"

Jinchul quickly dismissed Jongin's query. "Oh… No, it's nothing."

Jongin raised an eyebrow before facing forward. The sinister mana was coming from that direction, so they had to stay alert. Jongin thought about Hunter Sung being in the same position they were.

I hope we aren't too late……

There wasn't much else they could do for him at this point but move swiftly, keep their wits about them, and pray for his safety. They couldn't let the stress cloud their minds.

Jongin made conversation with Jinchul to ease the tension he felt. "How did Hunter Sung end up going inside?"

"I don't know the details, but according to witnesses, Hunter Sung seemed to already be aware that this gate had a double dungeon."

"Hmm." Jongin's forehead wrinkled.

"Any ideas on the matter?"

"No, but…… Something doesn't feel right."

"Oh?"

"I've done my share of research on Hunter Sung." Jongin was a guild

master, and one of his duties was to recruit high-level hunters. For obvious reasons, he had shown a great deal of interest in Jinwoo. "There was
a similar incident near here."

Jinchul himself had overseen the investigation, so he knew exactly
what Jongin was talking about. About six months ago, Jinwoo had
entered a double dungeon. And here he was again, seeking out another
after all this time. Those who knew of both incidents had a hard time
brushing this off as mere coincidence.

As Jinchul predicted, Jongin brought it up. "Double dungeons are
rare enough that most barely see one in their lifetime. Yet, Hunter Sung
has crossed paths with two of them. Not only that, but he also went
looking for the second. Isn't that odd?"

Jinchul didn't answer. Just as Jongin alluded, much about Jinwoo was
shrouded in mystery: the double dungeon, his reawakening, his unique
abilities...

But one thing was certain. The Hunter's Association—heck, all of
Korea—desperately needed Jinwoo Sung. That was why Jinchul had
asked the Hunters Guild for help right away without waiting for clear-
ance from his superiors. Hunter Sung's safety was to be secured by any
means necessary. There would be time to ask questions later.

Rousing himself from his thoughts, Jinchul raised his head.

We're here......

It would've taken almost an hour for most hunters to arrive, but it
only took about ten minutes for the elite strike squad and surveillance
team to travel the same distance on foot. The end of the tunnel was in
sight.

"I think that's it."

"Yes, I sense something." Jongin froze as he registered a menacing
presence. Thankfully, he could still sense Jinwoo's presence as well.

Everything's fine as long as Hunter Sung is okay.

Jinwoo's abilities combined with support from the elite hunters here
should have been sufficient to handle whatever kind of magic beast was
up ahead.

Reassured, Jongin called out to the group, "Let's hurry, everyone!"

The elite squad from the Hunters Guild and the association charged through the huge doorway resembling the entrance of an ancient castle. The sight that met them was unlike anything they'd ever laid eyes on.

"Wh-what on earth......?"

"What the hell is this place?"

There were countless broken stone statues littering the floor. Rubble was piled up throughout the room.

"L-look!"

One of the hunters pointed to a truly enormous statue of some unknown deity standing frozen in time, its hands interlocked in the middle of slamming the ground. Its head, with half its face blown off, caught their attention.

Jinchul's heart began to race as he recalled the testimonies of the survivors from the previous double dungeon incident.

They mentioned all this...... The statue of a god, the other stone guardians—everything......!

They'd each reported the same thing: This place was occupied by a monstrous statue that could vaporize a C-rank hunter with one look as well as innumerable stone statues whose movements could not be followed with the naked eye.

The entire area was scarred by an epic battle that had recently taken place here.

Wait, where is Hunter Sung?

With the threats neutralized, their priority was to confirm Hunter Sung's status. Jongin eventually spotted him farther into the room.

"He's over there."

Jinwoo was lying quietly on his back, as if asleep, just below the fists of the colossus.

"Hunter Sung!"

Haein raised both her arms to stop the hunters about to rush to his aid dead in their tracks. Jinchul impatiently turned to look at her and noticed how sweaty her face seemed.

"Hunter Cha......?"

She bit her lower lip. "There... There's something over there."

It was then that a certain stone statue kneeling next to Jinwoo slowly raised itself up. The wings on its back were shredded, and it was missing an arm.

"I don't remember inviting humans in here." The angel statue stood up straight and, having scanned the intruders, grinned.

"Ahhh......"

The hunters were rendered speechless.

Jongin didn't know what to say, but he was sure of one thing: This living statue was the source of the ominous energy he'd been feeling this entire time. The mana radiating from it was so strong that the space around it looked distorted. Jongin's entire body had goose bumps even as he gazed upon the statue from a distance.

He peeked at Jinwoo. Considering his opponent was such a being, he understood why Jinwoo was lying unconscious on the ground. He also understood that only Jinwoo could have destroyed all the other statues while simultaneously contending with the angel. Jongin was impressed beyond belief.

And now it's up to us.

A big drop of sweat dripped down the side of Jongin's face. He wasn't even sure whether this enemy was a magic beast, but it was definitely stronger than the monstrous ant from Jeju Island.

Jongin swallowed with difficulty. Haein and Jinchul had turned pale. They, too, could feel the immense power of the being before them and were appropriately distraught.

Meanwhile, the other hunters behind the trio were bowled over for another reason.

"Did that thing......just speak?"

"I'm not hearing things, right?"

"A magic beast that speaks our language?"

The hunters exchanged looks of disbelief. They were witnessing the impossible.

It was a well-established fact that intelligent magic beasts had their own language. When gates began to appear, people had tried learning their language, but their attempts failed due to the magic beasts' brutal natures. Those captured with much effort gradually went insane in the presence of the humans. Even when restrained, the beasts went berserk trying to kill their captors, not caring if they tore their own flesh or broke their own bones in the process. They eventually either mentally collapsed or were put out of their misery.

Humans and magic beasts cannot coexist, and communication with them is impossible.

This was the consensus among the scientific community that studied the creatures. Yet, here one stood, speaking Korean as if it was the most natural thing in the world. This magic beast could be considered the find of the century, but it filled the hearts of all the hunters with unexplainable dread. Their primal instincts sounded an alarm in each of them.

As the statue took a step forward, the hunters took a trembling step back. The angel's gaze slowly scanned from left to right as if relishing the fear and panic on their faces.

"Mighty humans…" Its eyes resembled those of a predator eyeing its next meal. "You'll make a sufficient first offering for His Highness."

Would a smiling snake look this creepy? The hunters were immobilized by the sight.

……His Highness?

Was there another magic beast?

Jongin was puzzled, but he didn't have time to parse what the creature's words. The angel statue ripped the arm off one of the statues on the ground.

Krrak!

What is it doing?

The bewildered hunters got their answer when the angel placed the severed arm on its right shoulder and the two parts melded together.

What the......?!

The angel leisurely stretched out its newly attached arm.

Zoom.

It appeared right in front of them. Before they could react, it threw a powerful punch with its new fist and crushed a hunter's face.

Pow!

Face crumpled, the hunter flew back and slammed into a wall. By the time his nearby colleagues attempted a counterattack, the angel had disappeared.

"Where......?"

"Over there!"

It had returned to its previous location as if it hadn't moved at all. It wiggled its fingers. The test of its new hand had been successful.

"Myungchul!"

"N-nooo!"

The cries of the hunters confirmed they had a casualty. He'd died on the spot. An A-rank tank from the best guild in Korea had been killed with one blow.

Jongin's eyes darted around in a panic.

Hunter Sung fought this thing all by himself......?

Jongin was more concerned with trying to find a way out of this situation than dealing with the pain of losing his colleague. However, not everyone could handle it as objectively.

"You son of bitch!" One of the female hunters in the group was the deceased hunter's lover, and she charged the statue, enraged. In each hand burned a ball of fire.

Before she could chuck them, though, someone grabbed her wrist. She turned her head to see Haein. She shook her arm and yelled at the S-rank hunter. "Let go of me!"

"Please. You have to control yourself."

"I said, let go!"

"Rein it in."

The woman took a proper look at Haein, who was biting her lower lip in grief.

"I promise, I'm holding back, too……"

The grim look on Haein's face gave the other woman pause. She was fully aware that since the magic beast had shown no further aggression following its first attack, it would be best not to provoke it. Still, she just couldn't stand there doing nothing when the beast had killed her beloved in such a gruesome manner.

She quietly sobbed. "Ngh……"

When she was certain her colleague wasn't about to do anything rash, Haein looked toward Jinwoo. She, too, was tamping down her anger. She had no idea why, but the magic beast had stopped attacking them, and Jinwoo was still breathing just fine. He looked peaceful, as if sleeping.

At this point……

The most they could do was buy time until Jinwoo recovered.

At that moment, the angel statue finished its warm-up stretches and burst out laughing. "Ha-ha." Its voice echoed in the empty lair as it focused on the hunters. "Time to have some fun."

Its eyes glowed red. Was it going to attack? The hunters tightened their grips on their weapons and braced for battle. With only one opponent, they might stand a chance. Their ranks included plenty of the best hunters in Korea, including two S ranks. Just as hope bloomed in their hearts…

Rrrrrrumble.

The interior of the dungeon quaked.

"Oh…… Oh no."

A shadow of despair fell over the hunters' faces.

One by one, the broken statues began to twitch. Statues without heads, statues with holes in their chests, and statues without arms or legs began hoisting themselves upright. But most worrisome of them all was the statue of the deity that could only be described as gargantuan.

"......Shit."

The statues rose to face their prey as if they had never been damaged. Their emotionless faces made them even more grotesque.

The hunters retreated until they bumped into something.

"Huh......?"

It was the door, which had firmly shut and locked while the hunters were distracted. The statues weren't going to let anyone out alive.

The angel spoke up. "Those of you still standing after my puppets have fallen will have the opportunity to witness the glorious rebirth of the king."

It had mentioned the king earlier as well.

What the hell is it talking about?

Jinchul frowned. He couldn't understand what the monster was blabbering about, but he was certain of one thing: It planned to kill everyone here.

He gritted his teeth. Jinchul had worked for the Hunter's Association for four years and had survived numerous dangerous situations by fighting tooth and nail. That was his plan today. He had no intention of laying down and dying.

But even if I don't make it......

Hunter Sung had to survive. When he gazed at Jinwoo, the angel statue coincidentally waved its hand at Jinwoo at the same time.

"This one took down my puppets in five minutes." It then pointed a finger at the other hunters. "I wonder how long it will take for all of you to die."

As soon as the angel finished that sentence, Jinchul shouted, "Everyone, duck!"

The hunters swiftly followed his orders as a red laser swept over their heads. It had been close, but miraculously, there were no casualties. The beam coming from the colossus slowly dissipated.

Oh?

The angel statue watched them with interest as it took a step back. They should prove amusing until the king opened his eyes.

"Huff, huff, huff!" Jinchul was breathing hard and sweating profusely.

He shuddered to consider what would've happened if he'd been less informed. They'd survived the first attack thanks to the testimonies provided by the previous survivors. But it wasn't over yet.

No, this is just the beginning.

Jinchul raised his head to see the statues advancing toward them. Had he not been a top A-rank hunter, he would have been unable to follow their movements. He jumped to his feet, wound up for a punch, and struck a statue with his specially made gauntlet.

Ka-pow!

His eyes widened.

......?

One strike should've been enough, but the statue was still standing. He'd assumed the statue's durability to be compromised due to its damaged shoulder, but he should've known better considering who'd caused said damage. The statue's head recoiled slightly, but it soon recovered from the impact and swung at Jinchul with its sword.

Tsk.

Jinchul tutted to himself. He'd put his full power into that punch without considering a counterattack, and the statue's speed and proximity left him with no room to dodge.

Kaboom!

An explosion sent the approaching statue flying to the side. Jinchul scrunched his features and shook his head to stop the ringing in his ears. A voice came from his right.

"Are you okay?" It was Jongin, the Ultimate Hunter.

Jinchul nodded to express his gratitude. There was no time for further conversation.

Stomp!

The colossus was on the move.

Tak, tak, tak, tak, tak!

The smaller statues already had the hunters surrounded.

"President Choi!" the tanks called. "Provocation skills don't work on them!"

"What?" Jongin's expressed hardened.

Without Provocation, the statues would instinctively go after the weakest hunters first—which usually meant the healers. With their healers down, their line of defense would soon fall apart and wouldn't last long.

To make matters worse, the colossus was raising its ginormous fist.

How are we going to get out of this alive?

They were trapped at the edge of the cliff, and there was only one possible way out of this mess: waking up the unconscious Hunter Sung.

That damn angel had said as much.

According to the statue, Hunter Sung dealt with all of them in just five minutes!

If the angel statue had previously defeated Jinwoo because he'd been weakened by the other statues, then the current situation was dramatically different. Dozens of excellent hunters had his back.

We need to wake him up.

A fireball appeared in Jongin's palm. He wasn't called the Ultimate Hunter for nothing. The power and accuracy of his fireballs were as good as any high-tech modern firearm.

This was their Hail Mary. Jongin shot the flames at Jinwoo. This type of magic might give Jinwoo a little jolt, but it wouldn't harm him. If he woke up from the impact, the hunters would have a shot at victory.

Please......!

The fireball left a long trail in the air.

Kaboom.

The angel statue slid between Jinwoo and the incoming projectile, and the fireball exploded against its torso.

......?

Jongin was startled by the angel's sudden defensive move. Its face was twisted and distorted.

"How dare you......" For the first time, the stone angel bared its teeth. "How dare you interrupt the king's sleep?"

The king? Who was it referring to?

Jongin couldn't make heads or tails of the angel's words. "What did you say......?"

The angel statue didn't bother replying. After all, did humans explain themselves to insects? Though it might have been stuck in its current form for various reasons, it nevertheless considered itself above humans and had no intention of explaining itself to them. Besides, if an insect was being bothersome, it just had to be squished.

The angel raised a fist and then hammered it down toward Jongin's head.

Hwoosh!

Jongin felt his heart sink, but just as he'd always told his guild members not to give up until the bitter end, he didn't turn away.

A flash of light temporarily blinded Jongin right before the blow connected.

Clang!

Jongin blinked to see the Sword of Light held before his very eyes.

"Hunter Cha!"

Haein stood her ground as she blocked the angel's fist with her Sword of Light. A second later, and Jongin's head would've been ripped off.

Jongin let out a tiny sigh of relief as Haein turned to him. "I've got this, so please give the others a hand, President Choi."

"I'm on it." Jongin dashed off to join the fray.

The angel regarded the sword encased in light with interest.

"Ha-ha." It was hard to believe there was another human besides Jinwoo who could block its attacks. "You're entertaining, very fun."

As the angel statue put pressure on its fist, Haein's knee dipped slightly. She wasn't sure how long she could hold out, but she'd give it everything she had.

"Ugh......" A feeble moan slipped out of her full lips, and her wrists shook.

"Let's see how long you can go?" The angel snickered as it turned up the heat. The stone floor beneath Haein's feet cracked under the weight. Even using just one arm, it possessed an unbelievable amount of strength.

Haein clenched her teeth.

I can't...take much more of this......

Realizing she wouldn't last much longer, Haein threw all her strength into pushing aside the fist. The burst of power forced the angel back a step.

It gave a pleased smile. "Ha-ha."

The statue had expected her to be a short distraction, but she proved far more amusing than it had originally anticipated. It appeared there was more fun to be had.

"How wonderful." This time, it focused its power in both hands.

Gulp.

Haein swallowed hard. Mana radiated in abundance from the angel's hands. If she could have, she would've run for it.

But......

With Jinwoo out of the picture, if she abandoned everyone, there would be no one left capable of fighting this creature. Her glare intensified.

The angel, on the other hand, smiled widely and took a big step forward. Standing nearly three meters tall, it towered over her. It commenced attacking in earnest. As it had against Jinwoo, the angel statue delivered a barrage of wild punches. It was regretful that it only had two arms left, but that was more than enough for a human of this caliber. The fists shot at Haein like a hail of bullets.

Pakpakpakpakpakpakpakpakpak!

Haein narrowed her eyes in concentration.

Sword Dance!

Her movements sped up significantly, and her sword drew elegant arcs in the air like she was dancing. But the blows were far too quick, and it took everything she had just to defend herself. Each strike was powerful enough to instantly end her life if she let it get past her.

Clang! Ka-clang! Clang! Clang! Clang! Cling! Cling! Clang! Ka-clang! Clang, clak! Clang! Ka-clang! Clang! Clang! Cling! Cling! Clang!

"That's it. Just like that. Ha-ha." The angel was enjoying relentlessly bombarding Haein with a torrent of punches that would be invisible to the average human.

Haein was pushed back little by little, and her body was drenched in sweat. Maybe it was the sweat, or maybe she'd reached her limit, but as her sweaty palms slipped, one of the angel's attacks slipped through. It was a painful mistake. The punch she had failed to block connected with her shoulder.

Crack!

"……!" Haein hastily backed away and gritted her teeth, but the bone was broken. Her shoulder went numb. She lamented the loss of her left arm as it dangled uselessly.

"Ha-ha. Is that it? Is this all you got?" The angel wasted no time and rushed at her, refusing to cut her any slack. The fight between the two resumed.

Clang! Ka-clang! Ka-clang!

Haein had barely survived these attacks using both hands, so she had difficulty fending off the angel statue with just one. As more punches connected, her body became battered and bruised.

Pow! Ka-pow! Pow!

Bones broke, and flesh tore. Then came a critical blow.

Wham!

The statue struck her hard in the stomach, lifting her feet off the ground as she coughed up blood.

"Urrk!" Doubled over, she flew into the air. Her forced ascension made it impossible for her to counter.

At this point, the angel lost interest in playing with the broken toy. It approached the falling Haein to deliver the final blow and gathered the fingers of its hand to form a blade aimed at her chest.

Suddenly, a blue glow swirled around her, and Haein's eyes shot open in the middle of her fall. She twisted her body and sword around, and the angel came to an abrupt stop, leaning its head back to avoid the blade. The tip of the sword brushed past its eyes.

Shink!

A thin line appeared across its face.

Tmp!

Having successfully landed an attack of her own, Haein regained her balance and landed with both feet on the ground. Thanks to the timely healing spell, she had dodged a bullet.

But what was good for one person wasn't always good for another.

Fwip!

The angel statue spun around to locate the source of the healing spell.

Shit. Haein yelled, "Get out of the way!"

The main healer, who had been casting spells from behind the tankers, flinched at Haein's warning. "Huh?"

But as he turned his head toward Haein, he came face-to-face with the angel statue.

"Oh......" The main healer's jaw dropped.

Without hesitation, the angel statue did to him what he'd planned to do to Jongin earlier.

Bam!

The healer's head slammed into the ground. His legs twitched a few times before becoming limp.

"No!"

The hunters surrounding the angel statue rushed toward it in anger, but their foe was an unstoppable force against which none of them could stand.

Pow, pow!

Each time the angel statue threw a punch, an A-rank hunter was helplessly defeated.

"This isn't fun. Not fun at all, humans." Once the superior being lost interest, it showed no mercy.

As the number of hunters dealing damage from the rear dwindled, the line of tanks enduring the assault of the other statues and the colossus crumbled in no time. It was pure pandemonium. The tide had turned in the blink of an eye.

Boom!

The giant statue avoided the tanks and slammed its huge fist down, crushing two other hunters. Stone statues brandishing weapons encircled those remaining and began closing in on them.

Dammit......!

Haein quickly cut down four of the statues and then jumped in front of the angel. Stopping it was her priority. But the angel effortlessly blocked her blade with its wrist and kicked her in her side.

Whap!

Now that the angel was hell-bent on ending this, she could no longer keep it at bay.

After seeing Haein fall, Jongin grabbed Jinchul by the shoulder. Jinchul, who had just taken out another statue, jolted in surprise.

"I'll draw their attention, and you wake up Hunter Sung. There's nothing else we can do."

"What? Isn't he unconscious?"

"Actually, he's asleep. His breathing and magic power are stable. And I don't think there's a single scratch on him."

Had someone cast a sleeping spell on him? Jongin had a theory that the angel statue might be protecting Jinwoo because it was worried what would happen if he woke up.

I have no idea what it means by the "king's sleep," but......

Considering how desperate the angel had been to defend Jinwoo, Jongin guessed that their fellow hunter waking would be a fatal blow.

"Hurry!"

Jinchul nodded in understanding.

Jongin gathered all his magic power, and soon a large halo of fire circling his hands spat flames in every direction. The burning projectiles exploded each time they struck something.

Fwoosh! Fwoosh!

Boom! Kaboom! Boom! Bam!

Naturally, the statues turned to see what all the noise was. While Jongin drew their attention, Jinchul rushed to Jinwoo. He prayed Jongin's theory was correct.

While Jongin and Jinchul teamed up to rouse Jinwoo, the angel statue loomed over Haein, who lay on the ground struggling to breathe. One side of her ribs had been broken by the kick, and as she struggled to reach for her fallen sword, the angel stepped on her arm.

Crack!

"Ahhhhh!" She grabbed her shattered arm and screamed in pain.

The angel statue had already done away with those who could heal, and this female was too injured to put up any kind of fight. The lone threat among the humans was about to be eliminated.

"Ha-ha." The angel raised its bladelike hand once more. "This is the end."

Haein continued breathing laboriously as she glared at her executioner. It was over for her, yet she refused to give up. She reminded the angel of Jinwoo Sung. During their first encounter, his eyes had burned with the same fire.

The corners of the angel's mouth arched upward as it thrust its hand toward Haein's chest...but it paused before it connected. The angel statue flinched and retreated a couple of steps.

A shadow soldier was hidden in the human's own shadow. Due to the rules of the chamber, said soldier was unable to emerge, but it was there nonetheless.

Haein was puzzled by clear surprise on her enemy's face.

......?

It could've killed her just now, but it seemed to be hesitating.

And indeed, it was. The king had placed a soldier in this human, but for what purpose? Of course, it could've been Jinwoo's doing and not the king's...

But the king and the human are fused together, even if only slightly.

How was the angel statue supposed to distinguish between the king's will and Jinwoo's? If the king had been the one to place the shadow soldier within Haein for whatever reason, the angel couldn't do whatever it wanted to her.

The angel demanded, "How did you find this place?"

"……" Haein didn't answer.

When the silence grew long, the angel changed its question. "What connection do you all have with Jinwoo Sung?"

"……"

Haein kept quiet, fully aware that she wasn't obliged to answer.

Realizing it wouldn't get anything out of her, the creature changed tack. The angel statue snapped its fingers, and the screaming hunters immediately went silent. As if on command, the colossus and the other stone statues paused and slowly headed to the far side of the lair.

The angel statue then extended its palm, and an invisible hand drove Jinchul, who had been making his way to Jinwoo, to the ground.

"Ugh!" Jinchul tried his best to resist this unseen force above him, but he couldn't move an inch. Jinchul clenched his fists and let out a huff.

The angel dropped its hand. Nothing in the lair escaped its notice. Struggle as the humans might, it had them all dancing to its whim. That was the difference between it, a superior being, and humans. There was no way to bridge that gap.

"I shall ask again." The angel statue pointed at Jinchul. "If you do not answer me this time, I shall kill that man as well as all your other colleagues."

"……Fine." Haein nodded. If this helped buy them time, that would be a huge help.

The angel statue stared as she struggled to sit up. "What is your relationship to Jinwoo Sung?"

"……We're friends."

"Why did you come here?"

She pondered her response before replying, "To save Hunter Sung."

The answer brought a smile to the angel's face. Just who was saving whom now? It was clear these humans had no idea what was truly going on. The angel was mortified for suspecting that the king might have a plan for this woman. These people had come to this place for the human Jinwoo Sung.

The stone angel couldn't contain its laughter. It then turned to Haein. "I shall bless you with an opportunity."

"......What opportunity?"

"Today, one of the noble sovereigns shall descend upon this world. I shall bless you with the opportunity to witness such a glorious moment in history."

Until the angel statue could confirm the king's intentions, it had to keep her alive. However, she was the sole exception; it didn't plan on letting the other humans go free.

"Every human except you..." Its smile had vanished, and the angel now looked downright maniacal. "...will die right here."

After all, it wasn't okay for these uninvited guests to be present for His Highness's majestic return.

A voice from behind challenged him. "Says who?"

"......?"

Before the angel statue could turn around, a fist connected with its face.

Ka-blam!

The statue slammed into the far wall.

Boom!

The impact shattered the wall, sending rubble tumbling down. Before the angel statue could collapse to the floor, Jinwoo appeared in front of it and grabbed it by the throat.

"You."

Jinwoo's other hand was on his own chest. Sure enough, it hadn't been just a dream. There was another heart beating on the right side of his chest.

Jinwoo squeezed the statue's neck as he growled, "What the hell did you do to my body?"

8

THE BLACK HEART

8

THE BLACK HEART

At some point while reliving the memory, Jinwoo had become the Shadow Monarch himself. In that moment, he came to the realization that a mana-powered heart that constantly radiated magic power had been beating inside his chest.

Was this all in his head? That was something he could easily check.

Stats.

Jinwoo called up the stat window with his hand still wrapped around the neck of the angel statue. Out of the many statistics tracked were his current reserves of magic power, which the system labeled as MP—or mana points.

[MP: 109,433]

Jinwoo was stunned.

A hundred thousand…?

He could hardly believe what he was seeing. The last time he'd checked his MP, which was immediately before departing for this very dungeon, it had only been around nine thousand. There was no mistake about it. His MP had increased over tenfold.

Something else caught his attention.

My title...

The title line blinked as if to indicate it had changed. Even though Jinwoo hadn't personally switched anything, the title had been revised. It now read DEMON HUNTER.

Jinwoo had simply ignored it until now because its information hadn't been revealed, so he went ahead and checked the details.

[TITLE: DEMON HUNTER]

The required conditions have been fulfilled.

You have recovered the memories of defeating Balan, the Demon Monarch of White Lightning. A great power has accepted the Player as its owner.

Buff: Black Heart: MP +100,000

The Black Heart!

That was the reason for the insane jump in MP. A hundred thousand more mana would be enough power to pretty much regenerate his shadow soldiers ad infinitum.

The image of the Shadow Monarch as he led the army of respawning soldiers against the silver soldiers who blotted out the sky sprang to mind. His soldiers had been in a never-ending cycle of death and rebirth that allowed them to gradually overwhelm their enemies.

The soldiers of the sky, although strong enough to push back an opposing force roughly the same size as their own army, couldn't keep up with the regenerating shadow soldiers and were ultimately forced to retreat. If not for the timely arrival of reinforcements, the silver soldiers would have been annihilated, and that was thanks to the Shadow Monarch's endless source of mana as seen in the system file.

If that's the case......

The Black Heart would make his shadow soldiers immortal! The thought gave him goose bumps.

"How...could you...?"

Jinwoo looked up at the stammering angel. For the first time, Jinwoo noted a look on the angel's face that wasn't a sickening smile or pure rage. It was fear.

The angel was staring at Jinwoo horror-struck. "How are you maintaining your own consciousness even as the Black Heart beats within you?"

Huh?

This question revealed two things to Jinwoo. One, the angel statue wasn't directly responsible for the Black Heart. And two, this outcome wasn't in its favor.

Krik!

Jinwoo tightened his grip on the angel's neck, causing cracks to form.

"Guh!" The architect's face twisted in pain.

"Tell me what a 'Player' is! What were you planning on doing to me?"

Jinwoo wouldn't relent, meaning he could break its neck at a moment's notice. Unfortunately, the angel wasn't in the right frame of mind to provide answers.

"No way…… Sh-Shadow Monarch, you……! Do you think the other monarchs will just sit back and let this happen?!" The angel statue glared at Jinwoo as it blathered.

Crack!

Jinwoo's finger punched a hole in the creature's neck. He could now break it with a single twitch of a finger.

The angel felt excruciating pain. "Arrrghh!" It let out an agonized screech toward the ceiling.

Jinwoo had so many things he wanted to ask. "Answer my question."

Having passed the test, Jinwoo had earned the right to interrogate the angel, so it was only fair for him to demand the reward that had been promised.

Instead, a bright-red light flashed from the angel.

"Ah!"

"What the—?"

The other hunters began screaming, prompting Jinwoo to look over his shoulder.

"Th-those things……!"

"They're coming!"

The colossus and the other statues had retreated to a corner of the lair earlier, but they now began moving again, their eyes glowing red.

"Ha-ha." The angel statue sounded pleased with itself. "If you kill me, there'll be no one to call off my puppets."

Will you kill me now? The angel was issuing a challenge to Jinwoo. Inferior beings had so many weaknesses, and if Jinwoo truly was a human, he'd have plenty to exploit. He must have had someone he deemed a friend among the hunters.

What's this......?

Contrary to the angel's expectations, Jinwoo grinned.

"What if I deal with the puppets after I kill you?"

Taken aback, the angel statue hurriedly answered, "If you kill me, then the architect of the system—"

"See, I've thought about that, too," Jinwoo interrupted. He looked at the angel with the same gaze it leveled at the humans. "You know, even if the architect of the system disappeared, I doubt the whole system would collapse."

Jinwoo called the statue's bluff. He knew everything it had purposefully omitted.

The angel had been careless and forgotten why it had chosen Jinwoo in the first place. He excelled at seeing through the rules.

You've forced my hand, then!

The angel statue played its last card.

Ping!

[System administrator access denied.]
[System administrator access denied.]
[System administrator access denied.]

Ping! Ping!

The chime went off several more times, but the same notification appeared.

* * *

[System administrator access denied.]

The angel froze. It had attempted to manipulate the system but had been rejected. When Jinwoo shrugged, the angel thrashed in his grip.

"You bastard! Gaaaaaaah!"

It apparently had no intention of providing Jinwoo with answers.

No reason to let you live, then.

Jinwoo released the angel's neck and threw a mana-powered left hook.

Ka-pow!

He not only punched through the statue's body but also left a gaping hole in the wall behind it.

Hwooo...

Silence immediately fell in his vicinity. An eye for an eye; a tooth for a tooth. Jinwoo had administered a punishment befitting the crime the angel had perpetrated. The statue's head and half its torso had been obliterated. What remained slowly slid down the wall.

It's too bad I couldn't get an answer.

But the angel had been tricking Jinwoo from the start, so how could he believe anything it said anyway?

This'll do.

He dusted off his left hand as if symbolically wiping away any regret.

An urgent voice yelled out to Jinwoo, "Hunter Sung!"

Oh, right.

Jinwoo turned. He'd been so focused on the angel that he'd forgotten about the rest of the statues, which were mercilessly attacking the humans as per the puppeteer's final instructions.

"Hunter Sung!" Jongin was frantically calling for Jinwoo while casting spells to defend against the onslaught.

Pow!

Jinchul stumbled after taking a punch to the chin. As he tried to steady his shaky legs, his eyes shifted from left to right. He took in the sight of blood and sweat spraying from his fellow hunters. His mind went blank. Hold on. What had he been doing just now…?

Oh yeah.

By the time he got his bearings, the statue was right in front of him. Jinchul confirmed he'd been struck with a book so thick that it looked like several encyclopedias combined. Since it was made of stone, it was no wonder his head was spinning.

Could a book…be counted as a weapon?

He remembered an episode of a courtroom drama involving a case that asked the same question and laughed in spite of himself. He didn't have the energy to block or dodge the stone tome, never mind the energy for a counterattack. Jinchul could only smile ruefully and drop his hands in surrender.

Kaboom!

The statue split in two at the waist and was tossed aside.

"Huh……?" Jinchul snapped back to attention. His eyes blinked, and he shook his head as a familiar man came up next to him.

"Are you okay?"

"Oh……!" Jinchul gasped.

It was Jinwoo.

Shocked, Jinchul could barely get out his question. "Did you just use your bare hands……?"

"Let's talk details later."

Jinwoo ran off, leaving his comrade behind. He looked around until light bouncing off metal finally caught his eye. It was his missing Demon Monarch's Dagger.

Found it!

Jinwoo stretched his hand out toward the blade, using his invisible hand to deliver it into his real one.

Tak!

The grip of this dagger always felt good in his hands.

Whap!

First, Jinwoo kicked aside a statue blocking his way and then started mowing down the others.

Hup.

As he did, he took a deep breath. He alone could move freely as time slowed. He vanished from view, and the only thing the other hunters could make out were the statues being destroyed.

Shhk!

Thud!

Four assailants fell to the ground simultaneously. Hunters whom Jinwoo had pulled from the brink of death stood there with their mouths agape.

"Huh......?"

Jinchul joined them and murmured, "He renders you speechless, doesn't he?"

"......Yes." The hunters nodded.

"It's the same for me." Despite having seen Jinwoo in action several times before, Jinchul was no less amazed. A bittersweet look crossed his face as he placed a cigarette between his lips.

One of the members of the surveillance team approached him. "Manager Woo, should we be standing around like this?"

"What do you mean?"

"Hunter Sung is fighting the beasts, and......" They trailed off as they got a proper look at Jinwoo. "Wh......?"

Jinchul stuck a cigarette into the hunter's open mouth and lit it for him. "Do you think there's room for us out there?"

"No, sir......"

"So let's stay out of his way and smoke."

"Yes, sir."

Other hunters who had also been watching Jinwoo in admiration gathered around Jinchul. He quickly ran out of cigarettes.

Suddenly, the tip of Jinchul's nose began to tingle.

I lost count of how many times I almost died here.

The statues had seemed undefeatable to him, so he was relieved and overjoyed to witness Jinwoo taking care of business all on his own.

"Manager Woo, are you crying?"

"No, of course not. I've got smoke in my eyes."

"Oh yeah, me too."

"Me too."

"Same."

There was so much cigarette smoke in the air, all the hunters were teary-eyed.

Bam!

Kihoon blocked the punch from the colossus with his shield and let out a grunt. "Ugh!"

His knees buckled. With no healer to help him, he had no choice but to endure the blows on his own, but he'd reached his limit.

"S-somebody, help......!" When he strained to see where his teammates were, he spotted them gathered leisurely to one side.

What the hell?

They weren't going to bother coming to his aid even though he was pouring out his blood, sweat, and tears to keep them safe. Pissed off, Kihoon bellowed, "What the hell are you all doing?!"

The other hunters responded by pointing at something above him. He took it as a warning of another impending attack, and he hefted his shield and braced for impact. But nothing came.

"......?" Kihoon abruptly noticed how quiet it was.

What now?

He surreptitiously sneaked a peek from under his shield and saw that the rest of the stone statues had been destroyed.

"What......?" Flabbergasted, he lowered his shield. It was only then that he could clearly see what everyone had been pointing at. There was the colossus, standing as tall as a skyscraper, and there was Jinwoo perched on its shoulder.

"Huh......?"

Kaboom!

Jinwoo punched the remaining half of the giant statue's face clear off. The headless behemoth began to teeter.

"Whoa, huh?" Every fiber of Kihoon's being told him he needed to run like the wind. Sure enough, the colossus came tumbling down right where he had been standing a second ago.

KROOM!

The entire area was blanketed by thick clouds of dust.

After a coughing fit, Jongin waved his hand in the air to clear the dust from his face as he approached Haein.

"Hunter Cha!"

"Sir……?"

"Are you okay? Can you get up?"

Haein gave a low moan and shook her head. Every inch of her body was screaming at her.

Jongin frowned sympathetically. "Let me help you. Take it easy, now……"

As Jongin tried to support her torso, Jinwoo appeared next to them after wrapping up his task. "May I help Hunter Cha?"

"Pardon?" As Jongin turned toward Jinwoo, he felt Haein gently push his hand aside. In his confusion, he agreed. "Oh, yes. Sure."

Jinwoo immediately lifted the blushing Haein in his arms. "Please hold on a little longer."

He ran to the exit and kicked the locked door.

Thud!

One kick was all it took. The door the high-rank hunters had struggled to open in vain was now in pieces.

On the other side, Jinwoo gently laid Haein on the ground. She was in bad shape, so he called up the shop, purchased a high-level healing potion, and poured it into her mouth.

Gulp, gulp.

Her wounds healed surprisingly quickly.

"How……?"

"Shhh." Jinwoo held up a finger. Now was not the best time to explain.

The other hunters exited the lair. It could have been worse, but while everyone looked awful, no one else appeared to need emergency treatment. Jinwoo closed the shop.

The hunters were surprised to see Haein get on her feet, unaware of the potion's existence.

"Hunter Cha? Just a few minutes ago……"

"The thing is……," Haein started to respond out of habit before changing the subject after a glance at Jinwoo. "There's no time to explain. Let's get out of here first."

The others agreed.

"Are there any more survivors?" Haein asked Jinwoo, since he had the best perception. Jinwoo scanned the inside of the lair and shook his head.

Seventeen people stood there. More than half the hunters who had entered were dead. The mood instantly shifted as everyone quietly grieved.

"I see."

As Haein turned away with a dark expression, Jinwoo took her by the wrist. She looked back at him. At this moment, he wasn't concerned about why the Hunters Guild was here. There was something he was more curious about.

"Um…… What happened in Japan?" Jinwoo had entered the lair right before the dungeon break occurred, so he had no idea how it had all turned out.

Haein searched for the right words. "Japan is doomed."

Yuri's plan to block the gate with a barrier spell had been a dangerous gamble to begin with considering this was an S-rank gate. When it came to both hunters and gates, the "S" meant that their power was impossible to evaluate or measure, which in turn meant that anything could happen. Nonetheless, Yuri had grossly overestimated his own abilities, and his arrogance had led to a disastrous result.

Jinwoo had mixed feelings. President Go had told him what the Japanese hunters had pulled on Jeju Island. While the members of the Hunter's Association of Korea had been unable to ascertain their ultimate goal, they had full knowledge of what had transpired on the island. If it hadn't been for Jinwoo, the Korean hunters would've had a tough time of it even without the monstrous ant in the mix. To make matters worse, the president of the Hunter's Association of Japan had had the nerve to come to Korea and threaten President Go.

They're getting what they deserve.

On the other hand, only the leaders and the top-ranked Japanese hunters had been aware of the plan. Despite some lingering tension over unresolved historical issues, no innocent Japanese citizens deserved to lose their lives.

A dungeon break in the middle of Seoul not too long ago had resulted in the deaths of nearly half the students at the school at the hands of orcs. But what if an S-rank gate opened in the middle of a metropolis of over thirteen million people? It would obviously be a horrendous tragedy.

Besides, the Hunter's Association of Japan itself was partially to blame for this disaster.

Things would've been different if their best hunters, like Ryuji Goto, were still alive.

Ryuji had been a powerhouse, strong enough to make even Jinwoo feel threatened. He'd managed to catch Jinwoo by surprise with an attack that had narrowly missed blinding him.

And he wasn't the only one. The Japanese hunters who were found dead on Jeju Island had all surpassed the Korean S-rank hunters in strength. Jinwoo didn't know anything about their combat abilities, but the amount of mana left in their bodies had been a good indicator. At the time, he hadn't wanted to turn innocent humans into undead shadow soldiers, but they'd been strong enough to momentarily tempt him.

If I'd known their true objective, I probably would've done it anyway!

He'd only learned the truth much later.

In any case, it was because of their scheming that Japan now lacked hunters of a caliber to deal with the S-rank gate. This wasn't an act of God; it was a man-made disaster caused by human greed.

"Hunter Sung?" Haein sounded concerned. Jinwoo hadn't let go of her wrist.

"I'm sorry. I was thinking of something else just now."

"Oh."

Jinwoo released her.

But Haein's worry lay in his grim expression. She couldn't help but wonder whether he had relatives or friends in Japan. Haein herself had no idea that the Japanese Hunter's Association had drawn up such a dastardly plan, so she viewed the events unfolding in Japan as a tragic accident.

With his most pressing question answered, Jinwoo now turned his attention to the other matter that had him curious. "So what brought you here anyway?"

Haein, Jongin, Jinchul, plus Kihoon and his team members, whom Jinwoo had met that time he fought Fang...side by side with members of the Hunters Guild and the surveillance team, two groups that didn't have much to do with each other, were gathered around him.

Jinchul finished checking on the injuries of his subordinates before stepping forward to speak. "We received a report about this gate and found out you had gone inside. But seeing how much magic power was seeping out..."

Jinwoo turned to look at Jinchul, who looked upset by the number of casualties. "We realized we couldn't handle it on our own, so we requested help from the Hunters Guild, who were already nearby."

The right to request assistance in case of emergency. It was the ultimate form of authority the association possessed over the guilds. Not even the Hunters Guild could have rejected the call. Jinwoo's heart ached as he realized how many people had come to his aid—and how many lives had been sacrificed as a result.

As Jinwoo fell silent, Jinchul gingerly inquired, "May I ask you a question, Hunter Sung?"

"Yes?"

"How did you know there was a double dungeon here?"

It was something weighing on many people's minds, including Jongin, who, as the president of the Hunters Guild, had suffered much loss today. How had Jinwoo known there was a double dungeon hidden within this C-rank gate or that there would be a beast beyond their wildest imagination waiting inside? They were curious to hear his side of the story.

Rrrrrumble...

A tremor signaled that the gate was closing, but everyone's attention was on Jinwoo.

He decided to tell them the truth. "The dungeon summoned me."

"It...summoned you?" Jinchul found this difficult to believe.

"Yes. I received a message to come here."

"May I see that message?"

Jinwoo shook his head and pointed to his temple. "I can only see it in my head."

The other hunters were at a loss for words at the unexpected explanation. While Jinwoo might have purposefully withheld some of the pertinent details, he wasn't lying. They didn't know what to make of his earnest expression.

Jinchul, who had known him the longest, shook his head a few times.

He's......he's someone I can't apply common sense to.

If the dungeon summoned him in his mind, maybe Jinwoo was a heavenly avatar sent to Earth to destroy every single dungeon.

Okay, now I'm just being silly......

While Jinchul huffed out a laugh, Jinwoo walked past him, through the door, and back into the lair.

In a panic, Haein called out to him. "Hunter Sung! We'll be in danger if we don't leave now!"

Hearing the worry in her voice, Jinwoo turned and answered, "I know."

Why wouldn't he know that? He had walked the entire length of the tunnel twice already. Doing so took almost an hour even at the walking pace of an average hunter, so if they wanted to get out before the gate closed, they were running out of time.

Furthermore, Jinwoo's father had gone missing inside a gate. He was told that his father, despite being gravely wounded, had helped his teammates out of the boss's lair only to end up trapped when the gate closed. Because nobody understood the dangers of a dungeon better than him, his reply to Haein was filled with conviction.

"I can't leave the hunters who came to my rescue behind."

Those assembled who were anxious to leave froze at his words. The people who had lost their lives in that lair were their precious colleagues and friends, and no one wished to leave them behind.

Unfortunately, there simply wasn't enough time to carry out their remains. Not only were the hunters exhausted, but they'd also have to take the time to locate and reclaim their friends' bodies from beneath the rubble of the lair. Hence, with tears in their eyes, they'd resolved to leave the fallen behind.

"I'm taking them back with me."

The statement hit everyone like a bolt of lightning. No one could bring themselves to argue that there was no time left and that they had to get out now. They watched him in a daze.

Jongin meekly asked, "Could we...please leave it to you?"

The guild members were like his family. He didn't want them rotting away in this icy cavern.

Jinwoo nodded and turned around.

Ba-dump, ba-dump!

His heart was beating quietly.

I need to focus on it more......

Essentially, his two hearts beat as one. It took every ounce of his concentration to separate the sound of the Black Heart from his regular heartbeat. Jinwoo gathered the mana pulsing from the Black Heart in his fingertips.

Is this how he did it?

Jinwoo mimicked Shadow Monarch's hand gesture and raised his hand with his palm up, as if holding something. He could feel the powerful magic in his hand. He was certain he could do this.

Jinwoo quickly located the deceased hunters' bodies through their mana signatures. His eyes were aglow as he broke the silence in the lair.

"Ruler's Authority."

Rrrumble…

Bodies rose into the air from under the rubble.

"Whoa!"

"No way!"

The hunters who were holding their breath as they watched Jinwoo now exhaled in amazement. Not only had Jinwoo instantly located the deceased hunters, but he dug them out without laying a finger on the bodies. It was like a superpower one would see in a movie.

The floating bodies levitated out the door.

Wow……

How is that even possible?

In the same way the average person was fascinated by a hunter's powers, these elite hunters were astonished by Jinwoo's abilities. Jongin, who held extensive knowledge about magic power, couldn't believe what he was seeing with his own eyes.

What kind of skill is that?

He had never seen or heard of this kind of ability before, but after watching Jinwoo's display, Jongin realized he'd been misunderstanding something. When he'd first laid eyes on the angel statue, he'd been convinced that it had defeated Jinwoo. He was totally wrong. What magic beast stood a chance against a hunter wielding such a mighty power?

Jongin shook his head.

It'd be impossible……

Heck, Jinwoo had taken down the angel as soon as he woke up. How could anyone not be amazed by that?

Jinwoo carefully moved the lifeless bodies to one side, and he summoned his shadow soldiers, which he was allowed to do outside of the temple. The shadow soldiers scooped up the bodies in their arms.

The living gawked at Jinwoo as he addressed them. "Let's get out of here."

The hunters nodded as the dungeon trembled once more. The shadow soldiers followed right behind the humans, and Jinwoo hung back to watch them before he turned to face the unmoving Haein.

Although fully healed, she looked drained.

Of course she is.

The angel statue was a creature he'd had trouble contending with, so Haein would definitely be exhausted after fending it off single-handedly.

Jinwoo approached her. "Would you like to lean on me?"

Haein gave a wan smile and shook her head.

He took her by the wrist again as she quietly looked up at him. He spoke softly to put her at ease. "We should get going, too."

She wordlessly nodded as she mourned the deaths of her colleagues.

* * *

Hunters began emerging from the gate. No one waiting outside had any idea of the scale of what had transpired on the inside, but the sight of the deceased hunters being carried out by the shadow soldiers made it clear that something awful had happened.

"Oh my God……"

"Are those all……?"

The members of the Bravery Guild who had reported this matter and the employees from the association who had been standing by all paled as they watched the procession. The number of casualties was simply far too high. They were elite hunters, the very best of the Hunters Guild and the surveillance team, and yet…

Jinwoo and Haein were the last ones to step out into the night. Enough time had passed that it was now dark.

The reporter, Kim, had stayed the entire time to keep an eye on the situation. His eyes widened as he took in the condition of the two S-rank hunters: caked blood, tattered clothing, and disheveled hair—the markings of an epic battle. Sure, Hunter Cha still looked quite lovely even in that state, but Hunter Sung looked like he'd been to hell and back.

That's it…… That's the shot!

Kim raised his camera, his hands trembling. The reason he'd become a reporter in the first place was for this very reason: to document events such as this.

He wanted to let people know that while everyone had been focused on Japan, certain individuals had willingly put their lives on the line to fight for their own country. Close to twenty of Korea's top hunters had perished today. If this dungeon had broken, it would've meant an even greater loss of life and destruction on an unimaginable scale. These people had made the ultimate sacrifice to prevent an even bigger tragedy.

If Kim hadn't been here to report the heroic deeds of these people, would the public ever have heard their tale? He stalked the association to stumble upon stories like this.

Ka-shak, ka-shak!

He was so moved that tears welled in his eyes as he busily snapped away.

Jinchul's legs finally gave out on him, and he sat to rest just outside the gate, which was where Jinwoo found him.

"…Hunter Sung."

Jinchul tried to get up, but Jinwoo stopped him and gestured at the reporter in the distance.

"Is he allowed to take my picture?"

Jinchul had to laugh. "Taking your picture outside of work is prohibited, but just like the Jeju Island raid, it's impossible to stop them from reporting these incidents."

Jinwoo nodded in understanding.

His mother might freak out if she saw him in this state. But while that did worry him, he couldn't force the reporter to stop doing his job, either.

Besides, he also wanted someone to let the world know of the ultimate price these hunters had paid and how they'd prevented another tragedy.

A quiet wind blew, carrying the sound of distant ambulance sirens with it.

The following morning, the front page of every newspaper carried a headline about the dungeon break in Japan. Only one publication reported on the news about the double dungeon incident.

That newspaper sold the most copies that day.

9
BLANK CHECK

9

BLANK CHECK

The Hunter Command Center of America dispatched agents stationed in Asia to assess the situation in Japan. A helicopter left the safe zone and entered Tokyo's airspace.

The senior agent who had volunteered to risk his life looked down and sucked his teeth.

"This is ghastly."

Tokyo was worse off than he'd thought. The dungeon break had left the city in ruins. Buildings had lost their shape, cars were crumbled like paper, streetlights were bent in half, and there was fire, smoke, and ash where structures once stood. *Ghastly* was an appropriate word to describe it. The agent furrowed his brow. He now knew what hell looked like.

However, he hadn't come here to mourn the decimated city. He had a job to do. He inspected the carnage as he took footage from their bird's-eye view.

He turned to the Japanese representative sitting next to him. "Considering all this damage, it's hard to spot any bodies."

His training at the Hunter Command Center had included learning about the S-rank dungeon break on Jeju Island. In all the videos and photographs, the streets of Jeju had been littered with the bodies of residents who'd failed to escape the island. It was one of the worst tragedies in human history, so the Hunter Command Center kept detailed records of the event. Yet, despite the utter devastation here, there were no corpses in sight. In fact, there wasn't even a hint of the dead to be found.

The Japanese representative explained. "Of course. The giants ate everyone."

It was obvious from his bloodshot eyes and unshaven face that this young man working for the Hunter's Association of Japan had been through a lot lately.

With a worried expression, he continued. "It's like they're trying to erase every trace of humanity from the place. They knock down buildings, eat humans, and even uproot trees planted along the sidewalks."

The agent agreed with his assessment.

The giants from the S-rank gate were different from other magic beasts. Typically, beasts' sole aim was to kill humans, while these giant beasts were destroying everything in sight. No matter where they looked, there wasn't a single building or house left standing in the giants' wake.

"But thanks to that, we were able to buy some time."

The association personnel gave a wry smile, unsure whether he should be grateful or sad that some people were able to escape with their lives because the giants were so thorough in their destruction. The warring emotions were on full display on his face.

As he looked at the man next to him, the agent thought.

It's amazing he hasn't gone crazy.

The capital city of this man's country had been wiped out in an instant. But the agent was able to empathize with this feeling of loss caused by magic beasts. It was only eight years ago that the magic beast Kamish had emerged from an S-rank gate and destroyed part of the American west coast.

Additionally, Japan's neighboring country of Korea had been forced to cede its biggest island to magic beasts for four years, and it had only recently been reclaimed. The agent had seen footage of the fierce battle. Despite having no ties to Korea, he also couldn't help but cheer when a young Korean hunter swooped in to save the day.

It wasn't because he was stationed in Asia. He considered the Jeju Island raid not as a simple fight between a small country against invading magic beasts but a battle between humanity and their mortal enemy. And now, here in Japan, yet another epic battle raged between humankind and these predators.

And this is the result......

Takakakakakakakakakakakakaka!

The helicopter was making an incredible racket, but the situation on the ground was so bad that the agent hardly noticed. He felt angry and frustrated, but he was powerless to help. All he could do was carry out the mission he'd been given.

The agent continued filming as he asked his Japanese counterpart the questions that popped into his head. But then he saw something that had him falling out of his seat in shock. "Oh! Th-that's......!"

The American yelled in fright as the Japanese representative helped him back onto his seat.

"So you saw it."

"O-over there! There's still a giant over there!"

"Yes, one stayed. Well, no, more like it's refusing to budge from that spot."

The young Japanese man shifted his gaze outside the window. The American agent wiped the cold sweat from his brow and did the same. A huge magic beast, bigger and taller than any living thing the agent had ever set eyes on, stood imposingly in a decimated section of downtown Tokyo.

So that's a giant......

The agent paled as the representative gave instructions to fly closer.

"A-are you sure that's safe?"

He'd been told that all the giants had left Tokyo, so it was perfectly safe. This wasn't what he'd signed up for.

The Japanese representative calmly explained. "It's fine. As long as we stay high enough beyond its reach, it's a hundred percent safe. Trust me—we've determined this through multiple reconnaissance missions."

Gulp!

The agent swallowed hard.

Did he say multiple?

The young Japanese man sounded so nonchalant about it, but how many people had been sacrificed for this intel? A chill ran up the agent's spine as he thought of what might have happened to those who'd gotten too close. Nonetheless, this was helpful data, as the agent's duty was to collect information on the S-rank magic beasts and report on the situation in Japan.

He opened his eyes wide and looked down at the giant. The beast looked rather familiar.

That's right......

It was the giant that had broken through Yuri Orlov's magic force field. While the other giants had spread out, this one, which many considered to be the boss, chose to remain.

The Japanese employee spoke bitterly. "Do you also believe that the giant is guarding the gate?"

"Um...... Well..."

"This is my third time seeing it this close, and I think something different every time."

"What about this time?"

"It looks to me like..." The Japanese man took his time completing his response. "It's like it's waiting for someone."

"I......see."

The agent's eyes shifted back over to the giant. That was certainly a plausible conclusion. He didn't think it was much of a stretch for the Japanese employee to assess the current situation in this manner.

As the two men discussed the boss-rank magic beast, the helicopter reached the limit of the safe area. Even with a helicopter buzzing overhead, the giant didn't flinch, like it didn't register the presence of the man-made contraption. It remained perfectly docile.

However, according to the employee, this was its choice. "The beast will attack anything within a certain proximity. Whether the target is a person or a machine, there's no escape."

How many flybys had it taken to reach this conclusion, though?

As the young man spoke, the agent thought about Yuri Orlov. The instant the magic beast boss broke through the barrier and snatched up Yuri, viewers had been aghast. His final moments had been broadcast live all over the world.

Yuri Orlov had been described in the Hunter Command Center's report as:

A man who seeks fortune and fame.

In the end, he never got any money from Japan, but he did gain global notoriety.

Though that might not have been quite what he had in mind.

As the agent recalled Yuri's dying moments, the association personnel spoke up. "This is just my personal opinion, but…"

The man's theory about the magic beast waiting for something made sense, so the agent was interested in his perspective. "Go on."

The representative continued at the agent's encouragement. "When I look at this beast, it doesn't feel like it's alive. Sure, it breathes and moves, but it seems more like a programmed machine."

"A machine……"

Unfortunately, the agent didn't agree with this theory. Up close, the giant was extremely imposing. This suffocating pressure wasn't something a machine could generate.

The giant's eye shifted in their direction.

"Yikes!"

Whump!

The agent fell out of his seat again. The Japanese representative promptly moved to calm him and helped settle his nerves. "It's just looking at us. If we keep our distance, it won't hurt us."

The agent nodded. He felt as if his heart had sunk to the floor. After a beat, he raised his camera, though the shakiness of the footage was a result of more than just the speed of the helicopter.

After he was finished, the agent asked, "How many giants came out of the gate?"

"Thirty-one. All of them except the boss headed off in different directions."

".......How many have you killed?"

"Just two."

"That leaves twenty-eight out there destroying Japan?"

"There aren't many hunters left to fight them. Everyone is busy running away." The representative's facial expression grew solemn.

On the day of the dungeon break, the hunters who fought the giants had laid down their lives to give the residents of Tokyo enough time to evacuate. They were able to kill two of the giants in the process, but there was no way to stop the remaining twenty-eight.

This was why the Japanese representative had agreed to accompany the American despite all the fires he was busy putting out.

"Wh-what are you doing?" The agent tried to stop the Japanese man as he dropped to his knees and pressed his forehead to the floor. Neither pride nor dignity mattered any longer. If that was the only price to pay, he was more than willing to do so.

The representative pleaded. "Please help the Japanese people."

The American agent paused at his handler's distraught tone. The representative switched to speaking in fluent English for emphasis.

"If America doesn't help us, then Japan as a nation is doomed. Japan is a trusted ally of the United States. Please consider making this sacrifice just this once for Japan!"

Whether the words came from the representative's own heart or the Hunter's Association of Japan, the desperation in the young man's voice was his own.

The agent chewed his lower lip as he thought about it for a second before replying with some difficulty. "I'll put in a request."

"Thank you! Thank you so much!"

As his Japanese guide bowed to him several times, the American didn't have the heart to tell him not to get his hopes up. The Hunter Command Center had become extremely strict regarding their hunters' welfare after losing so many high-rank assets to Kamish, so would they take such a risk for the sake of another country?

I'm pretty sure they won't.

Even so, how could the agent break it to the young man lowering himself for the sake of his people that his beloved country was as good as dead?

We can only leave it to the heavens......

The agent gazed upward. Unfortunately, there was only silence, just as there had been in the beginning, as there was now, and as there always would be.

He continued to stare at the empty sky as he muttered to himself, "Heaven help us......"

* * *

Jinwoo woke up early and took a light jog to the guild office.

I knew it.

He kept his eyes trained on something slightly above eye level, happy to see his progress on the screen.

Ping!

[Total distance run: 10 km.]
[You have completed running 10 km.]

Even though he'd eliminated the so-called architect of the system, nothing had changed. So far, the system continued to function as it had before, with the daily quests arriving as soon as he opened his eyes in the morning.

He was also in peak physical condition ever since the Black Heart had taken root within his body. Even though he was deliberately going slowly, each step was light as air.

Unfortunately, the architect's death left a ton of unanswered questions.

What exactly was that file I saw?

Watching the file had been one of the conditions to unlock the Black Heart, but everything else about it remained a mystery.

He was deep in thought when a loud clamor ahead snapped him out of it.

"Excuse me! Hello!"

"Mr. Yoo! I'd like to ask you some questions!"

Jinwoo looked up and saw reporters had gathered in front of the guild office building, and they'd caught Jinho on his morning commute. He was being inundated with questions.

"Mr. Yoo, were you aware of the recent incident involving the Hunters Guild?"

"Can we get an official statement from you as the vice president of the Ahjin Guild?"

"How did Hunter Sung end up at that gate?"

"What are Hunter Sung's thoughts on the crisis in Japan? Is he planning to help them?"

Jinwoo raised an eyebrow. The reporters couldn't interview him personally, so they'd resorted to latching on to Jinho, who was an easy target. He was about to step forward and fish out Jinho, but something gave him pause.

Hmm......?

For some reason, Jinho didn't look upset. He'd put on a troubled expression, but Jinwoo's keen eyesight caught him suppressing a smile every now and then.

Heh! He's enjoying this.

Dumbfounded, Jinwoo couldn't help but chuckle. There was no need to break up the party.

So what should I do now......?

Should he stealthily drag Jinho into the office or come back later and let Jinho have his fun? As Jinwoo considered his options, a car rolled to a stop behind him. Its window rolled down.

"Are you Hunter Jinwoo Sung?"

Jinwoo instinctively turned at the familiar voice.

Huh?

He blinked in confusion when he saw who it was.

"Ah, it's you." The man got out of the car as he confirmed Jinwoo's identity.

For his part, Jinwoo recognized him from his many TV appearances regarding business and economic news.

"I'm Myunghan Yoo from Yoojin Construction. It's nice to meet you, Hunter Sung." Chairman Yoo straightened his posture and nodded lightly. The greeting was neither disrespectful nor servile.

Chairman Yoo's introduction was disciplined and refined, the perfect example of how to greet someone. It took Jinwoo by surprise being treated like that by the head of a big company on their first encounter. Jinwoo was polite in turn.

"Jinwoo Sung. Nice to meet you."

With the pleasantries out of the way, Myunghan got straight to the point. "Pardon the sudden visit, but may I please have a moment of your time?"

If he wanted to contact me......?

It would've been more convenient for Myunghan to go through his son, Jinho, instead of coming out here.

Jinwoo kept the thought to himself. "How can I help you?"

Myunghan looked apologetic, as if he had no choice but to approach Jinwoo in this manner. "It isn't something I can discuss with you here."

Jinwoo wore a comfortable tracksuit with the hood raised so no one recognized him, but Chairman Yoo was starting to attract some attention. The frequent foot traffic didn't make this place exactly conducive to a serious discussion. Jinwoo understood that, but the problem was...

I have no idea what Chairman Yoo would want with me.

He couldn't even begin to guess. If he absolutely had to come up with a reason, he would assume it was about Jinho.

More people began recognizing Chairman Yoo, and some took out their phones to try to get a picture of him. As he attracted more attention, Myunghan grew a bit anxious.

If I miss this chance, it'll only become harder to get an audience with him.

He needed to meet with Jinwoo no matter what, so he gathered the courage to press him a little harder. "I apologize, but could you come with me, Hunter Sung? I promise not to speak of anything that might offend you."

Jinwoo glanced over his shoulder. He caught sight of Jinho basking in the attention from the reporters and swallowed a laugh.

Jinho seems preoccupied.

Plus, since he'd recently been monopolizing high-rank dungeons in the area with permission from the large guilds nearby, he thought it might be a good time to take a break from raids.

He acquiesced. "All right then."

"Thank you." Myunghan bowed his head in thanks and opened the passenger-side door for Jinwoo as a chauffeur might. "Please get in."

Myunghan climbed in via the other passenger door and sat beside Jinwoo. The car was so big that there was plenty of room between the two grown men.

Before the car started moving, Jinwoo asked, "Where are we heading?"

"I don't have a specific destination in mind. If you would like to go somewhere..."

Jinwoo shook his head as the car took off.

Myunghan made a suggestion. "I know a place where we can talk without distraction. We can go there."

Jinwoo leaned back in his seat. He found it quite comfortable, as expected of a luxury car. After a smooth, quiet drive, they arrived at their destination.

"Here we are, Hunter Sung."

When the driver approached Myunghan's door, he shook his head. The driver then walked over to Jinwoo's side and opened the car door for him. Jinwoo got out and looked up at the high-rise building before him.

This is where we're going to talk......?

As Jinwoo stood there speechless, half a dozen members of Myunghan's staff swooped in around them and gave perfect ninety-degree bows.

"Welcome, Chairman Yoo!"

"Welcome, Chairman Yoo!"

Jinwoo was impressed by the simultaneous greeting of the six staffers. He could only imagine how many times they would've had to practice to become so synchronized.

"Please follow me, Hunter Sung." Chairman Yoo casually led the way inside the building.

The words YOOJIN CONSTRUCTION adorned the top.

......

Eventually, Jinwoo followed Yoo inside. The chairman waited for his guest to catch up and then matched his pace.

"This way."

Every employee they came across politely welcomed Myunghan. Though stone-faced, he acknowledged every greeting with a nod. Jinwoo got a vibe from Chairman Yoo that was very similar to President Go of the Hunter's Association. The respectful gazes his employees gave him spoke to his character.

Jinwoo walked in silence behind Myunghan, and he quickly caught the employees' attention.

Who is he?

Wait. Is that......?

No way......!

He had taken off his hood as he entered the building, so people recognized him and were floored. The best hunter in Korea and the best entrepreneur in Korea—the sight of them walking the halls of Yoojin Construction together was surprising to all who saw them.

Whoa!

Everyone's eyes popped out of their heads. The hearts of female employees palpitated, and male employees nodded in respect. Nobody knew why he was with the chairman, but as leaders in their respective fields, the two looked good standing side by side. They were revered by everyone watching them.

The two men got in the executive elevator awaiting them at the end of the gauntlet of gawkers. Chairman Yoo's staff came to a stop, and the elevator doors closed, leaving Jinwoo and Chairman Yoo alone.

"......"

"......"

Jinwoo followed Chairman Yoo's example and kept silent. The elevator went directly to the floor where Myunghan's office was located.

Ding!

Secretary Kim was waiting for them at the entrance. He quickly nodded in greeting at Jinwoo and bowed to Chairman Yoo.

"My apologies, sir. You have a guest waiting for you inside."

"A guest?" Chairman Yoo's expression hardened. "Didn't I tell you not to let anyone in while I was out?"

Secretary Kim rarely made mistakes, so Chairman Yoo was more surprised than upset.

Seemingly at a loss, Secretary Kim blurted out, "I told him, sir, but he was quite insistent, so......"

"Hmm." Myunghan immediately knew who his visitor was. He shook his head and gestured toward his office. "Nothing to be worried about. Please, this way."

Wmmm.

The door to the chairman's office opened to reveal a middle-aged man sitting on the couch perusing a newspaper to kill time. He looked up at them.

"Why is it so hard to reach you, my dear elder brother? And after suddenly canceling our plans for today, too."

The man with the receding hairline was Seokho, younger brother of Chairman Yoo. He moved to stand, happy to see his elder brother, but Chairman Yoo glared at him.

"Didn't I tell you that I have important business to attend to? I'm busy, so come back later."

"I know your whole schedule! What's so import—?" Seokho finally caught sight of Jinwoo and stopped talking. "Huh? What?"

While others remembered Jinwoo from pictures in newspapers or on TV, Seokho recognized him from his daughter's social media post.

Is he the real Hunter Jinwoo Sung?

Seokho held up the picture on the front page of the newspaper in his hand to compare it to Jinwoo's face. It was a bit awkward for the hunter, but strangely, he didn't feel annoyed.

Maybe because his eyes resemble Jinho's?

If Jinho grew bald with age, would he look just like his uncle? In Jinwoo's mind, he'd already registered Seokho as "old Jinho."

Ignoring his brother's glare, Seokho stuck his hand out and smiled brightly. "Why, hello, Hunter Sung!"

"Oh." Jinwoo found himself returning the gesture.

Seokho shook Jinwoo's hand firmly as if greeting an old friend as he introduced himself. "I'm sure you've already heard a ton about me, but I'm Seokho Yoo of Yooil Pharmaceutical."

"……?"

Heard a lot about him from who…? Jinwoo didn't want to embarrass the man who'd so enthusiastically welcomed him.

"Oh, yes. Lovely to meet you."

Chairman Yoo had been anxiously watching their exchange and was now taken aback as Seokho pulled his shoulders back and puffed up his chest.

You saw that? My daughter has great taste in men, doesn't she?

Chairman Yoo's daughter was a musical prodigy, which always made Seokho feel a bit inferior to this elder brother. But now Seokho could stand tall. After all, Jinwoo was the most eligible bachelor in Korea.

……Seokho's social circle is larger than I thought.

Chairman Yoo had been planning to read his brother the riot act once Jinwoo left, but his irritation melted away. Their talk might go better if Jinwoo and Seokho knew each other.

"Oh geez, what am I doing?" Seokho finally released Jinwoo's hand. "You two have something to discuss, right? I'll get out of your hair."

He looked satisfied as he made to leave the chairman's office, but he stopped next to Jinwoo. "By the way, Hunter Sung."

"Yes?"

"Please come over anytime. My house is your house."

"......?"

Come over anytime? His house is my house?

"Ha-ha-ha-ha!"

And just like that, the bright middle-aged man who talked nonsense was gone like the wind. While Jinwoo wasn't offended or anything by Seokho's booming voice and sunny disposition, he did strike the hunter as a strange man.

Chairman Yoo carefully asked his bemused guest, "So how do you know my younger brother......?"

There was no need for Jinwoo to keep up the act now that the man himself was gone. Jinwoo calmly replied, "I've never seen him before in my life."

Chairman Yoo's expression darkened at the response.

Damn you, Seokho......

Myunghan should've known better. But he had a visitor now, so the man nicknamed Poker Face erased the irritation from his face as he gestured for Jinwoo to sit. "Have a seat."

He positioned himself across from Jinwoo.

As if on cue, Secretary Kim entered the room. "Would you like some tea?"

"I'm fine. Hunter Sung?"

"I'm okay." Jinwoo shook his head.

Chairman Yoo addressed the secretary. "We have an important matter to discuss, so if you could wait outside."

"Yes, sir." Secretary Kim exited the room and closed the door, guarding the entrance as he had been ordered to do in advance. Even the president of Korea would've been barred access, as this was a matter of grave importance.

"......"

"......"

Silence surrounded Jinwoo and Yoo just like it had in the elevator. The weight of this silence was different, though. Chairman Yoo needed to take his time, as it was a difficult subject to broach. By the time he finally opened his mouth, Jinwoo was feeling a little bored.

"Hunter Sung."

Jinwoo had been waiting patiently. "Yes."

Chairman Yoo removed a check from his inner pocket. It had been issued under Myunghan Yoo's name by the main bank used by Yoojin Construction. However, this was no regular check; it was a blank.

"Here." Myunghan pushed it toward Jinwoo.

Jinwoo looked down at it for a beat before looking up again.

Chairman Yoo spoke with much difficulty. "I'm not arrogant enough to believe that money can buy anything, especially with regard to an S-rank hunter."

His mouth felt dry, and he was more nervous than when he'd assumed the business after his father's passing, or the first time he'd had to make a speech in front of tens of thousands of employees, or the time he'd been hounded by hundreds of reporters.

This was more important than anything he'd ever dealt with in his entire life. His own life, the future of the company he had worked hard for, and a father's desire to see his children grow a little older were all hanging in the balance.

"I would be grateful if you considered this as a token of my appreciation." Chairman Yoo had a strong look of determination in his eyes.

Jinwoo guessed why Myunghan had chosen this place for their discussion. Whatever he was about to tell him was never to be made public.

This isn't about joining his guild.

Myunghan had chosen this place for their talk because, barring a natural disaster, he could control the entire environment.

Jinwoo was very intuitive, so he cut to the chase. "What would you like to buy from me, Mr. Yoo?"

10
HIS RESOLVE

10

HIS RESOLVE

Chairman Yoo laid all his cards on the table. "The truth is, I have the same illness that your mother suffered from."

Jinwoo was completely caught off guard. "Does Jinho know?"

Myunghan shook his head. "Other than my doctor, only three people know: my wife, my secretary, and me."

"And I'm the fourth."

"That's right."

Jinwoo nodded as he finally understood why Chairman Yoo had approached him directly in secret instead of going through Jinho. He wanted to hide his illness from his family.

I mean, tens of thousands of employees rely on him……

The stock of a company fluctuated depending on the well-being of its chairman, and even a single cough could trigger a drastic change. If it ever got out that Chairman Yoo's days were numbered, Yoojin Construction and its subsidiaries would be in trouble. For this reason, Myunghan was keeping his illness under wraps even from his own family. His way of accepting this reality was to bear the weight of the world solely on his shoulders.

Even so……

He shared it with me.

It was probably a calculated risk. Myunghan was a businessman—and not just any businessman but a stellar one who didn't know the meaning of the word *failure*. There was no way an executive of his caliber would risk anything without a reward.

Jinwoo had a rough idea of what Myunghan wanted to ask of him, and sure enough, the chairman resolutely continued. "I've searched the world over for a cure, but I've only discovered one patient who has been freed from this illness."

Yes, just as Jinwoo had thought.

"I don't believe it's a coincidence that the only person ever cured of the Eternal Sleep Disease is your mother, Hunter Sung."

Jinwoo had astonished many with mysterious, never-before-seen abilities. Chairman Yoo had thoroughly done his research and come to a reasonable conclusion: Jinwoo might have cured his mother with one of those abilities.

……

He did not acknowledge whether the chairman was right. Instead, he observed him in silence.

Chairman Yoo swallowed hard.

I can't afford any missteps here.

If everything up to this point had been a warm-up, it was now time for the actual match. It was the moment of truth. Myunghan exhaled briefly and spoke with conviction.

"I swear that everything I'm telling you now is the truth."

He pushed the check forward a little more.

"This token of my appreciation is not all that I'm willing to offer you."

The blank check was only a part of the payment, as Myunghan could give Jinwoo more than just money.

"If you help me, I will forever be in your debt."

The tiger of the financial jungle was bowing his head and pleading for Jinwoo's help. Those who knew Chairman Yoo would have been flabbergasted at the sight. On the other hand, Jinwoo maintained his calm as he studied the whole man.

I don't think he's lying.

The chairman's racing heart, heavy breathing, and desperation hidden beneath a facade of calm told Jinwoo everything he needed to know. Chairman Yoo was telling the truth.

However, earnestly wishing for something didn't guarantee that it would come true.

Jinwoo deliberated for a bit before making his choice. "I'm sorry."

Those two short words devastated Myunghan.

"I can't help you with this matter."

"But...then..." His hopes had been so high going into this discussion that Myunghan was having trouble accepting Jinwoo's rejection. "How was your mother cured, Hunter Sung?"

"Sir." Jinwoo's expression turned rather serious.

A sudden chill in the air reminded Myunghan exactly who he was dealing with.

Jinwoo continued. "If I knew how to cure the sleeping disease and wanted to profit from it, then I would've already done so."

A handful of possible scenarios ran through Chairman Yoo's mind. Did Jinwoo fear being targeted by someone powerful? No, not possible. Myunghan immediately dismissed that one. Jinwoo was an active S-rank hunter—and an especially powerful one at that. The notion that someone would threaten him was ridiculous.

Then, did Jinwoo want something other than money? Chairman Yoo rejected that idea as well. Hunter Sung could achieve fame and popularity if he so desired, but he didn't.

Oh......

Chairman Yoo belatedly realized his mistake. The key to negotiating was finding out what one's counterpart desired. "Give them what they wanted to get what you wanted" was the basis of negotiating. However, Chairman Yoo had no idea what Jinwoo desired, so it was doomed to fail.

It's one of two cases.

Either Jinwoo really didn't know the cure, or he didn't really want anything. Either way, the situation remained desperate for Myunghan.

"......I see." Chairman Yoo didn't try to keep Jinwoo any longer. "Well, then."

Myunghan awkwardly rose when Jinwoo did and called for his secretary, who hurried into the room.

"Sir—" As soon as Kim set foot inside, he felt the tension between Jinwoo and Chairman Yoo. His face turned grim, as this meeting had been their last hope.

"Sir, you called?"

Myunghan nodded weakly. "Hunter Sung is leaving, so please escort him home."

"Oh, no, thank you." Jinwoo politely declined the ride and got in the elevator alone after a short bow to Chairman Yoo and his secretary.

Wmmm.

The elevator moved rapidly from the highest floor to the lowest. Jinwoo hadn't realized it before, but the elevator was way too big and empty for just one person.

He let out a large sigh. "Haah…"

Jinwoo felt uncomfortable about rejecting Chairman Yoo, as he was the father of someone he considered a brother. Jinwoo could've let his compassion get the best of him and helped the old man, but…

I don't know him personally.

Jinwoo had no idea what kind of person Chairman Yoo was—or whether he really had the illness or was harboring another motive. The Elixir of Life Jinwoo had used to cure his mother was potent but in limited supply, so he had to be selective using it. The chairman's offer had been unconventional but hadn't been enough to persuade him.

Ding!

The elevator doors opened on the first floor, and Jinwoo got off with his hood back up. Unlike earlier, when he'd been accompanied by Myunghan, nobody seemed to recognize him. He did get some curious glances from people wondering why he had used the executive elevator, but Jinwoo paid them no heed and headed for the exit. The security guard spotted his approach and held the door open for him, but Jinwoo stopped in his tracks as he heard a voice across the lobby.

"This is the latest news regarding Japan."

Jinwoo turned toward the sound. The giant TV monitor in the lobby had been turned off on his arrival but was currently on and broadcasting a live feed from Japan about the dungeon break and the quickly spreading disaster left in its wake.

Jinwoo walked up to the monitor. The footage of the city captured by the news helicopter was horrifying. Giants were destroying buildings and snatching up humans to swallow them whole. What remained of the army deployed weapons against the giants in vain. It was impossible to defeat magic beasts without the power of hunters. While not exact, the death toll was estimated at well over a million. It was the very definition of a tragedy.

"……"

Jinwoo was stunned. This was the first time he'd seen any footage from Japan because after he'd left Jinchul to wrap up things at the double dungeon, he'd gone straight home and passed out.

The situation in Japan was much worse than he expected, and it reminded him of the nightmare that had occurred at Jeju Island four years ago. The one good thing about that incident had been it had happened on an island, preventing the problem from spreading throughout mainland Korea. But it was a different story for Japan. The country itself was on the verge of total annihilation.

Ba-dump, ba-dump, ba-dump!

Jinwoo's heart quickened, and he was starting to feel irritated. The thought of such weaklings devouring humans like that disgusted him.

Wait a sec……

Jinwoo jolted in surprise. Did he just think of them as "weaklings"? He had never fought these giants before, nor could he detect their magic energy from the TV. So what made him so naturally deem the giants his inferiors? Was he being overconfident?

Jinwoo tilted his head this way and that before shaking it.

There's so much going on that I can't think straight.

Jinwoo turned, slipped past the worried employees crowding around to watch the broadcast, and hastily exited the building.

* * *

It was day two of the dungeon break, and the whole world's eyes were on Japan. What was their plan? Was there any hope left for Japan? Would the United States intervene? Would the giants cross the ocean and invade other countries once they were done there? Concern grew as Japan continued to collapse. Even its worst detractors expressed sympathy for them, no matter how superficial their words.

However, the country did not need pity; they needed concrete action and the power to deal with the magic beasts. As the United States continued to delay making an official statement, news broke that a tenth of Japan had already been destroyed. Videos of evacuees flooding the highways aired on TV. People had left their homes to escape to the outskirts of the nation, but they would eventually hit the literal end of the road, where they would have to come to grips with their own ends…

More and more questions were raised as the world bore witness to the unfolding horror.

└What the hell is Korea doing?
└Why isn't Korea helping Japan?
└Doesn't Korea know what compassion is?

The Jeju Island raid had only been a few weeks earlier. Japan had lost half of their S-rank hunters because of it, so why hadn't Korea returned the aid? As the number of fatalities increased by the hour, so did the people's grief and anger. As the sympathizers with Japan increased, so did the criticism toward Korea.

* * *

└Make your move, Korea!
└Does loyalty mean nothing to them?
└Did Korea forget Jeju Island?

It was a hot topic globally. To add fuel to the fire, people began growing suspicious of Japan's seeming willingness to ask everyone but Korea for help.

Then, on day three, President Go finally decided it was time to call a press conference. He looked to the reporters and cameras that filled the room and quietly spoke. "First, I would like to extend my condolences to the people of Japan during these trying times. Now, allow me to state the position of the Hunter's Association of Korea."

Prior to Korea's press conference, the Hunter Command Center also announced their decision.

In the pressroom at the Hunter Command Center, the United States addressed the issue of the dungeon break for the first time.

"Hunters are assembling as we speak."

Was the United States finally moving to help Japan? The throng of reporters in attendance cheered as if they were the ones being rescued, as none of them wished for the countless deaths that would otherwise occur.

But as the atmosphere in the room heated up, the spokesperson shook their head. "However, this is not in relation to Japan."

What? The reporters murmured among themselves and exchanged looks. No one had been briefed in advance, so they looked to one another for clarification.

The spokesperson gestured to the screen behind them.

"Whoa!"

"No......!"

The reporters' jaw dropped at what was being shown on the screen. A hush fell over the room, though an occasional moan could be heard here and there. The footage being presented was shocking.

"This gate was discovered today in the state of Maryland."

Although smaller than the one in Japan, the gate was still abnormally large. And while there was no direct correlation between the size of a gate and its rank, a huge gate never led to a low-rank dungeon.

The spokesperson explained. "According to the evaluation done by our investigative team, this gate is an S rank just like the one in Japan. Our top hunters will do their best to clear this dungeon."

Reporters expressed their despair by covering their faces with their hands, shaking their heads, or groaning loudly. It was unprecedented for two S-rank gates to appear around the same time. Of course, the United States had nothing to worry about because they had several dozen S-rank hunters scouted from all over the world to take care of it. But this spelled bad news for Japan.

The US has no firepower to spare for Japan.

When the news broke that the help they'd been desperately waiting for was not coming, the Japanese people plummeted into anguish. It was the end. The giant magic beasts destroyed everything in sight as they advanced to the south, and the people who escaped north were running out of places to flee.

This was the current state of things when Korea held its press conference.

President Go announced, "Korea will not be getting involved with the matters in Japan."

* * *

The day before the press conference, two people, Jinwoo and Jinho, were the only ones present in the huge office of the Ahjin Guild.

Jinho's eyes twinkled with excitement. "Boss, there's a B-rank gate. Should I book it?"

"Is that gate on the Hunters Guild's turf?"

"Hmm? Oh, yes, it is, boss."

"No, I'll pass."

"Oh...... Got it."

The Hunters Guild had enough on their plates after having lost many of their elite members. Taking advantage of the situation and booking the gate wouldn't be a good look.

Jinho turned to Jinwoo. "Boss, what have you been looking at so intensely?"

Jinwoo took his eyes from the monitor and leaned back in his chair. "Hey, Jinho."

"Yes, boss?"

"Should I go to Japan?"

"Excuse me?" Jinho was caught off guard.

He knew who he was talking to. He'd had a front-row seat to Jinwoo's fighting more times than anyone else. However, S-rank gates were another story. They were impossible to measure, so anything could happen. Just as there was a huge range in power among S-rank hunters, no one could predict how dangerous the magic beasts emerging from an S-rank gate could be. That was why Jinho couldn't bring himself to brush off his boss's words.

Jinho glanced at Jinwoo's monitor.

Ah......

It was filled with breaking news about the dungeon break. So the situation had been troubling him. Jinwoo possessed great power, and with it came great stress.

"Hang on, boss."

"Hmm?"

The question had been put to him casually, yet Jinho was taking it very seriously. He got up and pulled a scrapbook out of a cabinet. He opened it to reveal a vast collection of printouts and newspaper clippings.

What's this......?

They were all articles about Jinwoo. The Red Gate incident, which the media still didn't know Jinwoo had been involved in, the Jeju Island raid, the traffic jam he'd cleared, and even his recent adventure with the Hunters Guild in dealing with the stone statues.

Jinwoo could only stare. "You've been saving stuff like this?"

"Yes, boss." Jinho blushed slightly.

"But why are you suddenly showing me these?"

"Do you know what these articles have in common, boss?"

"Well......?"

The fact that they all related to Jinwoo was too obvious for that to be what his friend meant.

Jinho responded as quietly as a mouse. "I'm not in any of them, boss."

If not for his heightened hearing, Jinwoo wouldn't have been able to make out his words.

"Huh?"

Jinho raised his head and met Jinwoo's eyes. "Boss, if you go to Japan, please take me with you."

"......?"

Jinwoo was baffled. He'd figured Jinho would either try to stop him or encourage him, not ask to accompany him. But Jinho was dead serious.

"This is kind of embarrassing to admit, but you're my pride, boss. You're the only thing I have that I can boast about."

"But—" Jinwoo snapped his mouth shut.

On the outside, Jinho looked like he had it all, but money and material possessions were more of a burden to him, not things he could be proud of. But meeting Jinwoo and establishing the Ahjin Guild was something Jinho had done himself. Jinwoo understood why he felt so strongly about it.

"That's why I'd like to be there with you, boss. Please take me along."

"You realize where I'm going, right?"

Jinho may have been somewhat naive and immature, but even he had to be aware of what was happening in Japan. It was hell on earth, where giants were deciding the fate of the country.

Regardless, Jinho nodded resolutely. "As long as you don't get hurt, I'll be fine. And if you do get hurt somehow... Gah, I don't even want to think about that!"

His big, bright eyes were full of the kind of unwavering trust that touched Jinwoo's heart. He playfully tousled the smaller man's hair.

Jinho was bewildered but didn't resist. "B-boss…?"

"I was only joking. Why would I go to Japan at a time like this?" Jinwoo rose to his feet. "Let's call it a day. Good work today."

"Huh? You're leaving already, boss?" As Jinwoo waved good-bye, Jinho bowed deeply at the waist. "I'll see you tomorrow, boss!"

* * *

Kerchak!

Jinwoo entered his apartment. The smell of his mother's cooking reached his nose and made his mouth water. He took a moment to enjoy the aroma.

So good…

The best part of his mother being home again was having someone there to welcome him when he came through the door. Gone was the dark and lonely house from before.

"Is that you, son?" Kyunghye's voice came from the kitchen.

"Yes, Mom." Jinwoo quickly took off his shoes and headed over to her. He greeted his mother with a smile. "I'm home."

"You haven't eaten yet, right?"

"No. How about Jinah?"

"She said she doesn't have an appetite."

Jinwoo stopped in the middle of pulling out a chair. "Again?"

"She couldn't sleep at all last night, so she just passed out now."

"……" Jinwoo noiselessly opened the door to Jinah's room.

"Hnn… Nnn…" His sister was restlessly tossing and turning in her sleep.

Though she had maintained her bright personality, it seemed she was still suffering heavily from her trauma.

Well…… She has been through a lot.

Every time he saw his sister anguishing, it made his blood boil and elicited an even deeper hatred of the magic beasts. What made them terrorize humans so relentlessly?

Just then, he recalled the silver soldiers who had swept away the monsters. It had been an army of countless soldiers with a similar burning hatred. What if they really existed?

Would they be our allies?

The enemy of my enemy is my friend and all that.

Jinwoo watched his sister a bit longer before closing the door.

And later…

"Thanks for dinner, Mom."

Jinwoo headed to the gym at the Hunter's Association to work out after dinner. Posting a shadow soldier there proved convenient. At times like this, when his mind was a jumble of too many thoughts, exercising was the best way to clear his head. It had been a while since he'd properly worked up a sweat.

He summoned Beru. As he did some light stretching, the former Ant King respectfully kneeled and bowed before him.

"My king……"

Beru was the only soldier in Jinwoo's shadow army who had any chance of withstanding his attacks. Yet, even he flinched, sensing that Jinwoo's power had grown.

"Congratulations, my king. I can feel that you have become much stronger."

The incredible amount of magic power emanating from the Black Heart sent a chill down Beru's spine, and he was visibly trembling. However, Jinwoo hadn't summoned his soldier to show off his buff. He gestured for Beru to stand.

"……?" Beru appeared puzzled by the worried look on Jinwoo's face, an expression he had never seen since joining the shadow army.

Jinwoo spoke in a hushed tone. "You need to attack me with everything you've got."

"My king, how could I dare……?"

"It's all right. I want to get a proper workout, and you're the only one who can do this."

"I... I am ever so grate—"

Jinwoo leveled a suspicious glare at Beru as he made to kneel in a show of gratitude. "Your vocabulary is improving. You didn't eat a human somewhere, did you?"

Beru shrank back, so Jinwoo dropped it. He clenched his fists and repeated his order. "Do your worst."

"It shall be as you command, Your Majesty......" Beru raised his head and elongated his claws. "Skraaaaaa!"

He unsheathed his talons fully, knowing they wouldn't harm Jinwoo anyway.

The hunter grinned and gave a satisfied nod.

"Skree!" With a loud roar that shook the whole gym, Beru jumped at him.

Bam!

Beru was slammed to the floor and splayed out on his back. "Kree......"

One hundred and twenty-seven losses out of one hundred and twenty-seven fights. Beru had taken his best shot but couldn't touch a hair on Jinwoo's head. In the few days since he'd seen Jinwoo, his master had grown much stronger. His respect for his king's power and loyalty toward him soared.

Beru struggled to sit up as Jinwoo flopped down beside him. A few beads of sweat were visible on his master's forehead, but that was the best the ant could do. Any more, and the gym would've come crumbing down around them.

Jinwoo sat on the floor in silence, staring into space.

Beru carefully propped himself on his knees. "My king...... Is something troubling you?"

"Troubling me?"

"Part of our minds are connected to yours, my king. Your distress causes us pain."

"......"

Jinwoo couldn't believe he was being consoled by a shadow soldier. And not just any shadow soldier but a former insect. He couldn't suppress a smile.

Normally, he would brush off Beru's concern, but he couldn't this time. "There's something I want to do, but I don't know how to go about it."

What was happening in Japan wasn't his concern, nor did he know for certain what kind of danger awaited him there. Besides, he couldn't take on all the world's problems by himself.

Then there were the complicated relations between the Hunter's Association of Korea and the Hunter's Association of Japan. Thinking about it all was giving him a headache.

Beru's head snapped up. "My king!"

Jinwoo was startled. This was the first time he'd heard Beru this emotional since transforming him into a shadow soldier.

"Nothing should stand in the king's way." Beru's voice was filled with conviction, and he sounded more like a longtime confidant than a magic beast turned shadow soldier. "He who does whatever he wants... That is a true king."

"That's why I told you I'm not a king."

The title Shadow Monarch was an arbitrary designation assigned to him by the system, after all.

Beru strongly disagreed. "With all due respect, you have enough power to do whatever you wish, my king."

Jinwoo's eyes widened.

Ba-dump!

For some reason, his heart responded to Beru's words.

"You are a king without a doubt," Beru repeated.

Strangely, Jinwoo was unable to calm his racing heart.

Whatever I want to do......

When he stared forward again, his eyes were as cold as steel.

* * *

The next day, after the United States issued their statement, President Go also announced the Hunter's Association of Korea's position regarding the situation in Japan.

"Korea will not be getting involved with the circumstances in Japan."

Ka-shak, ka-shak, ka-shak, ka-shak!

There was a flurry of flashing bulbs.

President Go then proceeded to reveal in detail the Japanese hunters' plans to thwart the Jeju Island raid. The evidence he presented was irrefutable, including the surveillance camera recording of Shigeo Matsumoto, president of the Hunter's Association of Japan, yelling at the top of his lungs at President Go and revealing his sinister schemes.

The Japanese reporters, who had been holding out hope that Korea would come to Japan's aid, were utterly devastated. Their hands holding the cameras dropped limply to their sides. The Americans had already declined to help mere mments before, and the ugly truth bomb dropped by the Koreans had been the final blow. Tears welled up in their eyes.

"......That is all I have." President Go concluded his presentation.

Normally, he would be flooded with questions at this point in a press conference, but every reporter in the room was rendered speechless by the shocking revelations. The stunned pressroom was broadcast live across the country as people finally realized why Korea had stayed silent about the tragedy unfolding within their neighbor's borders.

"However." President Go was about to leave the room but then turned back. "This is solely the decision of the Hunter's Association. We will not stop any individual hunters from taking action."

What did he mean by that? The reporters slowly stirred like animals waking from hibernation as they processed what President Go had just said.

"There is one such hunter who wishes to take on the giants."

Whoever could that be? Who would want to go to Japan by himself under these circumstances? The room quickly became a frenzy as even the teary-eyed Japanese reporters managed to reraise their cameras.

Please...... Please......!

Hope blossomed in their hearts once more.

One of the Korean reporters raised his hand high, and President Go pointed to him.

The reporter rushed to ask a question as if afraid of missing his shot. "Just who is this hunter?"

All eyes were trained on President Go. He waited a beat before leaning as close as he could to the mic.

"Hunter Jinwoo Sung."

Ka-shak, ka-shak, ka-shak, ka-shak!

Those three words were followed by an explosion of camera flashes.